'THE

OSTLER'S

DAUGHTER

by

Joseph B. Hodgkins

The Ostler's Daughter

Copyright © 2023 by Joseph B. Hodgkins

All Rights Reserved

ISBN (paperback): 978-1-7363849-8-5

ISBN (e-book): 978-1-7363849-9-2

Front cover: Looking east from the Morris Canal towpath in Denville, New Jersey, past the wooden truss bridge on Diamond Spring Road to Peer's General Store.

BRAGDON BOOKS

BOOKS BY THE SAME AUTHOR

The NoMO Killer

The Red Parka

The Reverend Elizabeth Williamson
& Church Gagne Crime Drama Series

Murder in the Apothecary

Lizzy's Jazz Joint

All titles are available in e-book or paperback in the
Kindle Store at amazon.com.
Search under the title or Joseph Hodgkins.

PROLOGUE

In 1860, Canal Ville was a flourishing unincorporated section of Rockaway Township in north-central Morris County. Initially settled in the late 1600s, the area had primarily been an agricultural community. Later, during the Revolutionary War, small ironworks and munitions industries emerged but didn't materially change the town's character. After the newly built Morris Canal was first used in 1829, light manufacturing and retail businesses developed along its hundred-mile route from the Delaware River to Jersey City and the Newark/New York City harbors. Now it bustled with ninety-foot canal boats hauling coal and iron ore eastward and wood, manufactured goods, beer, whiskey, bricks, and the like westward. Ports like Canal Ville, where the boats tied up overnight, had become particularly prosperous.

Peer's General Store, Eatery, and Tavern could be found on Grist Mill Road North, at the south side of Lock 8E. It was a hub of activity, employing boatwrights, ostlers, barmaids, cooks, and retail clerks. The establishment was popular with locals also and was chaotic this evening because the westbound *Zerubbabel* had tied up at sundown scarcely after the eastbound *Martha* had arrived. The mule drivers, steersmen, and bowmen were ready for a wash. Meals were served, drinks poured, and gradually, by nine o'clock, the crowd settled down to the hard-core drinkers and serious poker players. The ostler, Zeke Norris, had finished tending to the mules, had a sandwich and a beer, and was ready for cards.

Originally, Zeke had planned to leave work when his chores were done. But last night at the monthly communication of Canal Ville's Hospitality Lodge No. 17 of Free and Accepted Masons, he'd learned that twice past master Hank Conklin would be playing tonight. Conklin—in his fifties, a fatherless widower, and chief of police for the last fifteen years—was an excellent poker player. His reputation had been enhanced over the years because he'd accumulated a substantial net worth in real estate that he'd acquired instead of gambling debts. Hank held a sizable stack of Zeke's IOUs, secured by his fifty-acre farm situated a mile north of the wooden truss bridge that crossed the canal next to Peer's. Clara, Zeke's wife, had no idea of the extent of her husband's indebtedness but was wary of his gambling habits. So Clara had learned to stash the money she earned from taking in sewing in an envelope at the bottom of the rice canister—a rainy-day fund, she'd thought.

Tonight Zeke had a strategy. Earlier, he had taken Clara's hidden cash, which he'd discovered years before, withdrawn all but five dollars from their meager savings account, and with that stake, envisioned winning back all his IOUs. His tactics were simple: Zeke would have one beer, play conservatively until Hank became drunk, which he did most Friday nights, then strike.

But coincidently, Hank had a plan as well. He aimed to clean Zeke out, but not of his farm. So he gradually feigned increasing intoxication, folding with solid hands to let Zeke become comfortable. Finally, the scenario Hank had been waiting for came around. Zeke had considerable winnings on the table now and an excellent hand. But so did Hank: a royal flush. At length, Hank bid his entire pot—a pot greater than Zeke's.

"I'll call; let me have an IOU."

"No way, Zeke, I have too many of yours already. Shit, you'll never be able to pay them back anyway."

"That's not fair. Don't force me out."

"What's fairness gotta do with it? Christ, you'd probably put up your worthless farm again."

Zeke thought for a moment. *So that's what he wants.* "All right, I'll put up the entire farm."

Neither of the gamblers said anything. Four or five men were watching. One of them, Bobby, a steersman on the *Martha* and fellow Mason, who lived locally when he wasn't working the boats, said, "Zeke, fold. Quit while you're ahead—don't risk everything."

Zeke disregarded him, then looked at Hank. "You heard me."

"Fuck, your farm ain't worth shit. I need somethin' of value."

"I don't have anything else."

"Of course you do."

"Like what?"

"Evie."

Bobby reacted instantly. "That's not funny. His daughter—Jesus, she's barely fifteen."

"That's the deal."

"You're sure as shit not living up to your master Mason's obligation. Stop fuckin' around!" Bobby snapped.

The gamblers were quiet again before Zeke finally responded, "One night."

"No. I want Evie, period. Look at the bright side: you won't have to feed her anymore."

"Christ," Bobby persisted. "You're a prick, Hank."

"Tell you what I'll do, Zeke. If I win, I'll throw in all your IOUs . . . and marry her to boot."

***

Zeke stumbled along Grist Mill Road toward home, but his tottering gait wasn't from beer or the lack of moonlight after yesternight's full moon. It was from tears, and the IOUs stuffed in his jacket pocket were no solace. *What the hell am I gonna tell Clara? Oh, Christ, what am I gonna tell Evie?*

It was a terrible night; no one got any sleep. Finally, Zeke left to intercept Hank, who'd said he would come to collect Evie and her belongings after sunrise but before he went on duty. Zeke had walked about halfway to the canal when he spotted the chief's horse and wagon crossing the bridge. Hank halted when they were abreast, carping, "What the fuck do you want?"

"We gotta talk . . . I can't do it. I'll give you your IOUs back— please."

"Fuck you. A deal's a deal," Hank snapped, and started driving on. Zeke reached up, grabbing his reins, trying to stop him. "Let go!" Hank shouted, but Zeke wouldn't. The chief couldn't shake free, and his horse began skittering, rearing, straining to bolt.

Hank yanked hard on the reins with his right hand and with the other drew his Colt Dragoon. He pistol-whipped Zeke until the ostler finally collapsed on the ground, stock-still.

Eventually, the horse calmed down and the chief jumped off, nudging the inert man with the toe of his boot. Nothing. Hank checked for a pulse. Naught there either. Zeke was dead.

They were adjacent to the construction site of their new lodge. Hank loaded Zeke on the wagon and drove in about twenty-five yards, stopping alongside the excavation, where the dry stacked-stone foundation walls had been started. Grabbing a nearby shovel, he descended a ladder and dug a makeshift grave. The chief returned to the wagon and dragged Zeke's corpse to the edge of the excavation, pushing it over the side. Then Hank moved the body into place before covering, tamping, and smoothing the spot with the handy tools.

The chief left, arriving at Zeke's farm later than he had intended yet still with enough time to take Evie home and report to the police station.

Clara and Evie looked like they'd been bawling all night. "Where's Zeke?" Clara cried. "He went to meet you."

"Didn't see him."

Clara stepped between Hank and Evie. "You're not taking her. Zeke said he would straighten this out."

"Clara, it's a done deal. This is for the best; you're debt-free now. And after we're married, you'll be family, and I'll help if necessary. I won't hurt Evie, honest." Hank picked up Evie's suitcase, and they left.

The chief tried to work all morning, yet something kept disturbing his concentration. It wasn't Zeke, since that had been self-defense. *The horse coulda stampeded . . . I coulda been killed, right?* Then, with a start, Hank looked at his hand. His eighteen-karat-gold past master's ring, which the lodge had given him after his second tenure as worshipful master, was gone.

Shit, it can only be one place!

It was near lunchtime, so the chief announced to the station, "I gotta run an errand. Be back in an hour." Then he drove to the construction site. As he walked over, he thought, *Damn it, they weren't supposed to be working today!*

"Checking up on us, Chief?" the foreman said, smiling.

"No . . . merely nosy."

"We were a bit behind schedule, so we're catching up today."

The chief looked over the work in process. He noticed the foundation stones were being moved into the pit and stacked atop Zeke's grave. He sighed silently but said, "Grand idea, moving the stones nearby." Then, pointing at a pile of dirt, he asked, "What do you do with all that?"

"Backfill the excavation. Shores up the foundation."

"Makes sense." Hank thanked the foreman, then drove back to town, thinking, *I know where the lodge bought the ring. I'll replace it, right down to the engraving inside the band. No one will ever notice the difference.*

CHAPTER ONE

Friday, May 13, 2022
Canal Ville, New Jersey

Karl and Klaus finished breakfast at Central Avenue's Canal Ville Coffee Shop. Then, leaning on their canes, they walked east toward Riverside Park, where they would sit and chat until nearly noon. Later, they'd walk to the public parking lot behind the coffee shop, get their cars, and head home. Weather permitting, this was their weekday routine. Both men had been born in Canal Ville, been widowed before they retired from the Morris and Essex line of the Delaware, Lackawanna and Western Railroad, and been Masons for over fifty years. This morning's conversation—that is, a discussion of when their subsequent communication would be—occurred frequently. That was because Klaus was still in a muddle, even after all these years. The difficulty was that their lodge was a moon one. That meant meetings were set according to the full moon, specifically on that date, unless the full moon fell on a Sunday, in which case the meeting would be the following day.

"Klaus, I don't know why you can't keep it straight. It isn't that hard."

"Well, maybe, but it's a relic of the past. We don't need moonlight to travel by anymore—plenty of streetlights."

"I kind of like it. Tradition."

"That's what I'm talking about. It takes an act of God to make any changes."

"No. A higher authority," Karl quipped. "The grand master."

"Yeah," Klaus chuckled, "it's all form over substance."

"Well, if you're so unhappy, why do you keep coming out?"

"Because I've been doing it for over fifty years. So when's the meeting?" Klaus persisted.

"Monday."

The men were quiet until they moved on to current Masonic events. Today's topic was the donation of the old lodge built in 1860. Several years ago, the Canal Ville Masons had erected a modern, energy-efficient, smaller building that accommodated a reduced membership, and as a goodwill gesture, they'd offered to donate the old facility to the town. But the township didn't want to accept the donation if they had to demolish the building. To resolve the impasse, the lodge secretary, Jan Vanderveer, who owned a construction company, was leveling and removing the old structure gratis.

"We've encountered another snag, and the worshipful master wants to bring it up to a vote on Monday night?" Karl said.

"I don't know anything about it."

"Didn't you receive his email?"

"Don't have email."

"Jesus, Klaus, you complain about the meeting date being a remnant of the past, yet you don't have email!"

Klaus shrugged his shoulders. "Well, the master used to call everyone. I liked it that way. Anyway, I thought Jan was taking care of everything."

"Well, he was, but now the town wants the old stone foundation removed also."

"Christ," Klaus remarked.

"Listen, there's a solution. That's what the master wants to vote on Monday. Here's the deal. You know the fashion model Petra, who's renovating and enlarging the old Norris place north of the lodge?"

"Yeah."

"Jan's doing the work for her. She's willing to buy the stones, because she thinks it would be cool to have him build a wall along the front of the house using them. It'll cover his removal costs. What do you think?" Karl asked.

"Great idea—problem solved. Have you seen her, by the way?"

"No."

"Oh my Lord, I ran into her at the Canal Ville Apothecary. Rajathi, the pharmacist, introduced us. Petra's a friggin' knockout—long, sleek, redheaded, and a ten in most men's eyes."

"You always did like them tall and skinny," Karl observed. "Wasn't she married to an NFL running back but didn't get any alimony because she made more than he did?"

"Yeah, that was the scuttlebutt. You can't make this shit up."

***

The following Tuesday, Jan called Petra. "I have good news for you. Last night, the lodge approved the sale of the stones. So we're all set."

"But don't you have to resubmit something to the town?"

"No," he chuckled. "Small miracles do occur. They already approved it, 'subject to.' I guess they figured we would come around. I confirmed it with the township council president before I called you."

"Terrific. When can you start?"

"I'm almost finished demolishing the old lodge, but we gotta talk."

"About what?"

"Well, to go over the additional costs. I don't want to surprise you. Plus I'm going to need a payment."

"I didn't think any more were due before the final one upon completion."

"I'll have over two hundred thousand of my own money in the project by the time I move those stones. I need you to work with me. So when can we have lunch?"

"This week isn't okay. How about the end of next?"

They made a date for the twenty-sixth, but as they hung up, Jan thought, *She's stalling.*

***

Petra wasn't happy with the pressure she was under. But this wasn't new. It had begun sixteen years ago when her mother, a moderately successful model in her day, became convinced Petra could be even more successful than she had been. True to her belief, Mom used her friends and contacts to wheedle an interview for her fourteen-year-old with the managing director of Ford's Paris office.

They came to Paris the afternoon before the appointment and stayed at a second-class hotel within walking distance of the office. Petra would never forget that morning before they left for the agency. Sitting beside her on the bed, Mom explained their declining finances after her father split. Then Petra was given a master class on the birds and the bees and what she might be expected to do for a job. Later, when the managing director's secretary came to fetch Petra, her mother whispered, "If it hurts, bite your lip."

Forty-five minutes after that, Petra came out all smiles and shaking hands, yet as they walked to the elevator, she grew glum. As they rode down, Mom asked, "So, how'd it go?"

"I bit my lip . . . and I'm not talking about it."

Then a whirlwind began. Fame and fortune: four *Vogue* covers along with a *Sports Illustrated* swimsuit cover; years of naked—black-and-white—TV commercials where she simply held a bottle of perfume without revealing anything; and much more. Mom handled her career until Petra turned eighteen, but following that, it had been chaos.

She tried to sort out what had happened. Sometimes it seemed like everything had passed at the speed of light: partying with drinking and drugs; spending; sex with men, women, and ménages à trois; anorexia and rehab; successfully kicking drugs. Afterward, there was more craziness: drinking and extravagance; marriage to a jock with his beatings and affairs; her affairs; rehab again; and finally, licking booze. But then it all came crashing down, and in a moment of mutual clarity, Petra and her husband met like adults, deciding that an uncontested divorce was the only way to survive. So they put on happy faces, but later, when Petra's husband discovered how broke she was, he gave her two hundred fifty thousand dollars on the down-low before they parted, looking for all the world like BFFs.

Then the phone calls stopped. Petra's shelf life had expired, and now she was left with her 2012 red Mercedes SLK 55 and, after taking on the Norris house project, scarcely five thousand dollars. Moreover, she was three weeks past due with the Hampton Inn's rent. To get by, Petra stocked up on individual Drake's coffee cakes from their continental breakfast. *Good thing I'm not diabetic.* Then she hustled guys for dinner a few times a week. And every morning, she examined her body in the floor-length mirror and checked her face in the makeup light. While mulling over a way out, Petra focused on the good news: *I'm sober, my weight's stable, and I still look great.*

On Thursday, May 26, Petra and Jan met for lunch at a local Irish pub on Central Avenue. After Petra's iced tea and Jan's stout had been ordered, Jan began. "Before we talk business, I have something for you that I found on the job," he said, passing her a clothbound volume. "It cropped up when we removed the wall between the living and dining rooms. It's a diary from 1860 through 1862 that a woman called Clara Norris kept. I skimmed a few pages at the beginning, and it seems like she was the woman of the house."

"That's cool," Petra said, thumbing it. "She has a neat hand. It's very readable. Thank you."

"I thought you would like it because it adds history to the house."

They ate lunch, and finally, Petra began lying. "Look, I know you need cash, but my money's tied up overseas. I should be able to make a substantial payment in about two weeks."

"What's substantial?"

"At least fifty thousand dollars."

"It's a little light. Try to do better if you can. If we can't straighten this out, I'll need to pull my guys off and start our next job; it has good up-front money."

"All right, but maybe you could give me advice. My solution might be a mortgage, since the land and house are debt-free. Where should I apply?"

"Well, you might try my bank here in town. See their mortgage officer, Titus Bolen. What you need is a construction/permanent loan. It's gonna take time, though."

"If they issued a commitment, could you borrow against it?"

"I don't know. First things first, however. Talk to them and let me know what they say."

***

Late in the afternoon, on the Tuesday after Memorial Day, Henry Conklin drove home from Newark on I-280 West. He had come from a meeting with Sal "Doc" Piscator, the former proprietor of the Canal Ville Apothecary, who was incarcerated in the Essex County Correctional Facility. Doc was awaiting prosecution on many state and federal charges, including the murder of Nancy Clarke, a part-timer at his pharmacy; kidnapping; rape; sex trafficking; money laundering; and flight to avoid prosecution. Not to mention that the Treasury Department was about to file charges for income tax evasion. The US attorney and the Morris County prosecutor, Jon Anderson, were proceeding aggressively. Doc had finally realized he needed a new attorney, and there were two in the state who fit the bill—Murray Kriegman and Henry. Both men were high-profile, successful criminal defense attorneys with national reputations. They were tough, shrewd, and square shooters, differing only in style; Kriegman was direct and confrontational, whereas Conklin was circuitous and charismatic. Murray wasn't available, since he was already representing Bobby Wagoner, another accomplice who had flipped on Doc in exchange for immunity.

The reasons for taking Doc on were obvious. It would be the highest-profile case of Henry's career, his fee would be enormous, and he had no doubt Doc had the money squirreled away. Yet Henry was ambivalent, because it was a brutal, despicable case, and Doc had no redeeming value, notwithstanding his public persona. Furthermore, Henry had spoken with the Morris County prosecutor, and the evidence was overwhelming. During Doc's years of operation, 2009 through Memorial Day 2019, approximately 325 women, predominately between thirteen and twenty-two years old, had been abducted from southern New Jersey, Maryland, Delaware, and eastern Pennsylvania. They had then been imprisoned in the basement of the Canal Ville Apothecary for up to two weeks before being auctioned on the dark web. Sales had been domestic and foreign, and for the years 2016 through 2018 alone, gross revenues had been nearly $20 million.

Add to that the damning testimony to be provided by Kriegman's collaborating witness, Bobby Wagoner, who was in the WITSEC program now. Wagoner had done many of the abductions and other grunt work. He had correctly surmised that the police—with the help of Elizabeth Williamson, rector of Saint Andrew's Episcopal Church; her then fiancée, retired CIA senior analyst Church Gagne; and Detective Ronnie Gruenburg of the Morris County Prosecutor's Office—were closing in on them. So Wagoner had abducted Williamson, then imprisoned, drugged, and raped her repeatedly for nearly a week while he negotiated her release in exchange for immunity. He'd even conned

Manny Martinez, who was Doc's number-two until he was assassinated, into selling her on the dark web to raise money for his new life. The buyer, a Frenchman, was already airborne to Morristown when the police rescued Elizabeth on Memorial Day 2019. And according to Anderson, "Wagoner is credible. He has all the nonfinancial details, and nobody can imagine he's bright enough to make up any of this shit."

Even though Doc hadn't been charged in either Manny's murder or Williamson's kidnapping, the best Henry thought he could do was avoid the death penalty. Nonetheless, he had unenthusiastically taken Doc on as a client. And it wouldn't be a secret long, since a News 12 TV crew had been hanging around when he left the jail and cornered him for a statement. Henry wished he could have talked to his wife, Hannah, because of her canny sense of how his actions would affect his career—notably, his secret ambition that the two of them had shared: Henry wanted to go into politics. But Hannah had passed away unexpectedly six years ago.

So now, as he approached the Morristown area, Henry decided, *I'll stop by Rod's Steak & Seafood at the Madison Hotel for a drink and dinner.*

***

That evening, Petra sat at the uncrowded bar in Rod's, watching TV and sipping a club soda with a twist of lime. She'd ordered it because it looked like a "real" drink and men assumed alcohol would make her amenable. She noticed a handsome man—an affluent type in his midforties—take a stool four or five from where she was sitting. Petra took another look, because she'd just seen him on TV being quizzed by reporters over a big case he'd taken. She'd also spotted him giving her the once-over.

No reason to mess around, Petra thought. She smiled as she called to him, "Didn't I see you on TV? You must be a lawyer."

Henry laughed. "Don't hold it against me, please."

"Oh, perish the thought."

Their chatter turned to flirting, and she moved to sit beside him. After a bit, he said, "Can you stay for dinner?"

Petra ate lightly, because she didn't want to be listless afterward. They got along well, and finally, Henry said, "May I get a room?"

"I didn't realize you were married."

"No. It's not that. I'm a widower. I have a fourteen-year-old daughter, Evie."

"I understand. It's a confusing age."

"Yes, she's conflicted with being daddy's little girl and a young woman."

"Do you need to call home?"

"No, I'll text Mrs. Olsen, our live-in housekeeper."

As they rode up the elevator, Petra said, "I wouldn't have minded if you were married. I simply like to know." Meanwhile, she was thinking, *Maybe Henry can help me with my financial difficulties?*

***

Even though they hadn't fallen asleep until three thirty, Henry was awake early the following day, while Petra slept on. He got out of bed, took a shower, and wrote her a note before leaving:

Petra:

I had a wonderful time. Sorry, I must leave—an early meeting. Charge breakfast to the room if you'd like; I'll tell the front desk.

Please call. I didn't get your number.

Then Henry jotted his own number down, signed the note, left, and arrived home a few minutes after Mrs. Olsen had started puttering in the kitchen.

"'Mornin', boss."

"And a fine morning it is, Mrs. Olsen," he joked, smiling broadly.

"Well, I guess so," she tittered. "Did you eat?"

"No, I showered. I'll have breakfast, change, then head to the office."

"Here's coffee. I saw you on TV last evening. If anyone deserves a comeuppance for what he's done, Doc Piscator surely does."

"I know. Don't worry; the best I can probably do is plead him down to life without parole." As Henry finished, Evie walked into the kitchen.

"'Mornin', Dad," she said, unsuccessfully quashing a perceptive smile.

"Wipe that smirk off your face, or you'll be in big trouble," her father joked.

"Dad, I know you need to be with women; it's good for you, and Mom would want you to date. You can bring them home, you know. I'm not a child anymore; I'll be fifteen in August."

Mrs. Olsen turned away, chuckling.

"Speaking of your birthday, what would you like to do?"

"You're changing the subject."

"Evie, this isn't a father–teenage daughter conversation."

"Well, would I like her?" Evie replied, folding her hands on the table and waiting while Henry paused.

"Maybe you're right. Yes, I think you would. You might even know who she is—Petra."

"You're kidding. The model?"

"She lives in town now and is renovating the old Norris place on Grist Mill Road."

"And did you . . . ?" Evie started to ask, then paused, searching for a way out of the question she'd stumbled into.

"Yes, and it was enjoyable."

Mrs. Olsen left the kitchen, stifling a giggle as Evie blushed and exclaimed, "Oh, Daddy!"

"Well, you asked," Henry laughed.

CHAPTER TWO

Thursday, June 2, 2022

Church Gagne sat in the kitchen of the Saint Andrew's rectory, drinking coffee and perusing the morning's paper. *Elizabeth's right*, he thought. *I'm a dinosaur; I can't adjust to reading the newspaper on the phone.* After a bit, he put it aside. Now that things had begun to recover from the pandemic, he'd felt the need to reminisce occasionally and reflect, hoping that life would return to the way it had been.

After twenty-two years with the CIA, Church had retired to Canal Ville a little over five years ago. His "official" rank had been senior analyst. But in actuality, he was, and had remained, a member of a special operations group whose members never fully retired. They carried on in a vague reserve status and were always recallable. As a result, he continued to hold a top-secret security clearance and carry a side arm. The group was nameless and didn't officially exist. It reported to the president and director. If he had to describe it, he would say they were blacker-than-black ops.

He chuckled, recalling stumbling into the CIA on a whim after graduating from Princeton with a degree in art history. Not long afterward, he thought he'd made a mistake while undergoing the Navy SEAL training required before beginning his duties. However, Church was tenacious, sucked it up, and toughed it out.

It was unfair to say he'd stumbled into Saint Andrew's on a whim, but it was hardly a grand plan either. By the end of his career, he'd become disillusioned about the legitimacy of his group's activities. When gravely wounded in the mountains of Zacatecas, Mexico, he wouldn't have survived if it hadn't been for an indigenous woman, a local drunkard of a doctor, and Father John, a Jesuit missionary, all of whom nursed him. After recovering, Church made Zacatecas his last mission, retired to his roots in New Jersey, followed Father John's counsel, sought a church, and discovered Elizabeth. She was bright, humorous, athletic, blonde, and easy on the eyes.

Although he'd visited several churches, he kept returning to Saint Andrew's, finally realizing it was because of Elizabeth. They flirted at coffee hour, and she invited him to Thanksgiving dinner. Not long after that, he spent his first night at the rectory. She put him on the spot when he came down the following morning. Elizabeth stated that she couldn't go further until he told her who he was. Silly inconsistencies in his story about being a traveling desk jockey, never home for holiday dinners and such, had been amusing until that morning, when she'd seen his back—a story in itself of torture and violence. Not to mention his carrying a side arm.

He made a quick decision, because he knew how he felt about her, and told her more than he should've. But it allowed Elizabeth to resolve her intrinsic conflict between her call to the priesthood and his profession. Following that, Church talked the CIA's director into designating him Do Not Recall; they were married, had Wee Billy, and made it through the pandemic.

Returning to the present, Church watched Billy, their toddler, happily attack Gerber's Very Berry Fruit and Yogurt in his high chair, with mixed results. Jacques, their chocolate Lab, had been let out and fed, and now Church heard Elizabeth stirring upstairs. In a few minutes, she came in. "'Mornin'," she said, greeting all with a smile before hugging and kissing Church. Then she moved to Jacques, who was seated sentinel-like alongside the high chair. Elizabeth scratched his head, receiving two loud thumps of his tail. Next, it was on to Wee Billy. "How's my big boy this morning?" Elizabeth asked, reaching for a baby wipe and cleaning him up before kissing him.

Dropping his spoon, the boy cheerfully slapped the chair's tray with his palms to a cadence of "Mommy, Mommy!"

"I think Billy's starting to get the hang of feeding himself," Church commented.

"Yes. His mess seems to be localized to his face and hands now," Elizabeth joked, and came to the table with coffee. "Anything exciting in the paper?"

"Well, it looks like Doc has a new attorney, Henry Conklin. Doesn't his daughter come to church?"

"Yes, Evie. She used to attend with her mother. But now that Hannah has passed away, Henry ferries her back and forth."

"How do you feel about him taking Doc on? Henry's a heavy hitter."

"I guess everyone's entitled to the best defense possible, but I still have trouble being objective."

"I don't think Doc stands much chance of getting off, especially with Bobby Wagoner's testimony."

"Don't get me started on Wagoner. It galls me he'll skate."

"Sorry . . . didn't mean to upset you."

"I'm not hiding from it anymore. If it comes up, I need to handle it. I keep telling myself it can't be tougher than dealing with my drinking, and I licked that."

"Yes, you did. But I'll change the subject anyway. Ronnie texted me last night after you went to bed."

"What's up?" Elizabeth asked.

"Lunch tomorrow. Says he has something to talk over."

"That's fine. You should take a break from house-husbanding. The office is closed, so I'll take Billy along while I polish my sermon. He amuses himself in the playpen with his Legos."

"I'll text Ronnie and suggest he pick me up at your office so you can say hello, and he can see Billy."

Ronnie Gruenburg was a bit of an enigma. Despite his Jewish last name, he identified as an Italian Catholic. This was because his mother had demanded that her irreligious fiancé agree that any children would be raised as she had been. Now retired, Ronnie had been an old-timer with over thirty years on the job—a vice and homicide detective in Newark. Later, he'd become a detective in the Essex County Prosecutor's Office. He'd been assigned to the department's distinguished Organized Crime Task Force before becoming an investigator with the Morris County Prosecutor's Office for his last ten years. Church had no illusions about him. He was not today's cop: he was hard as nails and used long-outdated practices—a throwback to a film noir private eye—though he concealed a caring nature. According to Tom Johnson, Canal Ville's chief of police, Ronnie was probably the best detective he'd ever met. The chief, Ronnie, Elizabeth, and Church had formed the task force that brought Doc Piscator to justice.

***

The same morning, Karl and Klaus, having finished their breakfast at the coffee shop, leaned on their canes as they ambled to their favorite park bench overlooking the Rockaway River. After settling, Karl commented, "There'll be plenty of light for this month's lodge meeting."

"I know, a strawberry moon. I circled it on my calendar—June fourteenth."

"Jesus, you're a fount of knowledge today. I read that before colonial times, the northeast Algonquin tribes named it that."

"Maybe because of harvesting time," Klaus observed.

"I guess. Are you coming to church Sunday?"

"Yes, I was too tired last week. I don't like to miss now that things are sort of back to normal, with COVID-19 winding down."

"I know. I started tearing up when I was a lay reader on Easter and looked out over the congregation. The church was nearly full, masks were optional, and there was hymn singing and communion."

"I thought you were a little emotional," Klaus admitted. "Reverend Elizabeth did a terrific job throughout the pandemic: the church closing, opening with limited capacity, a second shutdown, and parking lot and online services before it finally reopened. But despite Easter, attendance isn't back, so we gotta support her."

"It couldn't have been easy, especially with her having Billy in the fall before the lockdowns," Karl remarked.

"It must've scared the shit out of her and Church."

The Rockaway River

***

Henry was working at his desk Friday morning when his mobile rang. He didn't recognize the number yet answered nevertheless.

"'Morning," Petra said. "Sorry I didn't call yesterday, but I was busy visiting the bank, seeing about a mortgage. Thanks for your note; I had a terrific time too. I hope you don't mind, but I slept in and charged lunch to the room instead of breakfast."

"Not at all. I'm glad you called. If it's not too short notice, how would you feel about coming to the house for dinner tonight? Mrs. Olsen's a wonderful cook, and Evie would love to meet you."

"Did you tell her we spent the night together?"

"Yes, after she scolded me for not being straightforward."

"Any problems?"

"No. Very adult, talking about my needs until it sank in. Then she acted her age."

"I told you: it's a puzzling time. So should I bring a nightgown, or do you want to take it slow with Evie?"

"Let's not rush her. I'll pick you up at seven fifteen."

"But later, you'll stay over at the hotel with me?"

"Yes."

"See you tonight," Petra said, ringing off.

Shortly afterward, his secretary came in. "I have the governor's secretary on the phone."

"Huh . . . I've never met him. Wonder what he wants? Please, put him through."

"Counselor, it's nice to meet you, if only by phone," said the voice on the other end of the line. "I saw you on TV. I've kept up on the case through the US attorney and Jon Anderson. They think they have that bastard, Doc, dead bang. You have a challenge on your hands."

"Governor, it's a pleasure for me also. It was a tough decision to take on this case."

"Well, based on your reputation, I'm certain you'll acquit yourself admirably."

"Thank you, sir. How may I help?"

"I'll be direct. One of our state supreme court justices intends to retire at year end. Keep that under your hat. I want to nominate you for the spot. I've already started the vetting process and am convinced the loss of income won't be a hardship. Am I correct?"

"Yes, but I don't understand. Why would you want someone who has spent his career advocating for criminals? I'm a lifelong democrat, active in the party, and a contributor to your campaigns, but not enough to come to your attention."

"You've been generous, but that's irrelevant. Political expediency cannot often be married to doing the right thing. Your CV undoubtedly appeals to the progressive wing of the party and the factions who want to overhaul the judicial and law enforcement systems. Still, I have confidence in your dedication to the rule of law and the federal and state constitutions. You're well educated and experienced, well written and well spoken, and have a reputation for being fair. Not to mention you can charm the pants off a virgin." The governor chuckled.

"Well, I don't know about the last part," Henry responded, and thought quickly. *It's not the route Hannah and I envisioned. We were thinking US congressman or senator. Yet this appeals to me, because it's essential for me to be around for Evie, and commuting to Trenton instead of Washington, DC, will make that possible. Then, later, it's a path already trodden to the United States Supreme Court or the Office of the Attorney General. Now, those are positions I'd like.* "Thank you. I would be honored to serve."

"Terrific. Here's the big picture. I appoint the justices directly, but the state senate must confirm them. We have a twenty-four to sixteen majority, so it should be a no-brainer. The appointment lasts seven years; if reappointed, it's for life or until you reach seventy. I'll be out of the picture by then.

"The senate traditionally takes a summer recess for July through September. They're backed up on judicial confirmations, so they'll hold a few special sessions during the recess to get caught up. If your confirmation isn't done by the end of the year, it will automatically carry over into the second year, 2023, of this two-year legislative session. But I don't want that to happen, so we need to start moving. First, I'll send you a copy of my proposed press release. Check it over carefully for accuracy. I plan to announce your nomination and circulate the presser a week from today. Second, my legislative aide, Tammy, will call you. She'll walk you through the entire process; rely on her. You'll need to start meeting with the senators ASAP; do as many as possible before the recess. Tammy will tell you who your priorities are and help schedule appointments. And lastly, I need full disclosure. Are there any skeletons we need to be concerned with?"

Henry considered his answer. "Well . . . my life's a matter of public record."

***

Later that morning, before noon, Ronnie stopped by the Saint Andrew's office, met Church, and said hello to Elizabeth and Billy. After the two men were on the road, Ronnie asked, "Any ideas on where to have liverwurst-and-onion sandwiches now that Arthur's is closed for lunch?"

"The Jefferson Diner on Route 15 North has them. We can get a stout too."

"Excellent." When they were seated with their drafts and sandwiches ordered, Ronnie continued, "Billy has grown."

"You haven't seen him in a while. He's speaking in phrases now and walks steadily."

"He remembered me. That was cool, him pointing, laughing, and saying 'Wonnie, Wonnie!'"

"We tried teaching him 'Uncle Ronnie,' but it's a work in process."

"Speaking of that," Ronnie said, "how's Elizabeth handling her abduction and rape? She seems copacetic."

"Mostly."

"But occasionally still blames herself?"

"Yes. She knows it was the drugs but has bad emotional days filled with self-doubt," Church acknowledged. "The good news is that she only needs to see her therapist or go to AA ad hoc."

"You know she'll eventually put it behind her."

"I do."

"Elizabeth's one tough broad."

"Jesus, don't let her hear you say that!"

"I know, and don't call her Lizzie either," Ronnie laughed.

"Tom Johnson's the only one who gets away with calling Elizabeth that and doesn't know she hates it." Church chuckled. Tom was Canal Ville's first Black officer and had quickly worked his way up to chief. He was forty-one and had done ten years as an army ranger with multiple deployments to the Middle East, where he'd been a squadron leader before leaving the service.

"I'm on good behavior when Elizabeth's around," Ronnie continued.

"She knows that. In any case, she's fond of you."

"I never said Elizabeth had good taste. She married you, after all."

"Touché."

When the table was cleared and they'd ordered a second stout, Ronnie said, "I have a reason for our meeting—a proposition. Jon Anderson called because he's having trouble staffing investigators in the prosecutor's office, and the police departments are having difficulties too. The chiefs are all complaining."

"Why's that? I didn't think the defund movement had reached Morris County."

"It's the climate surrounding being a cop. They're tired of the bullshit and are putting their papers in at a greater rate than before, and recruitments are down materially. It's not a crisis yet, but Anderson is trying to stay ahead of the curve. He found a loophole. Although his regular hiring budget hasn't been increased, the one for consultants has. So he envisions bringing back retired officers to help with the caseload. They'll work in his office or at local PDs. Anderson is finalizing the details now. I told him I would give it a shot if he brought you aboard and we worked together. I don't know the pay, but I don't think we'll get rich. I gotta tell you, I'm bored. I miss the action," Ronnie finished up.

"Me too. Didn't at first, but now I do," Church said. "Don't tell Elizabeth, because I do most of the house-husbanding, so we'll have to work around that. Yet she's reasonable and will be involved in no time, because she loved playing detective when we investigated Doc."

***

That evening, in bed during their talking time, Elizabeth cuddled with Church. "We didn't have a chance to chat this evening. What's Ronnie up to?" she asked.

After Church filled her in, she said, "I think we can work with it. I'll take Billy to the office."

"And Amy doesn't mind helping you look after him?"

"No, she enjoys it. Says it breaks up the humdrum life of a church administrator," Elizabeth joked.

***

On Friday, June 10, the governor held his press conference and announced Henry Conklin's nomination as an associate justice to the Supreme Court of New Jersey. Evie and Petra called on Henry's mobile, and his office phone was busy with congratulatory wishes until late afternoon.

Meanwhile, Jan met with Petra. "How'd you make out with Titus?"

"It won't be easy," Petra said. "I filled out the mortgage papers, but they want an up-front fee of fifteen hundred dollars for a loan application, origination, credit reports, and appraisal fees. I don't have it until the money I'm waiting for comes through," she lied. "So they're sitting on it. Truthfully, I don't think it'll work out anyway. My credit has sucked since the divorce, and I don't have much income now. I thought they would mainly be looking at the property's value, not the ability to repay."

"Well, why did you start this project if you didn't have the dough?"

"That's not fair. I've paid you in cash all along. And your costs have been overrunning the contract—you know it!"

"Well, shit happens. It isn't an exact science."

"Precisely. I would never have gone ahead if I'd known my modeling jobs would dry up completely."

"So . . . what's your solution? You'll take a big hit if you don't finish the renovation and sell. And if we go to court, we both lose."

"I have a contiguous one-acre plot to the north. It can be subdivided into two building lots. I'll sell those," Petra offered.

"Yeah, but that takes time. You're seeing Henry Conklin, right? He's a lodge brother, and I know him well. Maybe he could help—give you a private bridge loan and take a mortgage back. Lord knows Henry has the cash."

"We've seen each other several times, and I like him. Plus I've met Evie, and we get along well. But I couldn't ask; it's way too soon. I'm not effing this up just because you ran over budget," Petra snapped.

"All right, let's not argue. What's done is done. Talk to some brokers and see what they say about listing your lot." *Shit, I gotta protect myself. I'm filing a construction lien immediately*, Jan thought as they parted.

***

Henry celebrated that evening, taking Evie and Mrs. Olsen to dinner. As it was winding down, Evie asked, "Is Petra coming to dinner Saturday evening?"

"Yes, why?"

"Well, I thought we could go to church together if she stayed over. Petra wants to meet Reverend Elizabeth. And then you could sleep in."

"I think it's a splendid idea. Tell you what: when we get home, why don't you make up the guest room's bed, and I'll call her."

"Daddy, sometimes you can be such a jerk!" Evie declared.

"Watch how you speak to your father," Mrs. Olsen scolded, and laughed with Henry.

Evie flushed, but Henry took her hand, squeezing it. "We're only teasing. I wouldn't ask Petra over if it bothered you."

***

When dinner was nearly over Saturday evening, Petra said, "Henry, I have something you might be interested in. Jan Vanderveer found it, and

40

I'm certain it's partly about your family." Then she told him about Clara Norris's diary, which recorded that her husband, Zeke, had gambled away their daughter, Evie, to Hank Conklin; that Hank had collected Evie, after which Zeke had vanished; and that the chief, a widower with no children, had married Evie and had one son.

Jesus, that isn't a family legacy I'm proud of, Henry thought.

"According to Clara, she was convinced there'd been foul play, yet the police never discovered anything. She also comments elsewhere that Hank had twice been a worshipful master of your lodge. I can make you a copy if you'd like," Petra finished.

"Yes, please. My wife did research on my family tree before she passed. I'm the sixth generation descended from Hank, who was born in 1808. He would be my four-times-great-grandfather, but I had never heard this story. I wonder if Dad has. According to Hannah's research, Hank married Evie, and all their descendants were boys, following in Hank's footsteps by becoming police chiefs in Canal Ville. I was the first to break with tradition. All of us were worshipful masters of Hospitality Lodge as well. Hank's past master's ring has been passed down—my father gave it to me after I completed my term as master—and I wear it now. The other thing I know is that Evie was a family name. That's why Hannah and I chose it."

"So my four-times-great-grandmother was Evie Norris, who was won in a card game. I don't know how I feel about that. How old was she?"

"Fifteen," Petra said, "but Evie, it was a different world for women then. You don't realize how much things have changed, even since I started."

"But how could a father do such a thing?" Evie continued. "Could she even be married that young?"

"Your mom and I talked about that, but I never looked it up before she passed," Henry said. "The answer was yes, until the governor signed a bill to ban child marriage in June 2018. It raised the minimum age to eighteen. Before that, children under sixteen could be married with parental consent and a judge's approval, while children between sixteen and eighteen needed only parental consent."

"I'll also bring you a copy of her diary; you should read it. Clara doesn't dwell on it, but Zeke is so far in debt to Hank that it's the only way to save the farm. Remember, it wasn't her choice. Zeke and Hank are at fault here, not Evie," Petra said.

"Petra's right, and Evie was a victim despite the legalities," Henry concluded.

Later in bed, Petra said, "I like Evie a lot. It never dawned on me that telling her about Evie Norris would upset her. It was thoughtless."

"Real life can be a shock sometimes, yet it's part of growing up. Evie will be fine. She needs a little time to process it, that's all."

"I think so as well," Petra said, cuddling closer, whispering, "I'm so glad we met."

"Me too," Henry answered, kissing her.

"Now, can I show you some of those things I learned in my checkered past . . . unless you're too tired?" Henry chuckled and hugged her tighter.

***

The following day, when Henry came into the kitchen around nine thirty, Evie and Petra were dressed for church, finishing breakfast, and Mrs. Olsen was puttering. He was greeted with an overlapping chorus of "'Mornin', Daddy," "'Morning, Henry," "'Morning, boss," before Evie said, "I thought you were sleeping in?"

"I was, but I'm wide awake." Henry looked at his watch. "You better get moving if you want to introduce Petra to Reverend Elizabeth before the service."

"We're staying for the coffee hour, if it's okay."

"Sure, but I didn't realize they had started it up again."

"Yes, I think last week was the first."

"Fine, be careful—take masks."

***

On Tuesday morning, June 14, Henry called Jan Vanderveer. "Will you be at the lodge this evening?"

"Of course. A secretary's work is never done," he joked in reply.

"Splendid. Can we meet in your office for half an hour before or after the communication?"

"Last month's minutes and tonight's agenda are finished. Let's do it after dinner, before the meeting."

That evening they went to Jan's office, and Henry said, "Do you mind if we close the door?"

"Not at all. The brothers will march right in if we don't. What's up?"

"I'm seeing Petra," Henry started.

"I heard. Lucky guy."

"I am. She gave me a copy of a portion of that Clara Norris diary you found."

"I didn't read it but thought Petra would like it."

"Well, it contains a little history about my family. Do our lodge records go back to 1860?"

"Yes. They go back even further. What do you need?"

"Clara writes that Hank Conklin was the chief of police and twice a past master of our lodge by 1860." Henry told Jan the rest and took off his past master's ring. "This was Hank's ring, passed down to me. Looking inside the band, you can see his initials with a date on each side: 1852 and 1857. I assume those were the years he was master."

"Let's have a look at your ring," Jan said. "That's neat; it's beautiful. I see the engraving you're talking about." Then, returning the ring to Henry, he went to the shelves on the rear wall. "You would've been out of luck back in the old building, because the minutes were stored all over the place—in boxes as well as lawn and leaf bags. But when we constructed this lodge, I insisted on a suitable office and built the shelves myself. It took me months to organize this shit. Here we are, the two years you're looking for." Jan handed over the volumes.

Henry flipped to the first meeting in each book. There was Hank, recorded as the worshipful master. "Do you mind if I look at these for a while?"

"No, take your time; just put them back when you're through. Henry, I'm glad we're meeting, because there's something you could help me with as well."

"Sure."

"I didn't want to bring it up, but I have a problem with Petra. We're nearly finished with her project, and I'd hate to see it get fucked up."

"What's the matter?"

"Frankly, I think she's running out of dough. Petra keeps stalling, saying her funds are tied up overseas. She talked to Titus at the bank, but a mortgage doesn't look feasible. So Petra intends to sell an acre lot; however, it needs a subdivision and will take time."

"How much are you looking for?"

"I already have two hundred thousand into the job; then there's another seventy-five to finish. But I could get by with a hundred fifty now."

"All right, I'll talk to her."

Despite his annoyance over Petra's finances, Henry spent fifteen minutes on a nostalgic trip through the minutiae of running a lodge in the mid-1800s. He chuckled. *Not much different than today, only than that the minutes were kept with pen and ink.*

CHAPTER THREE

Friday, June 17, 2022

Sunday, Evie had introduced Elizabeth to Petra, who had asked if they could talk.

"Fridays are best, because the office's closed, and that's when I fine-tune my sermon. Come after lunch; I'll be finished by then," Elizabeth suggested, "and we won't be disturbed."

Because the hotel's manager had been pestering Petra for payment, she eschewed the fitness center and lobby. Today she left by the side door, walking to the church for exercise. Petra tapped on Elizabeth's doorjamb.

"Perfect timing; I just finished. Come in . . . coffee?"

"Please." They went to the copy/storage room, where a Keurig coffeemaker and paraphernalia sat on a table. When they returned to the office, Elizabeth began to share her own story in order to encourage Petra to speak freely.

"I'm glad you wanted to talk," she said. "When we chatted Sunday, I suspected we might have common ground—struggling with substance abuse. I'm a recovering alcoholic."

"I had no idea. What happened?"

"When I was at Stanford in 2004 and 2005, I was a top-ranked NCAA championship tennis team member. I couldn't handle the pressures of school and an elite athletic program. But I had a boyfriend on the basketball team who hectored me into AA. I don't think I would've made it without him."

"You were lucky. How long have you been sober?"

"About seventeen years."

"Wow! I'm only a couple. Does it become easier?"

"Of course, but be wary. It can raise its ugly head anytime. So what can I help you with?"

"I grew up in the church, but before last week, I hadn't attended since I was fourteen. I'm plagued by many things, particularly how I've lived. You must've seen it in the papers and magazines?"

Elizabeth nodded.

"I'm also under financial pressure now and scared of falling back into drinking. I've been to rehab twice. I licked the drugs the first time but couldn't make it off the booze until the second trip. I've felt abandoned for years because my career boiled down to nothing more than drugs, alcohol, and whoring. I mean the last quite literally. My agents and others pimped me out to brand managers, editors, photographers, publishers, et cetera."

"Did you feel like you had a choice?"

"No."

"Then it isn't prostitution. A priest once told me, 'You can only be a prostitute if you can say no.' And it's not simply about being pimped. Consider drugs and alcohol as well: they trash your impulse control. Honestly, I think you were powerless to resist?"

"I never thought of it that way. Do you talk to your husband about the drinking and everything that went along?"

"Yes, Church never judges, and I can tell him anything. He's a big help."

"I wish I had someone like him."

"You do if you're willing to try."

"You mean the church. God."

"Yes."

"I'm not an Episcopal; I'm Catholic."

"It's irrelevant, but if it makes you feel better, the Catholic Church recognized Episcopal ordinations until Pope Leo XIII declared the Anglican ones invalid over a silly doctrinal squabble. But the masses remained similar until recently, when the Catholics modernized. I think you'd feel right at home."

"Any difficulties with Communion?"

"No."

"I don't know; maybe I'm not ready to commit yet."

"Everyone struggles with their faith and age-old questions like *Why do bad things happen to good people?* Isn't that what you're asking about when you say you feel abandoned?" Elizabeth asked rhetorically. "Here's what I suggest. Attend with Evie. Keep coming if you feel comfortable and think my sermons speak to you. That's all you need to do. The rest will grow naturally."

"And if I don't feel it's right for me?"

"Don't give up. Try other churches; I won't be offended. We don't have to settle it now. Have you had lunch?"

"No."

"Let's go, then. I have room in my evangelism budget."

They went to the Irish pub on Central Avenue. Petra looked over the menu.

"I'll be at Henry's for dinner tonight, so I'll have something light—a salad."

"Me too, because we usually have pizza Friday evening."

After they'd eaten, Elizabeth asked, "You said you were under financial pressure. Is there anything you'd like to discuss?"

Petra was becoming comfortable with Elizabeth and chose to reveal her financial situation. Afterward, Elizabeth remarked, "It's a mess. Henry is probably the right person to talk to, but I understand your reluctance."

"I have one possible source of income," Petra continued, "yet it won't be a quick fix either, and I don't know how Henry would react."

"What's that?"

"I finally talked to my agent. He waited to call me until things were more certain, but he has been speaking with one of those 'as told by' authors who write books for celebrities, athletes, and others. My agent thinks he's close to an agreement for a tell-all book on the modeling/fashion industry. Even in our current woke environment, the industry remains as always—still using the casting couch."

"Could your agent negotiate an advance?"

"I hope so, yet I don't know how much time it would buy me."

When they were in the car, Elizabeth asked, "You walked to the church, correct?"

"Yes."

"Okay, I'll drop you at your hotel, but I need to stop by my office for a minute."

When Elizabeth returned to the car, she handed Petra a check drawn on her rector's discretionary fund for a thousand dollars, made out to the Hampton Inn, and two hundred in cash. "Oh no, Elizabeth, I can't take this."

"This is what it's for—to help folks out. I wish it could be more, but this check will pay half of what you owe on your room."

"But I'm not even a parishioner."

"It doesn't matter. When you're on your feet, you can pay it back if you'd like. But you don't have to; there're no strings attached."

***

That evening, Petra knocked on Henry's front door, then opened it before calling out, "Hi . . . it's me."

"I'm in the kitchen. Come on through."

"Where's everyone?" Petra said, noticing only two places at the kitchen table and Mrs. Olsen's absence.

"Evie's sleeping over at a friend's; she'll return tomorrow morning. And I gave Mrs. Olsen the evening off. She's meeting her sister for supper and a movie."

"Henry, I think you're up to mischief tonight."

"Absolutely," he laughed. "Mrs. Olsen left jumbo shrimp marinating in the fridge—no alcohol. I thought I'd grill them before topping off a salad with the shrimp. Also, I picked up French bread from Anthony's."

"It sounds perfect. I'll make the salad."

"Fine. Are you in a hurry?"

"No."

"Let's have iced tea."

They sat at the kitchen table and chatted. Even though Henry hadn't planned it, this was an excellent opportunity to talk to Petra about Jan's problems. *I'm optimistic I can carry it off without offending her.*

But when he'd finished, Petra started tearing up. Realizing he'd misjudged the situation, Henry quickly added, "Don't be upset. Let me help you sort it out."

Petra sniffled briefly, then said, "Jan's right: I'm stalling. There is no fifty thousand dollars, because I'm dead broke." She continued, telling Henry about her situation, before concluding, "Jan has been pushing me to ask for your help. But I don't want to, because I don't mean to take advantage. I'll admit to hanging out at Rod's to hustle a dinner, but our relationship changed by the next morning. I don't know where we're heading, but I won't let this come between us."

"I had no idea."

"I work hard at keeping up my image, because if it seems like I'm down and out, there won't be any chance of a job."

"So, you have no solution?"

"Something is developing, but it won't be quick." Petra went on to tell him about the book deal.

"What's the timing on that?"

"In a perfect world, it would be online and in the stores before Christmas, but I'm told that's an aggressive timetable."

Henry thought, *I agree—Christmas is a pipe dream*. "All right," he said, "I don't think you should count on the book bailing you out unless there's an advance."

"Possibly, but not enough to make a real dent in what I owe Vanderveer."

Henry continued ruminating. *I'm leery about this book of Petra's. It's gonna be scandalous. Could it fowl up my confirmation . . . my career? I won't tolerate it getting in my way. But I haven't been this happy in years, and Evie unquestionably likes her. It's a conundrum. It might be a lesser evil if I talk her out of the book by taking collateral and financing her debt.* "Maybe I could help, if you're willing to give me a first mortgage on the property. It's debt-free, correct?"

"Yes."

"Here's my idea. I'll be in charge from behind the scenes and put you in touch with Murray Kriegman. He's a bulldog of an attorney. Don't worry about the costs; we scratch each other's backs. Confirm the numbers for me: you owe Jan two hundred thousand now, including the stones, following which there's another seventy-five due at completion?"

"Yes."

"And you have a contract?"

"Yes, although there've been cost overruns."

"But you've approved them verbally?"

"Yes."

"I think Jan will come down fifty thousand dollars—a bird in the hand. So Murray will offer him one hundred twenty-five now, then pay one hundred when we obtain the certificate of occupancy. We'll do a simple addendum to your contract, including the new terms, and tidy up the overruns. Jan won't be happy, but it's better than litigating, because I won't back you if he does." Henry got up and went to the den. When he returned, he handed Petra a thousand dollars in cash, saying, "You shouldn't have to bamboozle anyone for lunch or dinner if I'm not around. Also, get me a statement on your hotel room, and I'll take care of that too. These are gratis."

"How can I ever thank you?"

"You'll think of something later on," Henry joked.

Petra smiled and reached for him. "I ought to start before dinner . . . don't you think?"

***

On Saturday morning, June 25, Jan started removing the stone foundation from the old lodge using his backhoe. Now that he had Henry's check in the bank, he wanted to finish Petra's job quickly.

Time is fuckin' money, Jan thought as he worked. He wasn't happy. Jan had met with Petra and Murray Kriegman on Thursday. Kriegman had beaten him down fifty thousand dollars, and Jan had gotten twenty-five less up front than he'd told Petra he needed. Plus he'd had to sign a release of his construction lien. There was no doubt in his mind that Henry was pulling the strings. *Not very Masonic to treat a brother this way!*

Jan continued digging a wide trench inside the foundation's walls. It would make shifting the stones into the loader easier and uncover unused ones. The work was slow and tedious.

Near the northeast corner, something caught his eye. Jan jumped down, got a ladder, and went into the excavation. A few feet inside the wall, the wrist and hand of a skeleton were visible in the loose earth. He bent over and carefully brushed the soil away.

Farther along the arm, near the elbow, was something shiny. Clearing additional dirt, Jan saw a gold ring. *I wonder if this is like treasure . . . finders keepers?* he thought. *But I shouldn't move it; I'll leave it for the cops.*

Before making any calls, Jan photographed the ring from several angles. Then he found a number in his phone.

"Worshipful Master, it's Jan. I started clearing the old foundation this morning and uncovered a skeleton. It's inside at the base of the wall—probably been there since 1860."

"Did you call the cops?"

"Not yet. I didn't know if you wanted to come over first."

"All right, but I can't come. I'll call Henry Conklin. He'll know what to do. Hang tight." The master rang Henry. "Jan phoned; he's discovered a skeleton inside the foundation of the old lodge. I can't go; will you? And for Christ's sake, call the cops."

"He hasn't done that yet? Why not?"

"I guess he thought I might want to handle it differently."

"Jesus . . . okay, but I can't stay too long, because I'm on the way down to the shore for dinner with a senator. Pain in the ass on the weekend."

"Well, at least it isn't Friday's traffic. Thanks."

About a half hour later, Henry arrived at the scene. Jan was leaning against the backhoe, smoking a cigarette. "So let's see what you found," Henry said, and Jan pointed at the ladder.

"It's near the bottom—on the right."

Henry climbed down, spotting the ring immediately. Then, looking at it closely, he thought, *It's a Masonic ring—a past master's.* He examined it. *Christ, the exact engraving as mine; it's a duplicate of Hank's ring. Nothing good will come of this if the cops see it before I figure out what's happening.* So Henry pocketed the ring, saying, "Well, these bones sure as shit are part of a skeleton. You may need to remove additional soil, but we should let the police decide how to proceed. I'll call them."

When the dispatcher heard why Henry was calling, he said, "I'll put you through to Tom; he's on duty."

When Tom came on the line, he said, "So, Henry, you have a skeleton up there at the old lodge."

"Yeah, and no cracks about it being one of our sacrifices," Henry kidded. "Jan was removing the foundation and discovered it."

"Vanderveer?"

"Yes."

"Okay, hang out until we arrive, and don't touch anything. We're leaving now."

Two black-and-whites arrived in a few minutes. Tom went to the grave with another officer, who took pictures. When Tom returned, he said, "Removing and transporting the skeleton is above our pay grade, so I called the Morris County crime scene unit and medical examiner. You guys didn't touch anything, did you?"

Henry shook his head no, and Jan said, "I only brushed enough dirt away to see what it was."

"Fine, you can go," Tom responded. "Stop by HQ on Monday and make statements."

CHAPTER FOUR

Monday, June 27, 2022

The lads were in place by eight o'clock in the morning: Church at the kitchen table, reading the paper; Wee Billy in his high chair, playing with a bowl of dry Cheerios; and Jacques on duty beside Billy, after having been let out and fed. When Church's mobile rang, he picked it up quickly so as not to awaken Elizabeth, who was sleeping in on her day off. "What's up, Ronnie?"

"Tom called, and we have our first job reporting to him. Anderson wants us to handle this because he doesn't think diverting Canal Ville's officers from their regular duties for this case makes sense."

"Why?"

"Well"—Ronnie chuckled—"because a buried skeleton was discovered at the old Masonic lodge that's being demolished. Tom says it might date back to the 1860s when the building was erected."

"Jesus, talk about a cold case. What time does he want to meet?"

"You tell me; he'll be in all day."

"All right, I'll call you later this morning."

Elizabeth came down at about ten. After coffee and talking, Church told her about Ronnie's call.

"Wow, that's something you don't stumble upon every day," she responded. "Does Tom have any ideas?"

"No; it might date back to the lodge's construction. He wants to meet with Ronnie and me sometime today. How's your schedule?"

"Yesterday, after church, Petra, Evie, and I planned to go to the mall this afternoon, probably around two thirty. But I'm taking Billy in his stroller, so it shouldn't interfere if you want to meet after we leave."

***

Tom, Ronnie, and Church met at police headquarters at three thirty that afternoon. The chief brought them up to speed. "I don't have much information yet. As a starting point, we're assuming the skeleton was buried at the time of the lodge's construction. I checked; we don't have any records dating that far back. The body is at the Morris County medical examiner's now. He'll send bone samples to the FBI's lab at Quantico for carbon dating and DNA analysis. I'm assuming that'll take time. But for now, he can tell us that the body is a five-foot-eight male and the cause of death was multiple blunt-force traumas to the head, most likely from a narrow metal pipe or the like."

"So it's murder," Church commented.

"Yes."

"We shouldn't wait for the DNA results to establish an identity, because if the sample is too degraded, the results might not be conclusive," Ronnie said.

"If the lodge keeps its old minutes, perhaps we could narrow the date of death through committee reports on the progress of the lodge's construction. I'll call the worshipful master and see if he can help," Tom suggested.

"We ought to check old papers for news stories," Church added. "Judy might find it a challenge." Judy was Elizabeth's cousin, who had helped them on the sly with Doc Piscator's investigation. She had graduated from Carnegie Mellon University with honors in computer science, was a reformed world-class hacker, and now owned a private-sector firm working in antivirus, malware, and phishing protections.

"If Elizabeth and Judy come aboard"—Ronnie chuckled—"it'll feel like the ole band's back together again. That would be cool."

***

In the evening, after the kitchen was tidied up and Billy was tucked in, Church recounted their meeting for Elizabeth, concluding, "I was thinking Judy might help us again by researching old newspapers."

"Hmm . . . I don't know how, but she'll figure it out. We could have lunch with her at the diner near Princeton where we used to meet. But let's make a day of it as well, dropping Billy off at my parents' first. They would love an opportunity to spoil him, unbridled by us." Elizabeth chuckled. "Then we could stay for dinner. What do you think?"

"Why not?"

"I learned something this afternoon that might help you guys. Petra was talking about a diary that Jan Vanderveer found at her house. It covers 1860 through 1862." Elizabeth told Church the story of the card game at Peer's and the subsequent disappearance of Zeke Norris. "Everyone assumed he ran away because he couldn't face what he'd done, but Clara, his wife and the author of the diary, always suspected foul play. Maybe Judy could develop something that would add credibility to her belief."

"And if we can match the DNA to Zeke and the carbon dating checks out, we'd have our victim. So who's the killer and why?" Church wondered aloud.

***

On Wednesday afternoon, June 29, the grand master of Masons of the State of New Jersey answered his phone.

"Most Worshipful Sir," the master of Hospitality Lodge began, "I'd like your guidance on something."

"Certainly. What's up?" the grand master replied. The caller explained the discovery of a skeleton and Tom Johnson's request to have access to the lodge's minutes. "Good Lord, and you think it dates to the 1860s?"

"Yes."

"Thankfully, it isn't on our watch. Do you have minutes from that period?"

"Yes."

"Well, we can assume the police will eventually obtain access with a subpoena, so let's not fart around with it."

"Agreed."

"Is Jan still your secretary?"

"Yes."

"All right, see what he can find. After you review it, call me. I'll approve it if there's nothing confidential like blackballing, disciplinary actions, or such."

"I don't think Jan can Xerox the minutes, because they're in large bound volumes. But he could make a transcript, with redactions if necessary, and then certify them."

"If the police accept it, that's fine."

***

Henry intended to take the day off on Friday, July 1, and make it a four-day holiday weekend. Petra was coming over in the evening, and he'd decided to discuss their plans. His feelings were growing deeper, and the prospect of having her in his bed were pushing him toward suggesting that Petra move in until the renovations on the Evie Norris house, as she now called it, were complete.

Yet the difficulty of her long-term income remained. It was still anybody's guess. So even though he'd removed her immediate financial pressure, he wasn't convinced Petra intended to put her book on hold. *I'd better keep her close, close enough to influence her. And what better place than in my bed? Evie will be delighted too, and a persuasive ally if Petra's stubborn.*

That evening, at dinner, Henry raised the topic. "Petra, why don't you move in here until your construction is finished? It might make sense."

"Oh, Petra, that would be fun," Evie blurted out. "We'd be like a big sister/little sister."

"We would," Petra said, smiling. "I don't have a sister."

"Evie, you might've missed the point," Henry said kindly.

"Oh . . . I know, Dad." Evie flushed. "I'm just sayin' . . ."

"Well, if I say yes, you two will simply have to share me," Petra said, and they all laughed.

"There're benefits," Henry continued. "You'll save money on the hotel room, and meals too."

"It does sound like a swell idea. I'll consider it . . . give me some time."

"Please," Evie pleaded.

"Don't pressure Petra. It's a big change." *It couldn't have gone better if I'd rehearsed it with Evie.*

***

Later, in bed, Petra snuggled up to him. "Henry, you're serious about me moving in, right?"

"Yes. I want you here every night."

"Well, could I have a few nights off"—she giggled—"for girl talk with Evie after she gets ready for bed?"

"Seriously, I don't know where this is heading," Henry answered, "but I want to be with you whenever possible. Though if you need time, I understand."

"I feel the same. But I'm worried my past might embarrass you in your new job. I've been called a tramp, a trollop, and a whore by the tabloids more than once."

"Fuck them," Henry said, giving Petra the obligatory answer.

"Now love me: we'll talk about me moving in again later—promise."

***

Judy was glad Elizabeth had called earlier in the week, because even though her business was running smoothly, it wasn't providing the challenge it once had. Research through possibly long-out-of-business newspapers from the precomputer age might be fun. As she sat in the diner thinking about where to start, Elizabeth and Church walked in. "It's great to see you both, but you didn't bring Billy?"

"We dropped him at Mom and Dad's. Promise we'll bring him next time," Elizabeth said, looking at the menu.

"So you're back in the sleuthing game," Judy quipped.

"Quasi-officially this time," Church replied, explaining how he and Ronnie worked as prosecutor's office consultants. Then Church relayed what information they had.

"It's hard to believe a brutal murder like this could go unsolved all these years," Judy observed.

"I'm keeping an open mind," Church said.

"Then you have a hunch?"

"Well, an inkling."

After lunch, Elizabeth and Judy talked about family matters. Then Judy said, "I saw on TV that Doc has a high-powered attorney. Are you okay?" Church knew that Judy was a recovering alcoholic as well and always spoke candidly to Elizabeth.

"Yes. I'm fine. Not happy, but I haven't stubbed my toe yet."

"All right. You know you can always give me a shout," Judy said. "As for this case of yours, I have enough to begin. Call me with any dates you unearth in the Masons' minutes."

***

As Elizabeth drove to her parents' with Church, she said, "I didn't know you had an idea already."

"As usual, Judy's observation was on point."

"You mean, how could it go undetected?"

"Exactly," Church said. "And there's only one person in Clara's narrative with that clout—Hank Conklin. I think she had the same suspicion."

"I see where you're headed, and if you extrapolate, we run right into another powerful person—Henry Conklin."

"And at a sensitive time," Church observed. "But it's too early. We need additional evidence."

"And after all these years, what purpose would it serve to traduce someone five or six generations down the line?"

"It's a quandary," Church admitted.

***

On July 1, Jan called Chief Johnson and reported on his inquiry. "I found what you're looking for, but the minutes don't copy well, because they're in bound volumes."

"That was fast. Is it possible to have a transcript?"

"How about a letter, signed and sealed by me as secretary? I'll quote the relevant sections; they're not long."

"That should work."

"Okay, I'll email it this morning and confirm by snail mail." Jan addressed the letter to the Canal Ville chief of police, writing:

> *You have requested that I review the lodge's minutes for the spring of 1860 to see if there were any references to the construction of the foundation walls being raised for our new lodge on Grist Mill Road. I located two references as follows:*
>
> - *In the regular communication of April 5, 1860, the Building and Grounds Committee reported, "The excavation has been completed, and the construction of the foundation's walls began in the northeast corner on April 2, 1860."*
>
> - *In the regular communication of May 5, 1860, the Building and Grounds Committee reported, "The foundation has been finished, backfilled, and the building is being framed."*

Very truly yours,

Jan Vanderveer, Secretary

When he finished, he sent the email, stopped by the post office, and met Petra at the construction site, after which she took him to lunch. Notwithstanding what had happened with Henry and Murray Kriegman, Jan had decided it wouldn't interfere with business, at least not yet.

"'Mornin',"' he said, shaking hands and thinking, *You never know. What goes around usually comes around. I'll bide my time.*

"Wow, that's a big pile of stones," Petra said, pointing to the front yard.

"There's another pile at the old lodge. But I'm finished there once I haul them over here. That's what I want to talk about: how you'd like the wall built."

Walking along the front of the property, they chatted until Jan said, "Okay, it sounds like a plan; let's go to lunch."

After they were seated at the Canal Ville Coffee Shop, Jan continued, "Thanks for inviting me; I appreciate it."

"It's my pleasure," Petra said, wondering what was up. *Jan's being gracious. Why? I know he was pissed after our last meeting with the attorneys.* "I was afraid you might carry a grudge," she continued.

"Well, I admit I was peeved. But it wasn't your fault. Henry was doing what he thought was best. But I must tell you, I don't like Kriegman."

"Yes, he's aggressive. Anyway, I wanted to say I'm sorry if you feel like they screwed you out of fifty grand."

"I'll be fine—got it covered."

"How so?"

"I've picked up the pace on your job, because, as I mentioned, I can move on to a better-paying one when I'm through. The owner already has a construction/permanent mortgage commitment, so there won't be any payment problems."

"I'm glad."

"And I stumbled onto a windfall. Keep this to yourself. When I found the skeleton, a gold signet ring was visible in the soil, lying near the elbow. If the original owner doesn't claim it, well—you know, finders keepers."

"Did you take it?"

"No, I figured it was evidence. So I left it for the cops, but I took photos, see," Jan said, showing Petra one on his phone. "I'll go to the station next week and find out if I need to fill out a claim form. With today's gold prices, it must be worth a pretty penny."

"It can't be worth the money you lost on the job."

"I know, but it's a stroke of luck anyway."

I still don't think Jan should be this happy about everything. Well, go figure, Petra thought as she left the coffee shop.

CHAPTER FIVE

Tuesday, July 5, 2022

As Karl and Klaus left the coffee shop and ambled toward the park, Karl asked, "How was your Fourth?"

"Fine. My neighbors invited me to their barbecue."

"Did you watch the Yankees?"

"No. They were off yesterday but in Pittsburg this evening. Aaron Judge will be trying for his thirtieth homer," Klaus answered.

"Do you think he'll break Maris's 1961 record of sixty-one?"

"He's on pace. Did you have a good holiday as well?"

"Yes, I went to a picnic also, next door at Joan's."

"Were they talking about the skeleton Jan unearthed?"

"Naturally. The cops think it dates to when the lodge was built."

"We'll have to keep our ears to the ground at church, because the lodge is dark until September tenth," Klaus observed.

"Yes. We might find out something there. When I stopped by the office, Amy told me that Elizabeth's husband and a retired detective from the prosecutor's office were working as consultants. They also worked together on Doc's sex trafficking case. I never bought that Church was just a CIA analyst," Karl opined.

"Why?"

"There was talk that he'd been a black-ops guy."

"It was probably bullshit," Klaus said.

"Not sure; I heard that the director of the CIA called Tom Johnson to push through Church's concealed-carry permit when he retired. Also, Church was rumored to have reported to the director and president and was still on active/reserve duty."

"How'd you find all this out?"

"Same as I did about the skeleton—Joan. She works at the police station, issues gun permits when approved, and hears gossip. You gotta keep this to yourself," Karl finished.

***

On Friday morning, Elizabeth, Church, Ronnie, and Tom met at police headquarters. "'Morning," Ronnie announced as he walked in. "Elizabeth, glad to see you're joining us."

"I have a couple of items to report," she began. "First, I went to the mall with Evie Conklin and Petra on June twenty-seventh. Petra was talking about a diary Jan Vanderveer gave her." Elizabeth described what Clara's diary revealed. "After Church told me about the case, I called Petra; she made us a copy of the relevant parts, and I brought them along today. Next, Church and I met with Judy on the sixth, bringing her up to speed about searching newspapers from that era for missing persons. She's getting started but needs to know what dates the lodge turns up."

"Great," Tom said. "Jan already emailed me; I'll send those to you." Then Tom browsed through the diary's pages. "There's no word yet on the carbon dating or DNA, but according to this, it's possibly Zeke

Norris's skeleton. So if Judy's search confirms Clara's dates and doesn't turn up any other missing persons, we can assume that the victim was Zeke. Also, I saw the article in the *Star Ledger*. They had the whole story: the card game, Zeke's disappearance, the skeleton, Evie's marriage, everything except the murder."

"How'd they find out?" Ronnie asked.

"Well, it wasn't much of a secret, because Petra, Jan, Henry, Evie, and probably Mrs. Olsen all knew—not to mention Elizabeth and me," Church interjected.

Tom continued, "I'll do a press release to stop further speculation. Maybe we'll get lucky and somebody will have additional information."

"Okay, let's meet on an ad hoc basis from now on," Ronnie recommended as they broke up.

***

On Friday afternoon, Jan and Petra met at the old Norris house while the stonemasons worked on a column on one side of the driveway's entrance. "What do you think?" Jan asked. "I don't want to go too far without your approval."

"It looks terrific, exactly as I pictured."

"All right. We're running electrical inside the columns, so you can put lamps on top if you wish."

"I didn't think of that. It's a great idea." They talked for a while about finishing details inside the house. As Petra was about to leave, she asked, "How long do you think it'll be before I can move in?"

"We could be finished in three or four weeks, but it'll probably be closer to six, allowing for delays, waiting for the building inspector and the certificate of occupancy."

"Okay. How'd you make out with the police regarding the ring?"

"Jesus, I'm pissed—still trying to figure out what to do."

"Why?"

"Well, according to the cop I spoke to, they don't know anything about it. I asked to see their crime scene inventory and photos. He was pissy but finally showed me, and there wasn't any ring. I was about to produce my pics and demand to see the chief, but then I realized that was tantamount to accusing the cops of theft. I figured I should think it through before I created a hullabaloo. The chief's a straight shooter and would have started an investigation, and then it would've been out of my control."

"That's odd. How did you respond?"

"Made a joke of it. I told the cop it must've been a dream, and he seemed to buy it."

"I hope you solve it," Petra commiserated as she left.

Jan talked with the stonemasons, after which he inspected the house's interior and reviewed the open items with the workers. Yet the entire time, something kept nettling him about the missing ring. His photos proved that he hadn't dreamt it, but Jan was also having trouble buying that the cops were thieves. He kept returning to what was becoming an inescapable conclusion: Henry was the only other person who had been there before the cops arrived, and only Henry could've filched it. But why? He didn't need the money.

Jan took his phone and enlarged the pictures. *Hmm, it's a Masonic ring; I should've looked closer. Son of a bitch, it's like the past master's ring Henry showed me.* Then Jan smiled. *Perhaps what went around just came around.*

***

Later in the evening, after Evie had gone to her room, Petra and Henry talked over coffee. "How was your meeting with Jan?" Henry asked. "Is your house coming along?"

"Jan thinks I should be able to move in by the last week in August. By the way, he told me something you might be interested in today." Petra reported how Jan had found a ring beside the skeleton and later gone to the police. "He meant to find out about claiming it as treasure, but they told him there wasn't a ring and even showed him their inventory and photos. Jan's pissed. He didn't make a fuss because he thought the cops might think he was accusing them of stealing."

"That's curious, but I'd rather focus on your house. After it's finished, how would you feel about moving in with me . . . permanently?"

"That's sudden," Petra declared. "I've scarcely got my head around being here part-time. And what about my house?"

"You could sell it. It makes sense, because you could pay off your mortgage and have a wad of cash left over."

"But I wouldn't have the house anymore. Is this all about getting your money back?"

"No. That isn't what I mean. You wouldn't lose anything, because you'd have the cash equivalent. And it would provide liquidity while you try to resuscitate your career."

"Henry, we need to talk. I need to be self-sufficient. The house is a big part of that. And who knows if I'll ever be able to return to modeling? So my book is also important. If it sells, it's a step in the right direction and might help revive my career. You know I can still pass for a young twenty-something. I need a chance."

"I thought you were putting the book on hold."

"I know you did, and you're apprehensive about how it might affect you. But I've decided. I'm signing a deal next week. And it looks like a fifty-thousand-dollar advance."

"It's your decision. I'll support whatever you do, because you know how I feel."

"I do, but this isn't about you. Please, let me be myself. We don't have to solve everything tonight. I'll consider moving in, so don't get pissed."

They went to bed, but Petra was unresponsive when Henry reached around, cupping a breast. So he held her and thought, *What Petra told me is concerning; I'm worried she might learn too much. So now the three of us know about the ring, and Jan and Petra may eventually figure out I stole it. What if Jan makes allegations to the cops—pushes the issue? And all of this is on top of my embarrassing family history and her book deal. Can this get any more screwed up? Jesus, I need to corral her. Get her to move in here? This is more complicated than I anticipated. I can't let shit interfere with my career. I haven't before, and I won't now.*

***

On Monday morning, July 18, Elizabeth and Billy went to the diner near Princeton for lunch with Judy, who'd called the night before vis-à-vis the newspaper searches. When they arrived, Judy fussed over Billy until

Elizabeth settled him in a high chair with his Matchbox dump truck and Cheerios.

After they ordered, Judy began. "I have terrific news. This wasn't as time-consuming as I thought it might be. I searched for missing-person reports based on the dates the lodge supplied: the six months beginning on April first, 1860, and ending September thirtieth."

"So you were successful?"

"Partially; I'll explain. I started by looking into two current New Jersey mass-circulation newspapers. They were the *Daily Record*, Morristown, established in 1900, which I eliminated, and the *Star Ledger*, Newark, established in 1832. Next, I searched for local newspapers that were no longer in print. A few dated to 1797, but the only one published in 1860 was the *True Democratic Banner*. What I discovered corroborates Clara's diary. Here's a draft. If you're satisfied, I'll email you a final version." Judy handed Elizabeth a sheet of paper, on which she'd printed a bulleted list:

- *The* Star Ledger *is an amalgamation of mergers, acquisitions, and purchases. The original newspaper was the* Newark Daily Advertiser, *published daily except Sunday, between 1832 and 1904.*

  o *On April 19 and May 2, 1860, a story and a follow-up, respectively, ran about the disappearance of Zeke Norris and the ensuing missing-person investigation. No new facts and no suggestions of foul play were included.*

- *The* True Democratic Banner, *Morristown, was published weekly on Thursdays between 1844 and 1917.*

  o *On April 26, 1860, a story ran about the disappearance of Zeke Norris and the ensuing missing-person investigation. No new facts and no suggestions of foul play were included either.*

- *There were no other reports of missing persons.*

- *Note: There's no complete archive of these newspapers, but the Library of Congress maintains records of past editions with where they're located: museums, historical societies, and the like. The files are on microfiche, digitally scanned into a computer database, presenting like photos of newspaper pages. The only difficulty was that the files were unsearchable, so I had a fascinating browse through mid-nineteenth-century Americana.*

Judy finished with, "There aren't many surviving copies, but I think this gives you what you want."

"This is perfect," Elizabeth responded. "Did you have trouble gaining permission from the museums or others?"

"I wouldn't know."

"Oh . . . so I shouldn't tell Tom." Elizabeth chuckled.

***

On Tuesday morning, Tom Johnson decided to stop for a cup at the Canal Ville Coffee Shop. He hadn't been in for a while and liked to keep a presence with the town's merchants. The chief had planned to sit at the counter, but as he entered, he spotted Klaus sitting alone. *I wonder where Karl is?* "'Mornin', Klaus. May I join you?"

"Certainly, Chief. It's nice to see you."

"Same here. Where's your buddy? Is everything okay?"

"Yeah. He had a doctor's appointment this morning—just routine. By the way, how's the investigation into that skeleton found at the old lodge going? It must be slow, since it dates to the 1860s."

"It's slow, but we'll get there."

"Well, at least you have Church and Elizabeth helping, as they did with Doc Piscator's case."

"You're well informed, Klaus," Tom probed.

"Karl was at his neighbor Joan's picnic on the fourth. He said it was a big topic of conversation."

Tom thought for a moment. *I'm sure that must be Joan, who works at the station.* They chatted about baseball for a while, and when their checks came, Tom said, "I'll pay these."

"Thanks. I'll leave a tip."

"Okay. Do you want a ride to the park? It's nearly ninety out already," Tom said as they left.

"That'd be great."

Tom dropped Klaus off and returned to headquarters. He looked up Karl and Joan's addresses; they were next-door neighbors. After thinking a minute, he buzzed Joan. "Would you come in for a moment?" As Joan entered, he said, "Close the door, please."

"What's up, Chief?"

"I need your help with a delicate situation. I can rely on you because you're a long-time staffer."

"Sure. What do you need?"

"I've heard around town that there's chitchat about the skeleton's cold case."

"Well, it's fascinating."

"I know, but it seems like the gossip is more specific than expected. Do you think someone here is telling tales out of school?"

She hesitated briefly. "I don't think so."

"Okay, good. In any case, please, do me a favor. Keep your ear to the ground, and let me know if anyone's talking out of turn. What happens here stays here. Thanks."

"Will do, Chief," Joan said, and left.

Hopefully, that'll shut her up—solve the problem. However, bringing it up at our next staff meeting couldn't hurt. Maybe I should move the Conklin meetings to the church; I'll ask Lizzie.

***

On Wednesday, the governor called Henry.

"'Afternoon, Counselor; I met with Tammy yesterday. She says you've already knocked off a few meetings with the senators and reports receiving favorable feedback. This is going well."

"Thank you, sir. Tammy and I are already scheduling meetings for when the senate comes back in session."

"Fine. I saw that story in the *Star Ledger* about Zeke Norris's disappearance after your ancestor won his daughter in a card game. You certainly have a colorful family."

"I knew about my relationship with Hank Conklin but nothing about the rest. I asked Dad; he didn't know either."

"How's Charlie?"

Henry chuckled. "Never lets his cane slow him down. Governor, you should know that our local PD issued a press release yesterday. They're now treating the skeleton's case as murder. Do you think any of this will affect my confirmation?"

"They're still waiting on an ID, correct?"

"Yes, but it will likely be Zeke Norris."

The governor thought for a minute. "Look, none of this has anything to do with you, yet politics is a fickle mistress. Just be prepared to deal with it in your interviews. We'll know soon enough if the senators start avoiding you. Don't worry." And the governor rang off.

Another fuckin' thing to get in my way. And what about the murder investigation? The governor would sure as shit cut me loose if he knew I'd removed evidence; it's prosecutable!

***

On Friday the twenty-second, Tom Johnson gave Ronnie a call. "I received reports this morning from Quantico on the carbon dating and DNA."

"How'd we make out?"

"The carbon dating is right where it should be, between 1850 and 1870. But no luck with the DNA—no matches."

"So what's next?" Ronnie asked. "Check with Ancestry.com-type companies?"

"No. That's not practical, because cooperation isn't in their business model. Dot-coms fear objections from their clients and usually require a court order. Additionally, their technology isn't up to the FBI's standards. And if they choose to lend a hand, it's by back channels, and we can't use the information in court filings. But I have another idea. Hank Conklin married Zeke's daughter, so if the remains are his, we have another of Hank's relatives living in town: Charlie Conklin, Henry's father and my predecessor. I remember him talking about Hank's unbroken lineage of police chiefs until Henry entered the law."

"Do you think he'll give a sample?"

"Yes. I'll call him now."

Tom let the retired chief's phone ring. Charlie was slow, walking with a cane because of the injury that had disabled him on the job. "Chief, it's Tom Johnson."

"Tommy, how you doin'? It's been a long time."

"Too long. How's the leg?"

"The same. The only good thing about it is that I retired early."

"You'd be back in a minute if you could."

"Roger that."

"I'd like to catch up and ask a favor. How about lunch?"

"Definitely, but you're buying. This fuckin' inflation is raising havoc with us retirees."

"You're not fooling me, but you're on."

***

A few days later, the chief picked Charlie up. At lunch, they chatted casually until the coffee arrived, then Tom brought the retired chief up to date on the skeleton's investigation. "Henry told me, but I never knew anything about the card game and Hank winning Evie Norris. I only knew we were related." After Charlie mulled it over, he continued, "I assume you're looking for a DNA sample. If I figure correctly, I'm Zeke Norris's fifth-generation descendent. He would be my three-times-great-grandfather. We should share enough DNA to help you."

"Do you have time to swing by HQ now?"

"Sure."

Later, Tom dropped Charlie at his house, saying, "Thanks again, Chief. I'll let you know." Following that, Charlie settled into his recliner and called Henry.

"How's it going, son?"

"Fine, Dad. What's up?"

Charlie told him about his lunch with Tom.

"Did the chief have a warrant?"

"For my DNA—are you kidding?"

"He can't compel you to give a sample."

"Well, why the hell wouldn't I give him one? What's the matter with you? Do we need to talk about anything?"

"No. I guess it's my profession—a conditioned reflex. Sorry."

"Son, I understand why you'd be concerned about bad press with your pending confirmation. Trust me; it will look worse if we stonewall. So what if Hank wasn't one of God's noblest creatures? Lots of folks have horse thieves in their ancestry. Don't forget this has nothing to do with you. Put together a response so you don't appear flat-footed—that's all."

"You're correct. I'm blowing this out of proportion . . . thanks, Dad."

CHAPTER SIX

Monday, July 25, 2022

Since Jan had talked to the police about the ring, his frustrations had built. He cogitated but continued to believe that Tom Johnson was the only person besides Henry who would have had an opportunity to pilfer it. Yet that made no sense. So Jan was convinced he was correct and thought it was worth a gamble. After all, if Henry didn't understand, it wouldn't work. So, he aimed to call Henry. *I'll get my fifty thousand back—frig him!*

Before noon, Henry's secretary buzzed. "Jan Vanderveer's on the line. Shall I put him through?"

"Yes . . . What's up, Jan?"

"Do you have a few minutes today?"

"Today's NG, but I could stop by the lodge on the way home—about five thirty."

"See you then. I'll be in my office."

Later that afternoon, when Henry pulled into the parking lot, Jan's pickup truck was already there. Henry went upstairs to the secretary's office, and Jan didn't mince words. "Look, I'm pissed. As a Mason, I asked you for help with Petra in good faith. You screwed me over—didn't treat me like a brother."

"What do you mean? I don't see it that way."

"You cheated me out of fifty K."

"I didn't have anything to do with it. I referred Petra to an excellent attorney and offered to finance her settlement. That's all."

"Bullshit."

"Now it's you who isn't acting in a Masonic fashion, Jan. You're accusing me of lying."

"Don't lawyer me. You know goddamn well you were in charge."

"Well, what do you want? If you expect me to hand over fifty thousand dollars, you're out of your mind."

"That's exactly what I want."

Henry stood, then called over his shoulder as he left, "No way."

"Is that how you want to play it with your confirmation pending?"

Henry stopped. "What do you mean?"

"You know the ring. Removing it from a crime scene is prosecutable. Do you think the senators will sign off if it's made public? It doesn't have to come to that. Henry, use your head."

"That sounds like blackmail. But it won't work, because I don't know what the fuck you're talking about."

Then Jan explained how he found the ring. "You and Tom Johnson are the only people who could have taken it, and I ain't buyin' that the chief pinched it."

Henry deliberated. "This is nonsense. I'm out of here." He started to leave again, but Jan called after him.

"Henry, don't. We've been friends for too many years. I don't want to do it, but I'll go to the cops. You know Tom Johnson will poke around."

Henry stopped again and stood quietly before returning. *Gotta deal with this; Jan isn't backing off.* "Well, we sure as shit ain't friends anymore. There's nothing to your allegation, yet you're right about one thing. The mere suggestion that I'm guilty of a crime will quash my appointment. Perception is reality today. How do I know you won't be back repeatedly?"

"I'm not out to hurt you. I only want what I'm entitled to."

"All right, I'll get cash, but I need ten days."

***

Petra had been fussing all day Tuesday, because that evening, she meant to tell Henry how she pictured their relationship developing. He wouldn't be happy. For one thing, he opposed her book; that was clear. But Henry seemed to be making a mountain out of a molehill. After all, it wasn't about him. Petra had even thought of a solution that might work: he could write the introduction wearing two hats, the first as a lawyer commenting on the tacit acceptance of abusive behavior within the fashion industry, and the second as a friend who'd witnessed the painful toll on a victim. It might soften any criticism. She wouldn't mind if he subtly portrayed himself as a shining knight. But Petra wasn't satisfied that her book was the only thing behind their tension. Did it have something to do with that ring, or was there more? And what about his control issues? No question Henry was a type A. He tried too hard to rein her in, pulling on her bit. She cared a lot for Henry and daydreamed about spending the rest of her life with him, but not under his thumb—only as an equal partner. She'd put up with the other shit for long enough. First, there'd been Mom's control; then, once Petra had broken away, the pimps, booze, drugs, and her husband. All masters, all dominating her life. Now it was a fine line she needed to tread: establishing her identity while keeping Henry happy. That was crucial.

Evie was sleeping over at a girlfriend's, so Petra chose to begin after dinner. "Henry, I've been thinking over your suggestion about moving in. Let's not decide yet—"

"Have you thought about it carefully?" Henry interjected. "I think it's an excellent idea—"

"Henry, please, I have lots to talk about, okay?" Petra had decided to bring up the book's introduction last. It might calm things down. She continued, not letting Henry sidetrack her. "This is about getting my own life in order—as I said before, trying to stand on my own two feet. I don't want to feel enslaved or like a kept woman. So I need time for myself to work on the book. Here's what I've come up with. I'll spend three or four nights a week here. Now that my hotel bill is straightened out, I can stay there without having to sneak around. I want to use the fitness center's treadmill because I got out of the habit of exercising."

"I'll get you a treadmill here."

"Henry, this is what I'm talking about."

"I guess it's an occupational hazard. I'm used to giving clients advice and having them take it."

"I didn't say it was bad advice. It's just not what I want to do, and I better be more than a client," Petra stated.

"Of course you are."

"And when my house is finished, I'll spend my off nights there."

"Am I allowed to visit, at least?" Henry queried peevishly.

"You better. Don't you see? This gives me time to work on the book without interruptions."

"Or influences."

"Yes, that too. This is a new world for me, and I'm looking forward to it."

"Well, I guess I won't play as much of a part in it as I envisioned."

"Henry, stop it. You're not even considering that a few nights apart might enhance our time together."

"I hope you mean our sex life."

"Of course."

"Oh, I do appreciate your sacrifices."

"Henry, don't be a dick. By the way, I want you to be part of the book." Petra explained her idea for an introduction.

"I never considered that; it might work," Henry said, but he thought, *Not likely.*

***

The following day, Giuseppe Pappalardo thanked Rajathi Patel as he left the pharmacy. He lived in an upscale town near Canal Ville and, at sixty-nine, was tall and fit, with flowing white hair and a perpetual suntan. Giuseppe always dressed in conservative business suits with the whitest broadcloth shirts. Nonetheless, bright bow ties were a testament to his individuality. He had grown up in a comfortable Italian family who spoke a Sicilian dialect as well as English. His mother had wanted him to attend college. Instead, Giuseppe had opted for the "family business" and, as his father had been before him, became the DeCavalcantes' Morris County *capo*. This mob operated from Elizabeth and controlled northern New Jersey, Trenton, and Atlantic City. The DeCavalcantes were allied with the Genovese crime syndicate, one of the Five Families in New York City.

He heard someone call from behind as he continued to the dry cleaners. "Giuseppe, is that you?" Turning, he saw Henry Conklin. They'd become friends through the lawyer's representation of his crew. Early on, Henry used to play poker in Giuseppe's exclusive first-Wednesday-of-the-month card game and won consistently. But as time passed and his criminal defense practice flourished, Henry stopped playing, and Giuseppe understood Henry's apprehension about being considered a mob attorney. By this point, Henry had claimed his niche and never handled any mob business other than defending those indicted. It was an arrangement that worked well, but Giuseppe missed seeing him nonetheless.

"Counselor, it's been a while. How's the family?"

"Evie's turning fifteen this month," Henry responded. "It's hard to believe, but she'll be off to college before I know it. How's your wife?"

"She's well also. You've been making the papers lately, taking on Doc's case and the governor's appointment to the supreme court. It sounds like you're developing a conflict of interest."

"Yes, I'll be stepping down as Doc's attorney before the senate returns to session," Henry responded. "Giuseppe, I haven't visited Emil's place in a long time. We ought to have dinner, talk."

"Sounds great. Just the two of us . . . in back?" Giuseppe inquired, because he often entertained groups of legitimate associates in the kitchen's large alcove. At these get-togethers, talking business, politics, or religion was forbidden; only safe topics such as baseball, families, goomahs, and the stock market were allowed. But at other times, when Giuseppe met one-on-one, illicit business was on the menu.

"Yes, give my burner a ring, and we'll set a date," Henry answered, furnishing Giuseppe with the number before they parted.

Hmm . . . I wonder what's up? Giuseppe thought.

***

Elizabeth, Church, Ronnie, and Tom met at police headquarters before lunch on Wednesday, August 3. Tom began, "Charlie's DNA is back. We have a match with Zeke's consistent with the generations separating them. That, combined with the carbon dating and Judy's research of missing persons, make me comfortable with our identification."

"So we have a one-hundred-fifty-year-old-plus murder by blunt-force trauma to the head that was committed by a person or persons unknown," Church remarked. "Any ideas?"

"Speculation," Tom admitted. "If we accept that Clara's diary is accurate, Hank Conklin seems to be the likely killer. The narrative fits. We know he was coming to Norris's farm early in the morning to collect Evie. Before Hank arrives, Zeke leaves to straighten out the madness. We also know Hank would have been traveling along Grist Mill Road—across the canal bridge towards Zeke's farm. It's not hard to picture a confrontation near the construction site of the lodge they were building. My hunch is that the murder wasn't premeditated. There's no way to tell who initiated the scuffle. At best, we have manslaughter and maybe even self-defense. But whatever happened, Hank's the survivor and makes what seems to be a puzzling decision: he takes advantage of the lodge's construction, buries Zeke, and proceeds as if nothing had occurred."

"Maybe it isn't as baffling as you think. If Hank comes clean—even if he's exonerated—it will damage his reputation and quash any hope of getting hold of Evie. It strikes me that something powerful—probably lust—was driving him. He didn't know Evie well enough for his feelings to be genuine," Elizabeth inferred.

"You're probably right. So where does it leave us?" Church asked.

"I think it would be irresponsible to go public with our conjecture. Who knows what damage it might do to the Conklins' reputations, especially with Henry's pending confirmation?" Tom summed up. "We should leave well enough alone."

"Stop investigating the cold case?" Ronnie asked.

"Yes."

"I'm okay with that," he replied. "I have something else I would like to bounce off you guys. It probably doesn't have anything to do with this, however. Since my retirement, I've kept in touch with several confidential informants. Jon Anderson reimburses me for out-of-pocket expenses and throws me a few bucks if I find anything interesting. I met with one of my guys in the DeCavalcante mob. Giuseppe Pappalardo had dinner with Henry Conklin the other evening at Emil's restaurant on Route 10. It was on the down-low, in the kitchen."

"Giuseppe's the guy we suspected to have helped Doc escape to Mexico, correct?" Elizabeth asked.

"Yeah."

"Conklin's a defense attorney. Why is that strange?" Church said.

"Because he only represents indicted persons," Ronnie continued, "and as far as I know, Giuseppe isn't. Neither are any of his crew. Anderson has put the investigation of Giuseppe's relationship with Doc on hold because of a lack of evidence. So I'd like to know why they were meeting. Also, I learned that Massimino 'Massi' Rizzo, a supposed longshoremen's organizer and the DeCavalcantes' reputed acting *capo bastone*, or underboss, is talking about bringing Jimmy Zee back for a job."

"Who's Jimmy Zee?" Elizabeth asked.

"A bit of a shadowy figure who disappeared about seven years ago. He was the DeCavalcantes' number-one hit man but also freelanced for other crime families."

"What happened back then?"

"Don't know. The scuttlebutt was that he'd had enough, just picked up his ball and went home. He's believed to be retired down south somewhere. I'm trying to connect the dots."

"So the dots are that Giuseppe might be organizing a killing for Henry Conklin?" Tom observed.

"Yes. We always suspected he'd coordinated Manny Martinez's murder for Doc. In any case, it isn't Giuseppe's bailiwick, but he knows whom to call."

"It's a big jump. Any ideas why, Ronnie?" Church asked.

"No, it's purely a hunch. I'll meet with this CI and see if I can determine what they're up to."

"All right," Tom said, "keep working that angle. On another topic, I have some apprehension about leaks. I think I've nipped it in the bud, but I want us to meet at Saint Andrew's hereafter—if that's okay, Lizzie?"

"That's fine. We can use the big conference room."

***

That afternoon, Jan called Henry, speaking forthrightly. "Counselor, the time you asked for is nearly up."

"I know, but I've run into a delay. It should be here shortly."

"Don't fuck with me."

"There's no need to bully. I'll have your dough."

"Tell you what," Jan said. "I'm sending you a text. Maybe it'll motivate you to put your ass in gear."

He rang off. Almost immediately, Henry's phone chimed. Jan's text showed photos of Hank's ring sitting in the soil near the skeleton's elbow.

Shit. I didn't ask for Giuseppe's assistance too soon, Henry thought. *He needs to get me Jan's phone, chop-chop!*

CHAPTER SEVEN

Thursday, August 4, 2022
Kill Devil Hills, North Carolina

James Zappulla's mobile woke him at seven o'clock. He jumped out of bed, grabbing it from the dresser before it roused Olivia, who was still sleeping serenely.

"Hey, boss, what's up?" he greeted the acting underboss of the DeCavalcante crime family.

"Jimmy Zee, how you doin'? Still happy on the Outer Banks?"

"Yeah."

"How long have you been down there, anyway?"

"Seven years."

"Are you still with that broad, or did she finally give you the bum's rush?" Massimino joked.

"We've been together five years now."

"Jeez, who woulda thought? Listen, I need you to do a job."

"Boss, I'm retired."

"I know, I know, but I ain't asked before. My Morris County *capo* referred it. It must be done right—*capiche*? It'll be like old times."

"Yeah, and I really wanna walk down memory lane. When, by the way?" Then they talked for a few minutes before Jimmy finally agreed.

He hung up and stood gazing at Olivia, who was still naked atop the sheet. She'd been seventeen when they hooked up. The first time they'd made love, scarcely a few hours after their meeting, Jimmy worried it was merely a thank-you, an expression of her gratitude—but not so. He still marveled that a nearly twenty-three-year-old wasn't tired by now of a man twenty-five years her senior. Today he reflected wistfully on their first meeting.

Jimmy had driven his 1996 Bronco Sport to the beach from his rented oceanfront condo. As usual, he wore a Yankees cap, sunglasses, T-shirt, and a bathing suit, taking along lotion, a thermos of iced tea, and a portable beach chair. Some mornings he packed a surf casting rod and holder, but today he'd brought a folding beach umbrella and a couple of towels instead.

After taking a dip and settling under the umbrella, he heard a rumpus. Jimmy looked over and saw a take-your-breath-away blonde surrounded by five guys drawing closer and taunting her loudly. "Show us your tits! Show us your tits!" He'd heard about this on the local news. These bums would keep it up until the scared woman capitulated. Then, after a quick feel, they'd nick her top and run off in different directions, leaving the woman frightened, confused, and crying. The police were having no luck rounding up these assholes.

Jimmy had spotted the blonde when he arrived. He recalled thinking that she was hard to miss in her skimpy bikini. *Christ, her bottom half's barely a G-string.* Yet if she was frightened, blondie wasn't showing it. Instead, she clutched her arms across her chest, securing her top while cursing a blue streak. He smiled as he observed her defiance.

Jimmy decided this needed sorting and approached the thugs, who were all heavier and taller than his 195 pounds and five foot eight inches. He was okay with that, because it would lull the pricks into a false sense of security. *You have no idea what's gonna happen*, he thought.

When he was closer, Jimmy said quietly, "Hey, guys, give her a break. You're scaring the shit out of her."

The tallest bully turned, saying, "Mind your own fuckin' business, ole man," and shoved Jimmy.

It was a mistake.

"Son, keep your hands to yourself. I won't warn you again."

But the jerk didn't get it and started to throw a punch, shouting, "Up yours, assho—"

The bystanders found it hard to describe what happened next. One onlooker later reported, "The older man seemed to uncoil like a spring. And just like that, the big son of a bitch throwing the punch was on his knees, howling, 'You broke my wrist.' Then the next-closest thug was rolling on the ground, clutching his balls and puking. After that, the others turned tail and fled. I've never seen anything like it."

Someone called the cops, but the injured troublemakers managed to slink away before they arrived. After the police had spoken with him and the blonde, whose name was Olivia, Jimmy said, "Let's get your stuff." They collected her paraphernalia, and she took his hand as they walked to his umbrella. He continued, "Are you here alone?"

"I am now," Olivia responded. "I was on vacation with a girlfriend celebrating our graduation, but she left yesterday to prepare for college."

"Are you going also?"

"No, not yet; I don't know what I want to do."

Jimmy nodded as he spread a towel. "Take the chair. How about iced tea?"

"Yes, please. Do you think they'll come back?"

"Probably not, but you're safe with me," he answered, sitting on the towel and pouring their teas.

"Thanks. Wow, my heart's finally slowing down. You were wonderful," Olivia said, kissing him on the cheek.

"You weren't too shabby yourself."

"I was so pissed. I'd already chosen the big SOB, the one you tackled first. If any of them had laid a finger on me, I was going right for his eyes," she stated, showing Jimmy her fingernails.

"Wow, that's cruel," Jimmy chuckled. *Smart lady*.

"Do you think they would've raped me?"

"Don't know. But put it out of your mind, since it didn't happen."

They continued to talk and hit it off well. Jimmy liked her. He was wondering if he could see her again when Olivia leaned over and looked at his watch.

"Oh, I need to go," she said. "I'm heading home to New Jersey in a few hours."

"Where? I'm originally from Jersey as well."

"Demarest. It's in Bergen County."

"I've heard of it . . . never been there, though."

Olivia collected her stuff and put on her cover-up, yet seemed hesitant to leave.

Jimmy continued, "This has been great. Not the circumstances— I mean meeting you."

"I know . . . me too." She laughed and kissed him again.

"I can walk you back or give you a lift. I'm parked nearby."

"No, I'm fine—it's a block away."

"Okay, well, bye."

He watched her walk off. Olivia turned, they waved, and Jimmy felt like he'd lost someone special. He dozed for three-quarters of an hour. When he roused and focused his eyes, there was Olivia, dressed in shorts and a T-shirt, sitting on her duffel bag, watching him, and smiling.

"I want to stay with you."

Jimmy was flabbergasted. "W-what? Um . . . all right."

"That doesn't make a girl feel very welcome."

"No. I mean, absolutely—that's fantastic!"

"Much better. Are you ready to go yet?" Olivia asked. As they approached the Bronco, she continued, "I'll shower, because I just changed quickly. I didn't want to miss you, so I crammed everything in my bag and left."

When they reached the condo, Jimmy showed Olivia around and took her satchel to the guest room.

"There's the bathroom and shower." He pointed. "We'll go to lunch when you're ready."

Jimmy went to his room, pulled off his clothes, and turned on the shower. He hadn't stood under the water long when Olivia slid back the curtain and joined him. She put her arms around his neck, kissing him slowly before saying, "Love me."

In time, they moved to his bed, and Jimmy noticed that Olivia had already put her duffel alongside the dresser.

A few hours later, she announced, "I'm starving. Let's eat." They walked to a fish place the locals preferred, and after lunch they stayed all afternoon, talking and drinking espresso. Olivia never asked what he had done for a living or where he'd learned how to rout those beach bullies so easily. And Jimmy never asked how a seventeen-year-old had become so incredibly talented in bed.

On the way back to the condo, he asked, "Should you call your parents?"

Olivia grinned. "Oh, I already did . . . before I came back to the beach."

They had been together ever since, and now Olivia was rousing, drawing Jimmy away from his reminiscences as she smiled and patted the bed.

"Can't stay long," he said. "Gotta go to New Jersey this afternoon. Business."

After breakfast and Jimmy's shower, Olivia sat on the bed, watched him pack, and said, "We've never been apart except for the couple of times I visited my parents."

"I know. It's a special situation; I couldn't turn the boss down. I'll be back in less than a week." Then Jimmy went to a safe on the floor of his closet and removed two thousand dollars in twenties, a wallet with a driver's license and credit cards, and two new burner phones with chargers. He tossed Olivia the wallet, saying, "I'll be traveling as Nico Karras." As she scrutinized the wallet, Jimmy opened the phones, started charging, and continued. "We'll use these to talk."

"I never knew what you kept in there."

Jimmy joked, "It's on a need-to-know basis." Turning to her, he asked, "Are you down with this?"

"Yes. Would you like me to drive you to Norfolk?"

"No, I'll take my car. I can catch the twelve-thirty flight to Newark."

***

First thing Friday morning, the men met for breakfast at Clifton's Tick Tock diner. After their coffees arrived and their orders were placed, the underboss admitted, "Jimmy, I know you don't want to do this, but I need someone I can trust."

"Boss, you must have others."

"None with your track record. Look, I know you only get the name of the mark and the relevant details, but I'll tell you what's up this time." Then the underboss explained his long-term strategy, concluding,

"This thing has been dumped in our lap, so why not take advantage of it? But it's gotta look like an accident."

"What are you thinking?"

"A house burglary that went wrong," Massi suggested.

"Easy enough—how soon?"

"ASAP."

"I need a few days to reconnoiter."

"Sure."

"All right, give me the mark's information and get me a silenced nine-millimeter semiauto with jacketed hollow-point ammo. But this is the last time."

"Okay, here's a photo and the details," the boss said, passing Jimmy a number-ten envelope. "I'll call you before the gun's delivered."

***

Later the same morning, Petra and Jan met at the Norris house. Jan reported, "We're on schedule. You should be able to move in by the end of the month. The stonemasons are finishing up the wall and the front walk, and you can have the appliances delivered next week. We'll do a walk-through afterward, then any touch-ups. I'll have the landscaper seed the back and sod the front. We'll need to bring in a water truck for the sod, because I don't see this drought ending or the water restrictions lifting anytime soon. Finally, we'll blacktop the driveway. I hope to have the building inspector here the week of the twenty-second."

"That sounds great. After removing my stuff from storage, I'll stay here three or four times a week."

"How does Henry feel about that?"

"He could be happier but understands I need my own life."

"I kinda thought you two were a permanent item."

"Well, I hope we are, yet how it'll shake out is still a work in process," Petra joked.

"How about lunch?"

"Sure."

Later, as they chatted at the coffee shop, Petra asked, "By the way, are you all squared away with Henry on payments?"

"Yes, and it's working out better."

"How so?"

"I talked to Henry again—and threatened to bring him up on Masonic charges—and now I think he'll come through with all the money."

"Is that all it took?"

"Well, that and I texted him photos of the ring."

"I'm not certain I understood the implications of those photos at first," Petra commented. "Are you sure that was a good idea?"

"I'm having second thoughts now," Jan admitted. "Henry has a clientele who wouldn't mind busting heads. I've been thinking: Would you do me a favor? Can I text you those photos? I'd like to have them backed up."

"What about your nephew, Lucas, who works for you? Or you could put them on your laptop."

"I don't have one. I use the lodge's, and it's none of their business. The same for my nephew. I want as few people as possible to know about them."

"I'm not sure. It feels like I'm betraying Henry," Petra fretted.

"You don't have to do anything. Keep them safe until this is over."

"Oh, all right, but I want to delete them quickly."

***

Early Friday afternoon, Ronnie met his CI, Jackie, for lunch at an out-of-the-way Mexican spot, Nolvia's Restaurant, in Dover. Jackie had always provided Ronnie with valuable information. They chatted until Jackie finally asked, "So I hear you're interested in Jimmy Zee?"

"Yeah. Do you know anything?"

"Well, he's here. Arrived late Thursday evening. My boss had breakfast with him this morning."

"What name's Jimmy traveling under, and where's he staying?"

"Don't know."

"What're they up to?"

"Don't know either. But Jimmy ain't happy about the job; he's retired. The boss thinks it's important because he doesn't want to use a local. Risk a screwup."

"You must have a clue."

"All I overheard the boss say was that 'if this is handled properly, we'll be in clover.'"

"What's that mean?"

"I don't know yet."

"Is Giuseppe Pappalardo involved?"

"Maybe, but unconfirmed."

"Any mention of Henry Conklin?"

"The defense attorney? No, I haven't heard anything about him."

"Who's the contract on?"

"I don't know that either."

"You're no fuckin' help," Ronnie joked.

"Hey, I do what I can," Jackie answered.

"I know. Stay on it," Ronnie urged, handing him an envelope as they parted.

***

Later that afternoon, Jimmy Zee returned to his motel on NJ Route 10. Continuing to be careful, he wore a baseball cap pulled low and oversized sunglasses and avoided the CCTV. Jan Vanderveer's home in one of Canal Ville's lake communities was a few miles away, so Jimmy had an early dinner at a nearby diner on US 46, then set out to locate the house.

The residences were all converted summer homes that had expanded upward because of narrow lots. The property he sought was a two-story affair on the water with a living room overlooking the lake, attractive and up to date. Vanderveer's house was deep, and because of the other homes' proximities, staging a botched robbery could be problematic. Yet Jimmy had tackled more demanding assignments before.

That evening at seven thirty, while he watched from down the road, Vanderveer arrived, pulled into his driveway, and carried shopping bags inside. An hour later, he reemerged with wet, combed hair, wearing a change of clothes, and departed in his truck.

Jimmy followed discreetly as the mark made his way on NJ 53 to a tavern in Morris Plains. It turned out to be a dive with dartboards, craft beers on tap, and pepperoni bar pies. The patrons seemed like regulars, and the staff was friendly—*a comfortable place to drink.* Jimmy sat farther along the bar, out of the mark's line of sight. He didn't want to tip his hand, so once Vanderveer was settled, he returned to his SUV, scooching down in the front seat, and waited. About midnight, Jan came out, and Jimmy followed him home, watching from nearby until the lights were turned off.

On Saturday evening, he again surveilled Vanderveer, who kept to the same routine. *I'll finish scouting on Tuesday, then Wednesday will be go day.*

CHAPTER EIGHT

Sunday, August 7, 2022

After Evie and Petra had left for church on Sunday, Henry called Jan. He wanted the house to be empty in case their conversation was heated. Yet no matter what happened, Henry needed to buy some extra time.

"Jan, it's Henry."

"Counselor, I assume you're calling to arrange payment."

"Well, yes and no. I should have the money by Friday."

"The twelfth?"

"Yes."

"That's over a week past when we agreed upon."

"I know, but I'll be in Trenton Monday through Thursday. It's the best I can do."

"Jesus, Henry, will you stop fucking with me."

"I'm not. I want this over as well."

"All right, but this is it. If I don't have my money by then, I'll see Tom Johnson," Jan concluded.

Henry grinned, because he had talked to Giuseppe on Friday, who had told him to have an alibi for the following week. So after his call, Henry rang Tammy to arrange meetings with the governor and several senators. *Finally, it's coming together.*

***

Later that morning, after coffee hour, Elizabeth, Evie, and Petra chatted. "How's everything with Henry?" Elizabeth asked Petra.

"Fine; we're working out a routine. Now that my bill is up to date, I spend about three nights a week at the hotel. I'm meeting my writer there until the house is finished."

"Is that still on schedule?"

"Yes, toward the end of the month. Moreover, since I no longer need to avoid the hotel's manager, I've started using their treadmill again," Petra said.

"You should run with me sometimes," Elizabeth offered. "You too, Evie, if you'd like. One of us could pick you up."

"That would be fun. Where do you go?"

"My route is about a four-mile rectangle: running west to the end of Livingston Avenue, then turning south to Central. Next, east along Central Avenue—through town—then north on Grist Mill Road, and left on Livingston again before returning to the church and rectory. I have a variation also: continuing north along Grist Mill to the canal's abandoned towpath. It's on the left, running southwest through the woods back to Livingston. That adds three-quarters of a mile."

"Let's do it soon, because I'll be back in school. After that, I can only do it on weekends."

"We will. How's Wednesday morning this week?" Petra asked.

"Fine. Why don't you meet me at the rectory at seven o'clock?" Elizabeth concluded.

***

That afternoon, Jimmy had already decided not to surveil the house in the evening. It struck him that Sunday would be an atypical day. Instead, he meant to familiarize himself with the area and its community.

According to rules posted at the lake's entrance, boating was limited to canoes, rowboats, and small sailboats and powerboats. The houses were in all states of repair, ranging from nearly ramshackle to renovated and elaborately overbuilt. He circled, looking between the houses for glimpses of the water. Jimmy eventually spotted Vanderveer's property. It had a rowboat tied up alongside a small dock.

In the evening, he had supper at a fast-food joint before returning to his room.

Jimmy preferred to work alone. Even having the gun delivered irked him. Yet there was no way he could've flown to New Jersey carrying one, so delivery was necessary. Massi Rizzo had called during the afternoon, saying the package would be hand-delivered around eight o'clock.

Once the parcel was dropped off, Jimmy checked its contents: a Smith & Wesson compact nine-millimeter with two magazines, a silencer, and a box of hollow-point ammo. He cleaned and lubed the gun with supplies he'd already bought, then function-checked and loaded it.

Lastly, he needed to work out disposal of the goods he'd steal, so as to create the deception that the killing had resulted from an interrupted robbery. The underboss had offered a "cleaning crew," but that would be too many people in the loop, especially since there wouldn't be any need to get rid of the body. Seeing the rowboat this afternoon had given Jimmy an idea, and he intended to focus on it when he returned to his surveillance on Monday.

Jimmy fell asleep thinking, *I nearly have it all worked out.*

***

On Sunday evening at dinner, Henry told Evie and Petra he would be in Trenton from Monday through Thursday the eleventh. "Why so long, Dad?" Evie asked.

"The senators are still on recess but making time for me while they're in the capital on other business. Tammy has me scheduled for a breakfast meeting with one senator on Tuesday morning and another in the afternoon. Then the same drill on Wednesday. Finally, she booked me with the governor at nine on Thursday morning. It would be a pain in the ass to commute, but I should be home by midafternoon. Sorry."

Evie turned to Petra. "Will you stay here until Dad gets back, please?"

"Evie, don't pressure Petra. You have Mrs. Olsen."

"It's okay, Henry." Turning to Evie, Petra suggested, "How about I stay through Wednesday morning? We'll run with Elizabeth, and I'll drop you back here. I'm meeting with my writer on Wednesday afternoon, then again on Thursday, so I must be at the hotel."

"That's great," Evie said, and asked to be excused.

"You know, Evie wants us to be together all the time," Henry remarked.

"I know."

***

Elizabeth, Church, Ronnie, and Tom met at Saint Andrew's Monday morning. Ronnie began. "I had lunch with my CI Friday. He confirms that Jimmy Zee is here and met with the DeCavalcantes' underboss Friday morning. He doesn't know Jimmy's fake identity or where he's staying."

"Does he know how the hit's going down?" Elizabeth asked.

"No, because the underboss is handling it."

"Isn't it unusual for him to be directly involved?" Church said.

"Yes, they're keeping a tight lid on this. But whomever the hit's on," Ronnie opined, "he must be removed for the underboss's plan to work."

"We don't have enough to interrogate Henry yet," Tom began. "But it's no coincidence that he has dinner with Giuseppe and almost immediately Rizzo reaches out to Jimmy Zee, who gets here lickety-split. And everything is hush-hush. I'm comfortable hypothesizing that it's about Henry's senate confirmation. So what's our strategy?"

"I think a deep dive into Henry's background is at the top of the list," Church said.

"The attorney general's office must've done one before the governor made his announcement; any chance we could have a copy of that file?" Elizabeth wondered.

"We're on the same page," Ronnie responded. "But I don't think they'll disclose it without an official request, and if we do that, I'm fearful the AG would talk to the governor, and Henry Conklin would find out immediately. So I have an idea. There's this guy, Frosty Wicks; we go way back. He was an FBI agent in the Newark field office for over twenty years. Since then, he has been a detective in the New Jersey attorney general's office. Frosty's due to retire shortly, so now they have him twiddling his thumbs—he's bored. I'll give him a call."

"Frosty?" Elizabeth quipped.

Ronnie laughed. "No one knows why. We assumed it was because he had ice water in his veins. I'll talk to him and see where it goes; afterward, Church and I can follow up. Elizabeth, would you talk to Petra and see what you can learn? You two seem to get along well."

"Remember, I can't mislead Petra or cajole her into revealing things without telling her I'm working with the police. And if we're alone and she talks to me as a priest, it's privileged—confidential."

"Sorry, I wasn't considering your constraints," Ronnie replied.

"I know that she's stressed over her relationship with Henry. I could offer to counsel her and ask if she wants it to be off the record. That's the best I can do."

"All right," Tom concluded, "let's do that and meet as soon as we have further information."

***

It had been nearly a hundred degrees yesterday, but today, Wednesday, August 10, was more comfortable, particularly in the shade by the river. It was a little before noon, and Karl and Klaus were about to leave Riverside Park when a stranger, wearing a baseball cap, sunglasses, and carrying a bag from Luigi's Italian Deli, entered. He sat on the first bench along the river, nodding to the men as he unpacked his lunch: a sweet-soppressata, sharp-provolone, and caponata sub with a Dr. Pepper. Karl and Klaus acknowledged the nod. "I wonder who he is," Klaus speculated quietly. "I haven't seen him around."

"Me neither."

"We should be polite," Klaus prompted as they were leaving. "'Mornin'. Are you new in Canal Ville?"

"No, passing through on the way to Pennsylvania." *Might as well spread a little disinformation*, Jimmy thought, chuckling silently.

"Well, the Water Gap's less than an hour from here on I-80 West," Karl offered. "I see you already found our best deli."

"Yeah, great menu," Jimmy replied.

"If you have time before you leave, try Canal Ville Soft Ice Cream. It's next door to Luigi's and is always rated by the *Daily Record* as one of the state's top-three ice cream parlors," Klaus added.

"Sounds great, thanks," Jimmy responded as the men walked by.

***

Jimmy relaxed, ate his sandwich, and reviewed logistics. His surveillance was complete now. Each evening Vanderveer would leave his house between seven and seven thirty and return between midnight and one in the morning. So on Monday night, Jimmy had followed his mark to the dive, and after dark he'd gone back to Vanderveer's house, picked the side door's lock, and investigated both floors. On Tuesday night, Jimmy had returned and canvassed the grounds, which sloped down to the dock and the rowboat. He noticed that along the northern border, separating the houses, was a six-foot shadow fence. He sketched the property, then

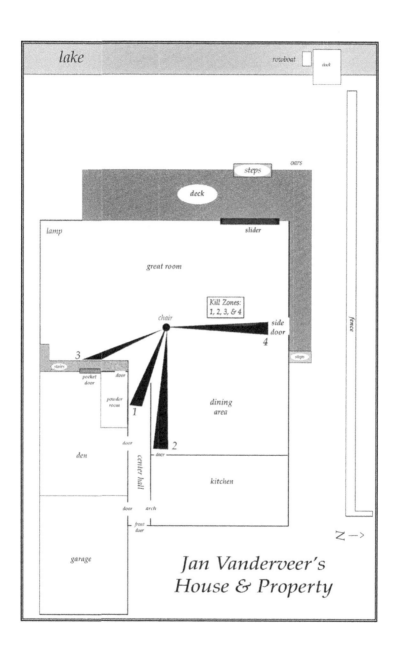

Jan Vanderveer's
House & Property

entered the house, adding the first floor's layout and four kill zones

Finally, this morning, Jimmy had stopped at a hardware store on Route 46, picking up the last thing he needed: heavy-duty wire cutters.

Now that tonight's plan was set, Jimmy continued relaxing on the bench, thinking of Olivia. After a while, he firmed up tomorrow's getaway. Before sunrise, he'd leave Vanderveer's house, stop at the Tick Tock for breakfast with the underboss, hand off the mark's phone, and collect the balance of his fee. Then he'd head to Newark Airport, drop off his rented SUV, and be on the 12:45 p.m. flight to Norfolk.

He walked back along Central Avenue, stopping for soft ice cream, before returning to the motel for a nap. It would be a long night.

***

At about the same time, Church, who'd been busy around the house all morning, rang Elizabeth. "I'm fixing lunch. Do you have time for a break?"

"Sure. I'm finished with the rough draft of my sermon. I want to talk to you about something too," Elizabeth replied before getting up from her desk and addressing Amy. "I'm off to the rectory for lunch. Won't be long."

"Okay, I brought a sandwich. Take your time."

Elizabeth left her office and walked across the parking lot to the rectory. Jacques greeted her as she entered the kitchen, then returned to his position beside Billy's playpen. Elizabeth rustled Billy's hair. "How's my little man?" she asked, picking him up for the hug he was reaching out for. Church was finishing preparing a lettuce and cold-vegetable salad and had set the table with French bread, cheese, and iced tea. "It looks nice," Elizabeth observed, nodding toward the table before returning Billy to his Legos.

While they were eating, Elizabeth began. "You know I ran early with Petra and Evie this morning. We decided to go out before the temperature reached eighty."

"Yes, how was it?"

"They're in better shape than I expected. We finished the entire run, albeit slower than I would have done alone. When we returned, Petra took me aside. She asked to talk again, so I invited her over after dinner. We could have coffee and cake. Then you could put Billy to bed and take Jacques for a long walk. Is that okay with you?"

"Yes, that's an excellent idea; you won't have to invent an excuse to talk with her."

"If we're lucky, maybe she won't mind if you're here. That would solve any questions about my confidentiality dilemma."

Petra arrived a bit past eight. The women sat in the living room chatting, and Church brought coffee and cake from the kitchen. In a few minutes, he said, "If you'll excuse me, I'll put Billy to bed, then take Jacques for a walk."

"You don't have to leave; I'd like a man's opinion," Petra said.

"All right, let me get Billy settled, then I'll be back."

When he returned, Petra started. "I need to talk about Henry and me. It's complicated, although I'm not worried about our love life—that's fine. It's other things that are straining our relationship."

"Such as?" Elizabeth asked.

"Well, it's perplexing. Henry has been looking for a permanent commitment from me, and I was also nearly there. But now it seems like he's having second thoughts. I think it's because of his appointment to the court. He's become overly concerned about my book. He wasn't like that at first; he appeared to relish my former risqué lifestyle. But now Henry's becoming increasingly controlling, pushing me to drop the book project, even though he knows how important it is to me. I don't know what to do," Petra concluded, looking at Church.

"It's never been a well-kept secret that men prefer their women to act like ladies during the day but prostitutes at night. It's a sentiment that men wouldn't express publicly today, but it's probably as true now as ever."

"Well, that certainly smacks of sexism," Elizabeth retorted sharply.

"I'm giving Petra a straight answer."

"I understand that feeling," Petra replied. "But I came up with what I thought was a solution." She described her idea of having Henry write the introduction. "But he can't accept that it isn't about him. I think he's afraid I'll be seen as a bad reflection on his judgment."

Putting aside her irritation at Church's comment, Elizabeth probed, "Even if all that's true, don't you think he's blowing it out of proportion? Could there be something else bothering him?"

"Possibly. Henry is embarrassed about his ancestor winning Evie Norris in a card game. And now that his dad's DNA is back, it's easy enough to infer that the probable murderer was Hank Conklin."

Church followed Elizabeth's tack. "Even a combination of those items would seem unlikely to interfere with a person of Henry's standing and track record. After all, none of it is his fault. I'm surprised he can't dismiss it as *shit happens*, albeit unlucky shit."

"You may be right, yet there's something else," Petra said, speaking to both of them. "Henry helped with my finances. He referred me to an attorney, Murray Kriegman, who renegotiated the remainder of my contract with Jan Vanderveer. Henry called the shots from the background. He had Jan by the balls because the builder badly needed the money." Then Petra reviewed the new deal. "I wasn't altogether happy with Henry's tactics. The men have been scrapping about it ever since. Although Jan recently told me that Henry had reconsidered his position but asked for a little time to pay the fifty grand."

"Why did Henry change his mind?" Church asked.

"I don't know," Petra answered, sidestepping Jan's blackmail.

"Most of this is out of your hands, so put it aside. You can focus on your book—do that," Elizabeth advised.

"Yes, but now I must choose between Henry and the book."

"That might be true. Yet I wouldn't give up on having Henry write the introduction. It sounds like a practical compromise. Remember, a compromise is what everyone can live with, but they don't necessarily have to be happy about it," Church quipped.

***

Later, in bed, Elizabeth asked Church, "Does Henry's concern make sense to you?"

"No."

"Do you think Petra knows what else is bothering him?"

"I don't know, but I'm convinced she was holding something back."

"If Ronnie's right and Jimmy Zee is here on Henry's behalf, we shouldn't minimize the squabble with Jan."

"Agreed, because people have killed for less than fifty K. And Henry might be stalling, waiting for the hit. Let's see what Ronnie turns up through Frosty," Church said. Jacques groaned from his braided rug at the foot of the bed. "We're keeping him awake."

Nuzzling closer, chuckling, Elizabeth whispered, "Well, we'll just need to be quiet, then."

CHAPTER NINE

Wednesday, August 10, 2022

Jimmy was chockablock full from lunch. He skipped supper and continued chilling. Eventually, he packed his bags, policed the room, and put his key and a fifty-dollar tip on the bed. Then he drove to the dive, parked, and slouched, watching.

The mark arrived a little after sundown. Jimmy waited until he was sure the target was settled before driving to Vanderveer's, where he parked down the street. He paused again, then checked his watch—nine o'clock. *Go time.* Jimmy donned disposable shoe covers and latex gloves, took his kit bag, and went to the side door. *No lock picking tonight; it has to look like a crude break-in.* He listened before folding a hand towel to fit the door's lower left pane. Next, holding the towel against the glass, he thwacked it with his right elbow. The shattered glass tinkled to the floor. Jimmy reached in for the doorknob and was inside in seconds.

The house's layout was like that of many lake properties. The front door opened into a center hall. On the left were the garage and den doors before the hall ended in a great room. Off the hall's right side was an arch to the kitchen, and from there was another arch into a dining area that opened onto the great room. Vanderveer had left a small lighted table lamp in the great room's southwest corner. The house's side door was in the north wall, and the west wall facing the lake was nearly all glass, with a slider to the wraparound deck. Along the room's east wall, stairs to the second floor climbed over a pocket door, the den's second point of entry, and another door to a powder room. Upstairs were two large bedrooms, each with a bath.

Jimmy took his bag, removed the nine-millimeter semiautomatic, attached the silencer, slipped in a loaded magazine, and racked the slide. He slid the gun underneath his waistband before taking out a flashlight and the wire cutters. Then he walked the ground floor, closing the curtains to a kitchen window that faced the street. Next, Jimmy went upstairs to the main bedroom. He opened several dresser drawers, ruffling clothes to leave the impression that they'd been searched. Afterward, he took a small box holding costume jewelry: tie bars, tacks, cuff links, and such. But it also contained a gold pocket watch and chain, which Jimmy put in his jeans before scattering the box's remaining contents across the dresser. Then he moved to a smart TV: unplugged it, cut the cable feed, tucked it under his arm, and went downstairs, placing it by the side door. Afterward, Jimmy followed the same procedure for a big-screen TV in the great room. Then he went to the den, cutting the power cord and removing a laptop he'd noticed during his earlier walk-through. He stacked all three items together.

Following that, he brought his bag to the chair alongside the table with the lit lamp and withdrew a 2.6-gallon garbage bag, putting the watch and chain inside before replacing the trash bag. Then Jimmy took out his Kindle and began reading.

About a half hour later, he stopped and went outside to reconnoiter. The lights were out in the house next door. *Good.* The oars he'd seen the day before were still around the corner, leaning against the deck. He took them to the rowboat and surveyed the lake.

The weather was as predicted: clear to partly cloudy, with a slight breeze and nearly a full moon. *Plenty of light.* Everything else looked in order.

When he returned to the house, Jimmy realized he was hungry. He looked through the kitchen, settling for a bowl of Grape-Nuts, a sliced banana, and milk. When Jimmy finished, he washed and dried everything, putting it away precisely as he had found before disposing of the banana's peal in his trash bag. He looked at his watch once again—eleven thirty. *Time to get into place in case the mark comes home early.*

Jimmy positioned a chair at the intersection of the kill zones, facing the center hall, then sat with his semiauto, waiting.

At about twelve fifteen, he heard Vanderveer's pickup pull into the driveway. Jimmy regulated his breathing. The mark unlocked the front door, put his keys on a sofa table in the hall, and nearly made it to the great room via kill zone number one before he spotted Jimmy. "What the fuc—!" the man began, but his speech was truncated by two *pop, pop*s before collapsing backward. Jimmy felt for the victim's pulse at both his neck and wrist—nada. His shots had been accurate: the first near the heart and the second in the middle of the forehead.

Jimmy picked up his brass and stole the man's phone, wristwatch, Masonic ring, and wallet. Then he pocketed the cash and dropped everything except the phone into the trash bag.

It was nearly twelve forty-five, so Jimmy read until three thirty. He had decided to stay there instead of driving around or hanging in a parking lot before meeting the underboss.

At length, he checked the alley outside the side door. All was quiet, so he made two trips with the TVs, laptop, and trash bag, loading them into the rowboat. Jimmy rowed toward the center of the lake and dropped everything overboard. He was back at the dock by four forty-five and replaced the oars where he'd found them. Then he policed the grounds and house.

Later, at about five, Jimmy walked to the dock and tossed the gun, silencer, and magazines into the lake. He was in his SUV a half hour before sunrise and drove away from Canal Ville.

That afternoon, after landing at Norfolk and collecting his car, Jimmy called Olivia, using the burner.

"Hi."

"Hi yourself," he responded. "I'm leaving long-term parking now."

"How was your trip?"

"All right. We'll discard these burners after I'm home."

"Okay. Do you want to eat out tonight, or should I cook?"

"I've been eating at diners, fast-food joints, and coffee shops since I left. Do you mind cooking?"

"No, I'll run to the store now. Anything you'd like?"

"Surprise me."

"Okay, love you."

"Me too."

CHAPTER TEN

Thursday, August 11, 2022

At seven in the morning, Lucas Groot had parked in front of Jan Vanderveer's house, where he was now unobtrusively tooting his horn. He was Jan's sister's boy and had worked for Unk since graduation. Yesterday, the men had decided Lucas would pick Jan up today, have breakfast, then head to the job site on Grist Mill Road.

He surfed his phone for a few minutes while waiting. It was unusual for his uncle not to be out the door immediately, so he tooted louder. When Unk still didn't appear, Lucas walked to the house, rang the bell, and paused before trying the door. It was unlocked, so he entered and was about to call out when he spied his uncle's body lying faceup in the hall.

Rushing over and kneeling, he noticed the bullet wounds. Even though he realized it was futile, Lucas checked for a pulse, then called 911. The Canal Ville police dispatcher summoned an ambulance, routed a patrol car to the scene, requested the medical examiner and crime scene unit, and notified Tom Johnson, who was finishing breakfast at home.

Driving to the murder scene, Tom rang Church, who was feeding Billy. As Elizabeth came in, Church ended the call. "All right, I'll be over."

"What's up?"

"Jan Vanderveer has been killed in his house. Tom wants me to meet him there."

"Oh, that's awful. Does he think it has anything to do with what Ronnie has been speculating about?"

"He didn't say. I don't think we can rule it out, though."

"All right, I'll take care of Billy. You'd better go."

On the way to the lake, Church notified Ronnie. "I have a doctor's appointment this morning, but I'll ring my CI and see if he knows anything—catch you later."

When Church arrived, he located the chief. "The CSU is here, and the medical examiner tentatively puts the time of death between eleven last night and three this morning. I have officers canvassing the neighbors on either side to establish if they heard or saw anything. At first glance, it looks like a robbery gone bad."

"It sounds like you're not convinced," Church commented.

"Ronnie's hunch about a hit man in the area bothers me. Here's where we're at: we've concluded that two smart TVs, a laptop, and Jan's wallet, wristwatch, phone, and a Masonic ring he wore are missing. Lucas's checking the house to see if anything else disappeared."

"How's he doing?"

"He was shaken, finding his uncle's body that way, but he'll be all right. Let's go over the crime scene together."

Later, after they'd finished in the house and walked the grounds, Church said, "I have a few thoughts. The broken glass makes it look like an unsophisticated entry, but it might be camouflage."

"Agreed," said Tom. "The CSU has already checked the locks, which don't appear to have been tampered with. But they'll do further analysis at the lab. There're no other signs of forced entry."

"Okay. But the pattern of the entry wounds looks professional," Church continued. "They weren't haphazard, as you would expect if an amateur were surprised. The medical examiner should analyze the entry angles to calculate the shooter's location."

"They look like nine-millimeter. No exit wounds, so they're most likely hollow-points. That might mess up further analysis."

"Possibly. That's all I noticed." Then Church added, "Ronnie's at the doctor this morning; he'll come by later."

"That's fine. I'll be here all day," Tom replied.

Lucas returned downstairs and, after Church extended condolences, reported, "Everything looks okay apart from Unk's grandfather's gold pocket watch and chain that he kept in his jewelry box. They're gone now."

"Do you know how old his laptop was?" Tom asked.

"It was the lodge's—old and beat up."

"So, why did the thief take it? It couldn't have had much value," Church observed.

"Not much. Unk always pissed and moaned about it."

"Okay, thanks," Tom said. Addressing Church, he added, "If you're around later this afternoon, let's meet with Ronnie at Saint Andrew's and review what we know."

"Okay, I'll see you then," Church replied as he headed to Elizabeth's office.

"How's Lucas?" she asked when Church arrived. "He must be upset."

"It's hard, but he's getting by. Even though it's still early, Ronnie, Tom, and I are meeting here later to compare notes. I'm keeping an open mind, but here're a few observations:

"The unsub entered the premises by breaking a glass pane in the side door at about nine p.m. A neighbor canvassed by the police stated that she'd heard a tinkling sound like breaking glass or wind chimes at that time. She remembers because *Hannity* had just come on the TV. Before I left, I checked Jan's and her property—no wind chimes.

"Then the medical examiner's initial finding is that the time of death was eleven p.m. or later. The house wasn't thoroughly turned over. Not much was taken, and it didn't seem to be of great value. So what was the unsub doing for at least two hours? I think he was waiting for Jan.

"And finally, the pattern of the kill shots was professional," Church concluded.

"Do you think it was Jimmy Zee?"

"That's my guess."

"Then he's already long gone?"

***

The same morning, after he met with the governor, Henry left Trenton. Tammy had sat in for the first part, reporting on Henry's conferences with the senators. Then they had gone over the timing for submitting Henry's nomination. The governor commented, "Well, everything's on schedule. Both of you have done a great job. I'm particularly pleased with the positive reactions from the senators thus far. Keep up the first-rate work." He paused, then said, "Tammy, would you give Henry and me a few minutes alone?" After she left, the governor continued, "I didn't want to mention this while Tammy was here, but I've had a few troubling calls from important senators with whom you haven't met yet."

"Is the Evie Norris story worrying them?"

"Remarkably, they don't seem concerned about the gambling aspect. They'd like to dismiss the whole thing, but they're still hung up on Zeke Norris's murder."

"How so?"

"We've never talked about it, but now that Zeke has been identified, isn't Hank the likely murderer? They're asking the same question."

"They can't honestly think I'm accountable for that."

"They say all the right things, telling me how open-minded they are, assuring me they're okay with it. However, they're becoming reluctant because of how it might play in the media."

"Are you thinking of pulling my appointment?"

"Not yet, but unless the crime is solved, exonerating Hank, you'll have to win them over. Those senators are concerned about the election and don't want to give the Republicans any additional ammo."

"Will you share with me who's hesitant?"

"I'd rather not. I don't want you to be defensive in your upcoming meetings."

Henry cogitated as he drove. *That son of a bitch is preparing to cut me loose. He isn't willing to invest more of his political capital. If I pull this off, he'll still be on board. But the first time I muck up, he'll tell me to withdraw!*

Before Henry could continue grumbling, his phone rang, and it was the worshipful master.

"Henry, Jan Vanderveer was murdered in his house this morning."

"My Lord, how'd you find out?"

"Tom Johnson called me from the crime scene."

"Why? Does he need something?"

"It looks like a bungled burglary. He thinks a laptop was taken and asked if it could be ours."

"Maybe; Jan used ours personally—he carried it back and forth. Did you tell the chief?"

"Yes . . . I need a favor. Would you take over as secretary until I can have a replacement appointed at September tenth's regular communication?"

"Jesus, I'm up to my ass in alligators between this pending supreme court appointment and arranging for Doc Piscator's replacement counsel. I want to pass."

"Look, Jan was up to date. We signed the checks for the end of July already. His minutes and grand lodge reports are current. And everything is backed up on a thumb drive in the office safe. Go to Best Buy or Staples and purchase a new laptop with a Microsoft Office Suite. Then I'll have the grand lodge download their software and issue you a password. I don't think we'll lose anything. You've done the job before and know what's involved. You'll need to prepare vouchers for a dozen checks, read the last communication's minutes, then take September's."

"Oh, all right. I'll do it, but only until then. Will you be calling Jan's family?"

"Yes. He doesn't have many relatives, though: his sister, her husband, and his nephew."

"We might need to prepare for some kind of service."

"I'll talk to his sister about that. Afterward. I'll email the brethren."

When they hung up, Henry continued pondering his situation. *The good news is that Jan Vanderveer's threat has been removed, yet difficulties remain. This Masonic bullshit will be a pain in the ass. Not to mention that Petra's book is still a friggin' sideshow!*

***

Later that afternoon, Tom, Ronnie, and Church met. Tom briefed them, concluding with. "The only thing new this afternoon was that a wider canvass of the neighbors turned up nothing else."

"Didn't anybody spot a strange vehicle parked nearby?" Ronnie asked.

"No."

"I can add one thing I noticed when I was leaving," Church said, reporting his observation about the wind chimes.

"So, we'll assume it was breaking glass—at the time of entry, about nine p.m."

"Yes." Then Church continued with the thoughts he'd shared with Elizabeth.

"I spoke with my snitch," Ronnie reported, when Church was finished, "and he has nothing to add other than that early this morning, the underboss had breakfast at the diner again; he doesn't know with whom. So are we on the same page that the robbery was a put-up job to cover the hit?"

Tom and Church nodded.

Ronnie continued, "Frosty called. He's obtained the AG's vetting of Henry Conklin and is sending it to Tom: nothing exciting. But here's what's noteworthy. Frosty has foreknowledge of Conklin. So Church, how would you feel about accompanying us to Stone Harbor tomorrow? We'll have lunch with Grant Allen. He's a retired chief of the Kearny PD."

"That's a hike."

"Yeah—about a hundred and fifty miles. It's a small seaside resort on Seven Mile Island south of Avalon. Frosty says it's complicated, but it won't be a waste of our time talking to the chief. We'll pick you up at seven."

***

On Friday morning, August 12, Ronnie drove to pick up Frosty and Church. After they were underway, Ronnie said, "I know you want us to hear it from the horse's mouth, but how about some background?"

"Okay," Frosty began. "We're meeting to discuss the March 16, 1998, disappearance of Roberta Allen. Her father, Grant, was the chief of police in Kearny. He and his wife had two children: Ewan, seventeen, a senior in high school, and Roberta, fifteen, a sophomore. After graduation, Ewan planned on a career in the Marines, while Roberta intended to study a business curriculum with no definite thought of what she might do afterward. She was charming and attractive, albeit shy and naive. Roberta's best girlfriend and alter ego, Carly Fraser, was an appealing and vivacious junior. But she was also a sexually active party girl. Carly carried out her shenanigans behind her parents' backs under the guise of studying at the library, babysitting, visiting girlfriends, and such. Eventually, she foisted her antics upon Roberta, convincing her friend that life was passing her by. So, intermittently, Roberta began hanging around with Carly, but she always made it home before her father's curfew. That changed after Roberta fell in love with Henry Conklin, who was at that time a first-year New York University School of Law student. Grant was suspicious that Conklin was involved in Roberta's disappearance, so when his department's investigation ran into a dead end, he asked if the FBI could help. I had met him on a case several years before, so I consulted with them, but nothing new turned up. I'll let Chief Allen tell you the rest," Frosty concluded.

As they made their way through Stone Harbor, Ronnie observed, "This is a high-rent district. How could a retired cop afford it?"

"He bought a small place years ago before shore properties skyrocketed, and I recall Grant's wife had a few bucks," Frosty answered.

They arrived and went to Nemo's Pizza and Restaurant on Third Avenue, where the retired chief was seated at a corner table facing the door.

"It's been a long time," Grant said, rising and shaking hands with Frosty, who introduced his colleagues. They sat, perused the menu, and ordered. While they waited, Frosty began.

"As I mentioned on the phone, Canal Ville's PD and the Morris County Prosecutor's Office are looking at Henry Conklin as a person of interest in an apparent contract killing. You have a history with him, so they're all ears."

"Did you fill them in?" the chief inquired.

"Just the basics."

"When Roberta disappeared," Allen stated, "my department investigated. An old-timer, Detective Sergeant Declan 'Dex' Murphy, caught the case. And as you can imagine, I monitored it closely."

"Is he still around, and if so, could we talk to him?" Church inquired.

"No, he passed. After the case went cold, we reviewed the file twice: once by Dex in 2006, then again by another of my men in 2012. That was just before my retirement—nada both times. I resigned myself to never knowing what happened to Roberta. But, Frosty, when you called, it reawakened hope. I'm seventy-five now, and there isn't much time left for closure.

"Here's a rundown of what happened: Roberta was a good kid, never gave us trouble, and did well in school. But things began changing during the fall of her second year in high school. That's when she started palling around with Carly Fraser. We discovered during our investigation what Carly was like: dating older boys with cars, staying out until the wee hours, and drinking."

Church interrupted. "Drugs?"

"I don't think so," Grant replied. "The situation deteriorated. Roberta wanted a cell phone and an email account on the PC that we'd just bought. We never agreed and squabbled continually. Then by Christmastime, unbeknownst to us, Roberta began accompanying Carly on some of her Friday and Saturday night jaunts. Before that, we'd never had a reason to distrust Roberta—her pretexts for being out seemed feasible, and she was home on time. Everything heated up after New Year's 1998, when she became serious with a boy. When he picked Roberta up, he never came in. Then Roberta started staying out later and later and frequently came home smelling of booze. My wife and I asked to meet her boyfriend and constantly quarreled with her. One Friday evening she was running late, so I went outside where he was waiting in his car and invited him in. That's when I met Henry Conklin. He was handsome, pleasant, and at ease with adults. Henry seemed okay, except he was at least seven years older than Roberta. That was a huge difference for a girl her age. The whole time I talked with him, I pictured what they were doing, which wasn't legal. When Roberta came down, she was mortified and dragged Henry out as quick as a wink. I waited up, and we had a donnybrook when she came home drunk. Afterward, I grounded her and forbade her to see him again."

"How'd that work out?" Ronnie asked.

"I think you know the answer. Roberta doubled down on seeing him, we fought constantly, and her poor mother tried to keep the peace. Finally, in early March, it blew up before spring break. She wanted to go to Florida with Henry. I said no, and she stormed out. Roberta was impossible to live with afterward. Then one Monday afternoon, she didn't come home from school. In time, we checked her room and discovered that Roberta hadn't packed a bag. It made no sense. We haven't seen or heard from her since."

"So how long was it from your 'donnybrook' until Roberta went missing?" Frosty asked.

"A couple of weeks. Conklin had an ironclad alibi: spring break with his roommate, confirmed by a Fort Lauderdale motel where they stayed. Nothing else ever developed. Here's a copy of Kearny PD's file. My son Ewan, who is the chief now, copied it. After Roberta went missing, he joined the force instead of the Marines. I guess he thought he could do better than his ole man." Grant laughed self-deprecatingly. "I've also included Dex's original notebook. Maybe fresh eyes can locate something in his notes. I'd be grateful if you guys turn up anything new."

Returning to Canal Ville, Church considered Roberta's relationship with her parents. "She seems like a typical middle adolescent, dealing with establishing her identity, privacy, and being treated like an adult. The phone and email issues are the tip-offs. But in any case, Carly begins leading her down the wrong path, then Conklin shows up." Frosty and Ronnie nodded in agreement before Ronnie called Tom.

"How was your meeting?" Tom answered.

"Fine. We have a copy of Kearny PD's file, and the original notebooks from the investigating officer and Frosty. Church and Elizabeth will review everything this weekend, and I'll contact all my confidential informants again. Let's get together on Monday afternoon. How's your schedule?"

"Three o'clock looks fine. Frosty, are you coming?"

"No, Monday's NG, but I'll be available on the phone if necessary."

"All right, see you at the church," Tom concluded.

***

On the afternoon of August 15, Elizabeth, Church, and Ronnie met with Tom. Church began, "Elizabeth and I spent time with Kearny's file and the notebooks. A lot is routine, as you'd expect. Here are the meaningful points:

"An Amber Alert was issued, and Roberta's disappearance was reported to the National Center for Missing and Exploited Children along with photos, fingerprints, and DNA for their databases. Since there was no crime scene, there wasn't any forensics other than what was sent to the NCMEC. To date, this hasn't turned up anything. Her parents and the police searched Roberta's room. She didn't take a bag; nothing else of interest was noted. There were no recent withdrawals from her small savings account either, and Roberta didn't have a phone, credit card, or email address. This happened before social media came into play. Interviews were conducted, and the statements from the Allen family conformed with what we learned from Frosty and Grant.

"Next, Henry Conklin was interrogated. He seemed to be upset about Roberta's disappearance and confirmed their dating. But because her father was determined to keep them apart, Conklin said he'd broken up with her before spring break, claiming that Roberta had taken it hard. Then he drove to Florida with his roommate, Thomas Bellotti. They left around noon on Friday, March thirteenth, and arrived the evening of the fourteenth, staying ten days. Henry hooked up with another girl, Hannah Finch, a sophomore at Princeton. She came from a wealthy Cape May family and later became his wife. Hannah was never interviewed."

Elizabeth interjected, "Hannah used to come to church with Evie but died from cancer several years ago."

Following that, Church continued, "They talked with Thomas Bellotti. As an aside, he's the son of Enzo Bellotti, the present *capo bastone*—underboss—of the Genovese crime family."

"It seems like Conklin has an affinity for villains," Ronnie interrupted.

"Could be." Church chuckled, adding, "Bellotti's account of their trip to Florida agrees, and Dex verified their stay at a Fort Lauderdale motel. They seemed to have been good friends and roomed together at Princeton before attending law school, where they shared an apartment in Greenwich Village."

"So you agree that Conklin's alibi is solid," Tom observed.

"Yes," Church responded. "After that, Dex interviewed students and teachers. Elizabeth will have more on this. Then I looked at the two file reviews Kearny PD did. Here are the highlights:

"Dex ran criminal background checks on Conklin and Bellotti in 2006, which turned up nothing. Then he met with Conklin again. After graduation, Conklin clerked for a judge in the federal district court for New Jersey, then joined a prominent Morristown firm before beginning his practice. Henry was polite but couldn't add anything to his previous statement. He said that in the future, the police should contact his attorney. Dex also interrogated Bellotti, who had gone to work for his father, representing the gangster's legitimate enterprises. Bellotti couldn't contribute anything further and referred future questions to his attorney. Carly Fraser was backpacking in Europe with a girlfriend. Dex left his card with her parents, asking that they have Carly contact him, but Dex didn't hear from her before he retired. Amara Marino, Roberta's gym teacher (more later), had left teaching shortly after Roberta's disappearance, and Dex couldn't locate her.

"In 2012, one of Grant's detectives worked the case again. Criminal background checks were run once more—nada. The investigator tried to interrogate Conklin, but, through his attorney, Conklin refused. Next, according to Enzo Bellotti's lawyer, father and son had become estranged. The younger Bellotti had left the area, and additional information was refused. Carly Fraser was questioned by phone but was evasive about her career. Notwithstanding that, the detective suspected that Carly was the kept woman of an older wealthy man. No new information was forthcoming from her, and Marino still couldn't be located."

After Church wrapped up, Elizabeth picked up the conversation. "I spent time on the itemized entries in Dex's notebook about his interviews with Roberta's friends and teachers. The final report didn't include those details, merely stating that the reasons for her upset varied. I discovered two items worth mentioning. The first was that the schoolkids all reported that Roberta had been acting out of sorts for a few weeks before disappearing. She complained about being pissed at Henry for not including her in his spring break plans, mad at her father for grounding her, disturbed over her father trying to break them up, and interestingly—but just to Carly—apprehensive over telling her parents that they planned to be married. The second involved the teachers' reports. They'd witnessed the same things the schoolkids had, except none of them brought up any mention of marriage. But then something new cropped up. Amara Marino told Dex she'd found Roberta crying in the locker room and offered help. Dex picked up on this, jotting an underlined reminder in his notebook. I want to follow up with Carly and Amara if we can locate them."

"Let's call Frosty and see if he can remember what he supposed Dex meant," Tom said.

After Frosty answered, he thought for a moment. "I checked with him. He didn't remember why he'd jotted down Marino's *help* comment, but I didn't think much about it then. Subsequently, I was told by my field office to stand down and catch a new case. Huh . . . I hope I didn't drop the ball."

"It's probably nothing," Elizabeth suggested, "but if you could track Carly and Amara Marino down, I'll follow up."

"Will do," Frosty answered, finishing the call.

Later, Church remarked to Elizabeth, "You don't think it's nothing, do you?"

"You're right. I think Frosty assumed that the teacher intended a referral to a therapist. But considering Carly's remark about marriage, I have a hunch that Roberta was pregnant. Amara may have meant a doctor or an abortion clinic instead of a mental health professional."

Church paused. "If so, why didn't Roberta get an abortion? *Roe versus Wade* had been in effect for many years."

"Maybe Roberta said no."

"Well, it sounds like a motive to me," Church said.

CHAPTER ELEVEN

Monday, August 15, 2022

At suppertime, the conversation among Petra, Evie, and Henry was about Jan's death. Notwithstanding Henry and Jan's quarrel over money, Henry seemed upset, as was Petra. Additionally, she was concerned about how it would affect the completion of her house.

Evie was bummed too, and Petra had an idea of what might make her happy. So as Evie cleared the table, Petra asked, "When does school start this fall?"

"On September first. Why?"

"Well, I thought we should go clothes shopping for you."

"That would be fun! Can we, Dad . . . please?"

"Sure! Do you think a hundred dollars will cover it?"

"You're being a jerk again," Evie chided with fake frustration as she scooted upstairs to make a list.

Henry laughed and said, "That was a hit. I lost track of time between work and my confirmation—nice save. Do some birthday shopping for her also. I'll give you my credit card."

"You've been distracted lately and probably didn't notice how Evie has been outgrowing her clothes. Are you okay, by the way?"

"Yeah, it's all the bullshit about orchestrating my confirmation. Let's not talk about it. How's your book progressing?"

"Well, I met with my writer several times while you were in Trenton. We've developed an outline about what to include and to whom we'll talk. Next, he'll start recording our sessions."

"How about your advance?"

"I should have a check next week."

"Fifty K?"

"Yes," Petra said. "But thinking about money, do you know how Jan's death will impact finishing my house? They haven't been working since the tenth, although I guess that's to be expected."

"I don't know. Jesus, I hope Jan had a will. Otherwise, everything will be screwed up. His attorney is Toby Jarndyce here in Canal Ville. You might give him a call."

"Jan told me his nephew signs checks on the business account, so I was thinking of calling Lucas."

"It makes sense. And don't forget, I'm still obligated for the final payment once the certificate of occupancy is issued. So if Lucas runs short of working capital, I can make a prepayment. That will cover you."

"Thanks. That means a lot to me."

***

Later, in bed, Petra was more loving than she had been. And now she was sleeping gently with her arm across Henry's chest and her head on his shoulder.

As Henry dozed, his mind wandered. *Petra's not backing down on her book. She's just as fuckin' muleheaded as Roberta was.* Suddenly, Henry wasn't drifting any longer. *Shit! I'm dredging up long-ago ire, wrath I thought I'd purged.* Maddening memories persisted until Henry finally fell into a restless sleep.

Hours later, Petra roused him softly, whispering in his ear. "Are you all right? You've been tossing, turning, and talking."

Groggily, Henry managed, "I'm fine . . . It must've been an anxiety dream."

"Don't worry; it'll be all right in the morning. By the way, who's Roberta?"

***

Wednesday morning, Frosty called Elizabeth. "Hi. I have the information you need on Carly Fraser and Amara Marino."

"That was fast."

"It turned out to be easier than I imagined. I was able to put together some background info for you as well. I Googled Carly. Her wedding announcement popped, and she's now Carly Johansen, living nearby in Mountain Lakes with her husband, a surgeon, and their two kids. Carly's a soccer mom now."

"Quite a change in character."

"Not entirely; her husband's ten years older."

"And Amara Marino?"

145

"The trouble was that Dex and Grant didn't know where to look. Here's the thirty-second version: She was from the wine country north of San Francisco and headed west to marry her high school sweetheart. But it didn't work out, so she returned to New Jersey six years ago. I found a landline under her maiden name. Amara lives in a high-rise apartment in Hackensack and manages a gym in Paramus. Here're their details."

"Thanks, Frosty," Elizabeth said. "This is great." She rang off.

***

A little before noon the same morning, Henry stopped by his secretary's desk as he was leaving. "I'll be gone an hour or so—errands."

"Okay, see you later."

When Henry was in his car, he headed for Morristown to meet with Giuseppe, who had called earlier. Henry pulled into the parking garage beneath the Headquarters Plaza building. Several levels lower, he parked and waited.

In a few minutes, Giuseppe approached, opened the passenger's side door, and got in.

"I didn't realize you were here already," Henry remarked.

"I watched for a few minutes to ensure you weren't followed. Here's the phone you requested," Giuseppe said, taking Jan's from his inside suit coat pocket. "I assume there's data on it that you don't want falling into the wrong hands. So remove the SD and SIM cards and destroy them before breaking up the rest of the phone."

"Thanks."

"Do you foresee any problems with the governor's appointment now?"

"Several senators are prickly over my ancestor's disgraceful poker-playing antics," Henry deflected, chuckling. "But I can handle it."

"Well, good luck. Call if you need anything."

On the way back to the office, Henry decided it was time to move ahead and call Murray Kriegman. "Murray, I have a couple of things to discuss with you. First, I need to arrange a replacement attorney for Doc Piscator. Are you interested if you can resolve your conflict with Bobby Wagoner?"

"Yes, his deal is all inked, and I can find competent counsel to babysit him through the rest."

"All right, I'll recommend you after you give me the go-ahead."

"Thanks. What else?"

"This is the main reason I called: Would you consider purchasing my practice? I must divest myself before I go on the bench."

"I was hoping that might be on your mind. I meant to call."

"You know my firm. I've always been small. Besides me, there's a receptionist, two paralegals, my secretary, a part-time file clerk, and Saul Blake, an independent private investigator I use."

"You're very profitable, though."

"Yes."

"I'm out of space here and thinking of expanding into bankruptcy," Murray said. "If I do, I must acquire space for two attorneys. How's your lease?"

"I have three years left, can sublet, and have a vacant office in my suite. Once I'm out of here, you could move in two lawyers."

"I'll call it the Conklin Group." Murray laughed.

"Let me know when you'd like to see the books. Another thing: I'd appreciate it if you could keep the staff on."

As Henry parked, he thought, *Good. Three fewer things to worry about now.*

***

Later in the afternoon, Tom called Church. "Something curious came up yesterday."

"What?"

"One of my officers was on vacation last week, returning late Monday evening. When he heard about Jan's death, he reported that he'd met with Vanderveer, who stopped by the station regarding a ring he'd found at Zeke's grave."

"What ring?"

"I don't know. Vanderveer alleged that there'd been a gold ring in the loose soil near the skeleton. He left it there, assuming it was evidence."

"Why did Jan come to the station?"

"He needed to find out about claiming it as found treasure."

"Finders keepers?"

"I guess. It's beside the point, since there wasn't any ring. I double-checked the crime scene inventory and photos," Tom said.

"Assuming Jan wasn't crazy, who would've had an opportunity to take it?"

"Only Jan and Henry Conklin were there when I arrived."

"Hmm, curiouser and curiouser," Church quipped. "Henry seems like the only one who could've nicked the ring. That's removing evidence from a crime scene—"

"And that's prosecutable. Not to mention a motive for murder."

"You mean if Jan was blackmailing Henry?"

"Yes. We need to revisit this case," Tom concluded.

***

During supper at Henry's on Wednesday, August 17, Petra updated Henry and Evie on the status of her house. "I called Lucas yesterday. Tomorrow he's bringing the crew back on the job and thinks there's still enough money in the checking account to finish up. Jan had already purchased most of the construction materials he needed, so henceforth, it's primarily payroll. Lucas will let us know if he runs low. And I should have my fifty K any day now. I could chip in too."

"Let's leave it the way it is, because if you pitch in, it will screw up the accounting. I don't want you to run short, either. Has he talked to Jarndyce yet?" Henry inquired.

"Yes, he's the executor. He told Lucas that Jan's will was straightforward. Lucas inherits the business, and his sister gets everything else. The lawyer doesn't see any reason Lucas shouldn't run the company while the will is probated."

"Do you think Jan's sister might object?" Evie asked.

"Jarndyce reported that at Jan's request, he sent her a copy of the will when it was updated, and she had no objection."

"So when do you think you'll be in your house?"

"Lucas says by the tenth of September."

***

Over the weekend, Henry had been mulling over Hank's story. The senators were concerned, and it didn't matter that Henry thought it was bullshit. Gradually, he realized he'd been looking at the situation incorrectly. *Instead of wishing the story would disappear, I'll embrace it: control the spin, offer help, and emulate a judicial temperament. I'll see Tom Johnson next week.*

***

On Tuesday, August 23, Elizabeth interviewed Carly Johansen and Amara Marino. Carly came to Elizabeth's office that morning, and after Elizabeth made coffee, Carly began, "I was glad when you called me about Roberta. I've wanted to come clean for a long time, but I didn't think it mattered anymore. When Detective Murphy questioned me afterward, I wasn't forthcoming. I never thought Roberta had disappeared—none of us did. We assumed she was getting even with her father and believed she'd be back in a few days, certainly no longer than a week."

"Didn't you think it was odd that Roberta never told you, her best friend? I even thought that she might've involved you."

"I wondered about that. Then, as time passed, it became harder to come forward. I was scared that I would get into difficulties."

"Why?"

"Well, unbeknownst to my parents, I'd been living a madcap lifestyle and was afraid it would all come out. Plus I felt guilty about involving Roberta in my fooling around."

"Why didn't you return Murphy's call in 2006?"

"I was still apprehensive about my parents. They thought I'd been in Europe with a girlfriend when I was with a guy."

"I hate to keep pressing, but why weren't you candid in 2012 when the Kearny PD finally caught up with you? Look, why not tell me? I'm a priest and have heard it all. I don't pass judgment. I can keep it confidential if you'd like, but I wish you wouldn't."

"Okay, it was simple: I was having too much fun letting wealthy, older guys take care of me."

"The detective who spoke with you supposed you were a . . . paramour."

"Well, I guess it's better than being called a mistress. Over the years, several older men kept me in an apartment and gave me an allowance."

"Not all at once, I hope?" Elizabeth joked.

"No, one at a time—mostly." Carly laughed. "I did begin dating my husband while still with another man, who cut me off once he discovered my cheating. My husband was single and asked me to move in, so I did. That was eight years ago; we've been married for six years now, have two great kids, and I've never been happier. He knows all about my past, doesn't care, and there's no reason not to tell you now.

"Roberta never said anything directly to me, just her comment about getting married. But I did wonder if she was pregnant. I kept quiet because I didn't want her to get into trouble. I even thought Roberta might've gone away for an abortion."

"Thanks for telling me. I'll keep it on a need-to-know basis. How did everything else work out?"

Carly smiled. "All's cool now, especially with my parents."

"I'm glad; grandkids will do that." Elizabeth chuckled. "I have a few more questions. Did you know Henry Conklin or Thomas Bellotti?"

"Yes, both."

"What did you think of them?"

"Tommy was nice, quiet. I met him once when he and a date joined us at a blues club on Route 9W along the Palisades."

"And Henry?"

"A charmer, but he wasn't serious."

"If Roberta was pregnant, do you think Henry was the father?"

"Yes."

"How do you know?"

"Girl talk. Henry was her first and only."

***

After lunch, Elizabeth drove to Paramus to question Amara Marino. They met in her office, and when they were settled, Elizabeth began, "I appreciate you seeing me so promptly."

"I was startled when you called, because I had no idea the police needed to talk to me again."

"Would you go over it one more time?"

"Sure. I was upset when I found Roberta in the girls' locker room. Although she was unintelligible about why she was crying, I tried to help. But Roberta disappeared before I could do anything. Then I moved at the end of the school year and lost track."

"Can you tell me what you thought happened?"

"Yes; two things came together. One of Roberta's classmates told me that she had also discovered Roberta crying in the girls' room and thought she'd been sick—vomiting. Then, after our encounter, I became convinced Roberta was pregnant."

"Then your offer of help wasn't about a therapist?"

"Well, yes, possibly—but mainly, I meant to take her to a clinic or a doctor to confirm my suspicions. If Roberta was pregnant, she needed to understand her options, and I intended to support her in whatever she chose."

"I can tell you that you were probably correct. We found a girlfriend who agrees with your opinion."

"Carly Fraser?"

"I can't say."

"That's ironic if it's Carly, because I would've thought she'd be the one in such a predicament. Do you have any idea what happened to Roberta? I keep jumping to awful conclusions: rape, murder, and such."

"Not yet."

"I hope you find out for her family's sake; it must be awful. Will you let me know if you solve it?"

"Of course. I'll tell you what I can, when I can." Then Elizabeth thanked Amara and was on the road ahead of the commuter traffic.

CHAPTER TWELVE

Thursday, August 25, 2022

Tom Johnson's interoffice extension rang at ten a.m. "Chief, Henry Conklin's here for his appointment," the desk sergeant reported.

"Thanks. Tell him I'll be with him shortly."

Tom waited ten minutes before meeting Conklin in reception. *I'm not sure why he's here, but letting him cool his heels for a while couldn't hurt.*

"'Mornin', Henry, sorry to keep you waiting. I couldn't get off a conference call."

"No problem." The men got coffee in the kitchen and proceeded to Tom's office.

"What can I help you with?" the chief continued.

"I've been thinking about the Zeke Norris case. I'm puzzled over why Hank gambled for Evie and can't overlook the implication that he might be Zeke's murderer. This has besmirched the family's name. I know it's a tall order, but we shouldn't leave any stone unturned. So I came to offer any assistance I could. If you need any family information—anything else—let me know."

It sounds like Henry's trying to get on the record—perhaps even do some fishing. "I appreciate your offer," Tom said. "May I speak bluntly?"

"Of course."

"Well, we've concluded that Hank had the hots for Evie and took advantage of an opportunity. I suppose I get it. Hank was a lonely widower, and grooming a young girl would've been a turn-on."

"Believe me; I've considered that. But it isn't something I would like to attribute to a relative, so I keep searching for another reason."

"I don't think there's anything else to it."

"I hope you're wrong. Regarding Zeke's murder, have you made any progress in identifying other persons of interest besides Hank?"

"No, we chose to close the case, but then something new turned up." Tom reported Jan's visit to the police about the ring and their analysis of who could've taken it.

Henry sat quietly before finally musing, "Huh . . . I didn't see any ring there. Are you positive Jan had it right?"

"Jan was insistent."

"Well then, I'll speak bluntly as well. I'm not pleased with your implications, although I can understand. Are you making allegations?"

"It's too early."

"I should hope so. It seems like we don't have anything else to talk about. My offer of assistance still stands."

"Hang on, Henry. I'm not finished yet. We've turned up something else I need to discuss."

Henry paused. "Am I to understand you're investigating me?"

"I can't disclose any details. Tell me about Roberta Allen."

"Good Christ," Henry replied, "that was over twenty-something years ago. And I was cleared."

"Not so. You weren't exonerated, just not prosecuted."

"Tom, be very careful. You're bordering on slander already. If you misstep, you know I have the means, connections, and skill to exact my pound of flesh. I'm done here."

***

Tom, Elizabeth, Church, and Ronnie met the following day. Ronnie reported that his informants had two bits of new information. One confirmed that Jimmy Zee had breakfasted with the underboss the morning after Jan's murder. Another had sourced additional information on Thomas Bellotti's disappearance; he had probably gone to work at a Philadelphia law firm. "I'll continue to work that angle," Ronnie said.

Elizabeth went next and discussed her interviews with Carly Johansen and Amara Marino. "I think there's a very high probability that Roberta was pregnant and that Henry Conklin was the father."

"I agree," Ronnie said. "We'll never know if an abortion was considered. But if Roberta refused, as Elizabeth suggests, it's motive to do away with her. A shotgun marriage before finishing law school would've stymied Henry's ambitions."

"Would Conklin have had the means and skill to pull off a murder, concealing it for over twenty years?" Elizabeth asked.

"That's why I'm interested in Thomas Bellotti. While he may not have been a mobster, he had the contacts to stage-manage it on behalf of his friend. And I'm confused about his disappearance. It seems like more than a dissatisfaction over working for his father. After all, I'm positive it was what they envisioned all along," Ronnie surmised.

"All right, keep working on that," Tom said, and continued, "I spoke with the New Jersey Human Trafficking Task Force. They report that the victim almost always knows who committed the abduction: family, friends, neighbors, or such. The rest are stranger abductions, mostly of women who will likely end up in the sex trade. Roberta's abduction might be a hybrid: a stranger hired by someone she knew.

"Regarding Jan's case, I'm still waiting for the last six months of his mobile carrier's records. Also, the forensic lab didn't turn up any helpful DNA at the crime scene. The only usable fingerprints were from Lucas and Jan. Apparently, Jan had no recent visitors. His bloodwork disclosed alcohol below the legal limit. Next, the bullets were hollow-point nine-millimeters, but they were too distorted for further ballistic analysis. No gunpowder stippling on his clothes, so Jan wasn't shot at close range. The entry angles were hard to determine accurately, but they were upward. So I think the shooter pulled a chair over in line with the center hall, sat, and waited. Afterward, he returned the chair to its place.

"Then the lab reexamined the locks and concluded that the side door had been recently professionally picked. So the broken glass was misdirection. I don't think there's any doubt now that we're dealing with a pro.

"And finally, I had an interesting phone call and meeting with Henry Conklin." Tom went on to describe what had occurred. "I'm confident I stressed him, although he handled it well. If we continue pressuring him, maybe Henry will screw up. Church, do you have anything to add?"

"We have two cases that Henry Conklin loosely links," Church began. "The first one is the probable murder of Roberta Allen to avoid an unwanted marriage. There's just one key to this crime: Thomas Bellotti. Ronnie's onto something.

"The second case is the ring theft/murder of Vanderveer. These crimes were probably committed because the ring would link Conklin's ancestor to Zeke's death and possibly upset Henry's appointment to the supreme court. There are four keys. The first three would prove that: Conklin stole the ring, Jan knew about it, and Jan was blackmailing Henry. If we're successful, Conklin can be prosecuted. The fourth key is tying Conklin to Jimmy Zee. That's harder. Unfortunately, we might only be able to prove the theft and obstruction of justice charges. But under the circumstances, I think Conklin would lose his appointment to the supreme court and draw jail time," Church said.

"None of us are willing to settle for that," Tom commented. "So I need to talk to Jon Anderson, for a few reasons. First, we're stumbling around in a twenty-plus-year-old cold case in Kearny's jurisdiction. I need to sort that out. Then I must convince Anderson that we have sufficient probable cause to obtain search warrants for Henry Conklin. The prosecutor may think we're still operating on too much conjecture. If that's the case, I'll ask for more horsepower. I'll see if Anderson will support having Frosty temporarily assigned to us from the attorney general's office. I don't think the AG will mind, because Frosty's coasting to retirement."

"If Anderson talks to the AG, won't it leak to the governor and then Henry in no time?" Ronnie asked.

"I've thought about what his approach might be," Tom responded. "If Anderson only reports that we're involved with an old missing-persons case in Kearny; that we're helping them locate a material witness, Thomas Bellotti, who has mob connections; and that

Ronnie recommends Frosty's help because he was involved in the case when he was with the FBI, I think it ought to fly."

"Agreed. And then Anderson could follow up, citing the short staff here and in Kearny," Ronnie added.

"Moreover, Conklin's name will never be mentioned," Elizabeth observed.

***

Henry reflected on Thursday's meeting with Tom Johnson. It was clear the cops were investigating him on a plethora of charges, including, after all these years, Roberta Allen's disappearance. Not surprisingly, Henry hadn't slept well last night. He had been confused and restless, but by early morning, he'd decided on an approach. First thing Friday, Henry would review everything—take a fresh look, make sure there weren't any loose ends. With that resolved, he'd finally been able to doze off.

Henry entered the office at nearly ten a.m. "'Mornin', Ella," he greeted his secretary. "I need to focus on some pleadings this morning, so hold my calls."

"Okay. Do you want coffee?"

"I'll get it myself—thanks."

Afterward, Henry checked his email. Nothing surfaced there that couldn't wait, so he began reviewing: *Jan knew about the ring, and the police were inclined to accept his story. But he's been terminated, his phone with the ring's pictures has been destroyed, and I deleted those photos from my phone. Giuseppe and I met three times: once outside the pharmacy, a while later for dinner at Emil's in Whippany, and finally, in the parking garage of Headquarters Plaza. We weren't observed by anyone who could cause trouble. Otherwise, we've only communicated by burners. And most important, Giuseppe's a professional. He'll know how to handle the cops if he's interrogated. Then, finally, the hitter was a pro from out of the area who staged a botched robbery.*

Henry concluded that there wasn't anything else to be done about those items; however, a few other things needed his attention.

I should switch to new burners and delete all my photos, logs, texts, emails, and internet activity from my smartphone. Next, the rings. I can tell them apart, because Hank's original has a distinctive scratch toward the back of its band. But I'm hesitant to do away with it because it's a family heirloom. I'll think about it. And I can't forget about Petra, yet I'm reluctant to do what probably needs to be done.

It was nearly lunchtime, so Henry left the office. He purchased several burners and picked up a sandwich before returning. Then he ate at his desk before turning his attention to Roberta. Petra's recent stubbornness, the dream, and the meeting with Chief Johnson had dragged everything up.

It all happened because of a chance conversation with my flatmate, Tommy. One evening he asked me if everything was all right, because I seemed down. I was surprised at how easily I unburdened myself. Roberta was pregnant, but her devout Scottish Catholicism wouldn't allow her to consider an abortion. I offered to pay and even found a doctor, but she meant to get married immediately.

Marriage to Roberta wasn't in my plans. I didn't love her and had set my sights much higher. I begged Roberta to be reasonable, but she threatened to tell her father if I didn't agree and agree fast. After that, it unfolded surreally.

Tommy went into his bedroom and made a call. He returned and said that his friend AJ, who worked for his dad, could help. Later, we met with AJ, who questioned me about Roberta and told me I needed an alibi. When Tommy mentioned that we were going to Fort Lauderdale on spring break, AJ said to be sure we were noticed: that was all we had to do.

On the way home, I asked how much. Tommy said, "It's gratis," adding that AJ would handle it off the books because they'd been friends all their lives.

Henry continued to cogitate about Roberta. Back then, he'd found it hard to accept responsibility, because it seemed like Tommy's fault, not his. Hell, Henry didn't even know what had happened. So, in short order, he'd suppressed any guilt. Then the Kearny investigation—with two follow-ups—hadn't shed any light on Roberta's disappearance either. So Henry had been lulled into thinking everything was hushed up. But now he wondered whether AJ and Tommy might be latent risks.

Although AJ probably isn't, since we're not associated with each other. Moreover, he's Enzo Bellotti's consigliere—hardly an amateur. But then there's Tommy. Even though he's in the same boat as I am, Saul needs to track him down on the q.t.—pronto. I have to evaluate how much of a threat he is.

CHAPTER THIRTEEN

Wednesday, August 31, 2022

Tom met with Ronnie, Church, and Elizabeth in her office. "I met with Anderson in Morristown yesterday," the chief began. "First, we spoke with the attorney general. He was interested in the politics of the case. He's concerned about Kearny's jurisdiction, so we had a conference call with the Hudson County prosecutor and Ewan Allen. The upshot was that they both felt too understaffed to take on the investigation but don't have a problem if we run with it. Next, I brought up Frosty Wicks, and the AG bought our approach. Ewan knows about Frosty through his dad, so he's okay. Afterward, we talked to Frosty, and he was on board.

"Finally, as anticipated, Anderson doesn't think we have enough evidence to apply for warrants on Conklin yet, so he wants us to search only what's in the public record. Much of that information, such as arrests, DUIs, the sex offender registry, and so on, are easily sourced online."

"And we should also expand our search to Thomas Bellotti," Church added.

"Agreed."

"It sounds like it went well," Elizabeth commented.

"It did. But I'm still concerned about leaks. So, Lizzie, will you ask your cousin to do the public record searches on Conklin and

Bellotti? I'll hire her as an independent contractor, and she can bill my department. It isn't hacking, so I don't think she'll have a problem."

"I'm positive Judy will help," Elizabeth replied.

"Ronnie, would you and Frosty concentrate on locating Thomas Bellotti? Lizzie, Church, and I will deal with the rest. This is working fine; we'll keep meeting at Saint Andrew's ad hoc," Tom said as they finished.

***

On Friday, September 2, Elizabeth and Church dropped Billy at her parents' before meeting Judy at the diner near Princeton. During lunch, they chatted about family matters; afterward, Church floated Tom's idea. "Judy, how about working for the Canal Ville PD as a contractor? Nothing like last time—all legal."

"Sure. What do you need?"

"We need publicly available information on Henry Conklin."

"The lawyer?"

"Yes, as well as another lawyer, Thomas Bellotti. He would have graduated from NYU's law school in 2000. Following that, for six years, he worked for his father, who is a Genovese crime family underboss."

"Was Thomas a mob lawyer, or did he handle the legitimate side?"

"The legit activity. All we know is that he and his father became estranged. Afterward, the younger Bellotti is rumored to have moved to Philadelphia, working for a law firm there. It probably would've been around fifteen years ago."

"Do you think he was trying to disappear, or did Bellotti simply fall off the grid?"

"Don't know. Thomas may have changed his name to avoid associating with his family, making it easier to obtain employment."

"It isn't too complicated. I'll also look for marriage, divorce, and name change filings and real estate transactions. But rather than using a third-party vendor, I'll source everything myself. I'll be in touch."

***

On Sunday the fourth, Evie caught up with Elizabeth at coffee hour. "May I talk to you for a few minutes?"

"Sure, let's go to my office. What's up?"

"I'm a bit bummed out. There's tension between Petra and my father. The first month they were together was great, so good that I hoped Petra might become my stepmom. Yet now things seem to be heading in the wrong direction."

"Well, it wasn't a very long time. Maybe you had unrealistic expectations? Do you know the causes?"

"I know Petra was jammed up with the finances on her house, and Dad helped out. Then Jan's death put its completion behind schedule for a week or so."

"How is her book coming along?"

"Petra meets regularly with her collaborator, and her agent is scheduling TV talk show appearances. She isn't broke, because she received an advance check about ten days ago."

"It doesn't sound too serious. Let's put Petra aside for now. What's bothering you about your dad?"

"He's stressed too. And it seems to grow worse all the time. I know he found the Hank Conklin story embarrassing and coming at a bad time. Then there's Petra's book. Dad has been apprehensive that it might screw up his confirmation."

"Do you think those are all of his problems?"

"Dad keeps grumbling about the politics surrounding his appointment. But he's always worked in a high-pressure environment. Do you think that could've thrown him for a loop?"

"It doesn't seem like it ought to have," Elizabeth admitted. "Is there anything else?"

"Well, Petra woke up one night with him having a bad dream. He was tossing, turning, and talking in his sleep. She said it wasn't like him. And a week ago, he went to police headquarters and seemed even more worried afterward."

"Why don't you talk to him about your feelings? Tell him you're concerned." Then Elizabeth asked, "Is school back in session yet?"

"Yes, we just went back on Thursday."

"You might try extracurricular activities. It could take your mind off things. Or run with me in the morning. And remember, focus on what you can control and dismiss the other stuff," Elizabeth counseled.

"I'll try—thanks. I want to run. Maybe we could work Petra in if it isn't too complicated."

"Sounds like a plan. Let's do that."

Later that evening, when Elizabeth and Church were chatting in bed, Elizabeth said, "Evie wanted to talk after church. She's down."

"Is it something you can disclose, or was it confidential?"

"She didn't ask me to keep it off the record," Elizabeth said, telling Church what they'd discussed. "The only thing new was that Henry may be more worried about his conversation with Tom Johnson than we realized."

"I'll keep it between us. What did you say?"

"I suggested distractions like extracurricular school activities and running with me in the morning. She likes that idea and wants Petra to run also, if possible. You'll have to wake me earlier if I need to fetch Evie."

"No problem. I'm always up with Billy and Jacques."

***

Karl and Klaus had breakfast at their usual spot on the day after Labor Day.

"Today's rain is welcome," Karl said.

"At least it was pleasant yesterday—not too hot either. How was your holiday?" Klaus asked.

"I went to Joan's again."

"Did you pick up any additional scuttlebutt about Jan's death?"

"No—all was quiet. Are you attending his memorial at the lodge on the tenth?"

"Yeah, it's gonna be a busy day. I heard Reverend Elizabeth would officiate because the family doesn't have a pastor. Do you know if we need to wear our aprons or go through the opening and closing rituals.?" Klaus asked.

"No, we don't need to, because it isn't a Masonic funeral or event."

"And then there's the regular communication at night."

"Right. By the way, how was your holiday?"

"I had a quiet afternoon—stayed home."

"Did you watch the Yankees?"

"Yeah, they beat Minnesota at the stadium. Five to two. And Judge hit his fifty-fourth homer."

"I think he might do it."

"Me too," Klaus agreed. "Let's skip the park today. It doesn't look like the rain will let up,"

"Okay, maybe we'll have better luck tomorrow."

***

On Saturday afternoon, Church headed to Amy's, dropping Billy off before he went to the lodge. Even though Elizabeth had planned a simple memorial service, she left early to review it with the worshipful master, organist, and chaplain, all of whom would participate. Next, she comforted the family and confirmed their parts in the service. By then, the lodge had filled with mourners, including Karl, Klaus, and other Masons; Henry, Evie, and Petra; and Church and Tom Johnson.

As two o'clock approached, Elizabeth moved behind the altar, where Jan's ashes sat in a small urn. The organist played "Amazing Grace," and when he had finished, Elizabeth began reading from *The Book of Common Prayer*:

> *I am Resurrection and I am Life, says the Lord.*
>
> *Whoever has faith in me shall have life, even though he die.*
>
> *And everyone who has life, and has committed himself to me in faith, shall not die for ever . . .*

Then, after a silence, Elizabeth resumed, "Most merciful God, whose wisdom is beyond our understanding: Deal graciously with Jan's family in their grief . . ."

Next, Jan's sister read from Ecclesiastes:

> *There is a time for everything.*
>
> *There is a time for everything that is done on earth.*
>
> *There is a time to be born.*
>
> *And there is a time to die . . .*

Afterward, the chaplain, in unison with the mourners, read a psalm, following which Elizabeth delivered John's Gospel:

> *Jesus said, "Do not let your hearts be troubled. Believe in God, believe also in me. In my Father's house there are many dwelling places . . ."*

Lucas eulogized his uncle, the worshipful master said a few words, and Elizabeth continued, "Father of all, we pray to you for Jan, and for all those whom we love but see no longer . . ." and began the commendation. Finally, the chaplain offered a closing prayer, Elizabeth proclaimed the blessing, and the organist finished with "What Wondrous Love Is This."

Many of the mourners repaired downstairs to the collation hall for a repast. Some Masons mingled, while others, including Karl, Klaus, and Henry, reminisced about how Jan had organized and cheffed the annual Saint Patrick's Day dinner—the lodge's primary fundraiser. The solemnity lightened as Jan's crew and several subcontractors traded humorous on-the-job yarns. Elizabeth spent time with Lucas's sister and her husband, and Petra and Evie chatted with a small group of women.

Tom and Church talked at the bar. "I reviewed Jan's phone records for the last six months," Tom said.

"Anything interesting?"

"A few calls with Henry. That may not be significant, since they were both active Masons. The last one—incoming—was on the afternoon of August seventh."

"What about emails and texts?" Church asked.

"They have different rules depending on how far back we go; I might need a warrant. Although a subpoena may work with Toby Jarndyce's consent."

"As Jan's executor?"

"Yes; I'll follow up. Also, Frosty called yesterday afternoon. He turned up something odd."

"What?"

"He spoke to the secretary of the managing partner at a Philadelphia law firm where Frosty had learned Thomas Bellotti worked. She said she wasn't authorized to provide any information and referred Frosty to her boss, who was out of the office."

"What's strange about that?" Church inquired.

"Nothing, aside from when Frosty continued chatting her up, the secretary let slip how a private investigator had also called about Bellotti the day before. The lawyer wasn't available to him either, so the PI said he'd call back but wouldn't leave his name."

"Hmm . . . so someone else is trying to track Bellotti down. I don't think it's the mob; they have their sources," Church observed. "Who's your best guess?"

"Probably the same as yours—Conklin. Let's schedule a meeting for Tuesday morning," Tom finished.

***

On the thirteenth, Tom, Church, Ronnie, Frosty, and Elizabeth met at Saint Andrew's. Tom began, updating them on the information from the mobile carrier. He concluded with, "I'll talk to Jarndyce and see about consent for emails and texts. I don't expect a problem. Afterward, I'll obtain a court order, and then we're probably looking at several weeks before we hear back. Frosty and Ronnie, would you update us on the Bellotti investigation?"

Ronnie went first. "I've been working my confidential informants in the Genovese and DeCavalcante organizations—nothing new. Frosty's following up on Judy's information; we thought an active detective might be more effective than a consultant."

Frosty picked up the debrief by reporting that a private detective, presumably Conklin's man, was investigating Thomas Bellotti also.

"If Conklin is behind it, he might be tidying up loose ends," Church observed.

"I don't think Conklin would hesitate to go after Bellotti," Ronnie admitted.

"Let's assume you're correct," Frosty continued. "Judy has been searching in New Jersey and Pennsylvania, and here's what she discovered: Bellotti graduated from NYU law school in 2000. Afterward, he worked in his father's legitimate businesses until 2006. There's a record of a name change to Thomas Bell filed in New Jersey in 2007. Next, he joined a white-shoe law firm in Philadelphia, and finally, there's a record of a DUI conviction in June 2010. His home address is an apartment in Lansdowne, PA, but Bell hasn't lived there since the end of that year. Next, Judy will search marriage, divorce, and real estate records. Tomorrow Ronnie and I are driving to Philadelphia. We'll camp out on the doorstep of the law firm Bell used to work for, because their managing partner is stonewalling."

***

On Wednesday morning, September 14, before leaving to meet Lucas at Tobias Jarndyce's law office, Petra and Henry signed a note and mortgage. Next, they stopped by the bank, where Henry purchased a cashier's check.

At length, when everyone was assembled in Jan's lawyer's conference room, Toby began. "Lucas tells me you've done a walk-through and the building inspector has issued your certificate of occupancy, correct?"

"Yes," Lucas replied. "But Petra and I will do another walk-through after her furniture is delivered from storage, just in case of any scuff-ups."

"Is that all right?" Jarndyce asked, addressing Petra and Henry, who each nodded their assent.

After reviewing the paperwork, Henry stated, "I brought the final payment for the renovations," and passed the bank check—made out to Jan's estate—across to Jarndyce.

When Petra and Henry had finished and were walking to the car, Henry suggested, "We ought to celebrate tonight. How about going out to dinner with Evie?"

"It's an excellent idea, and I'll stay over also."

"Not up to a sleeping bag on the new house's floor?" Henry teased.

Laughing, Petra agreed. "Not on your life."

***

Also that morning, Ronnie and Frosty set out for Philadelphia. The firm that had employed Thomas Bellotti, Wilson, Rush LLP, was located on Market Street and had been established before the Revolutionary War. It now had a national/international presence and employed over 250 lawyers.

Before calling on the managing partner, James Wilson III, Ronnie and Frosty had a late lunch at a nearby coffee shop. When they arrived at the offices, Frosty flashed his badge, and a stately receptionist with a silver-blue coiffure departed for the inner sanctum.

Following a drawn-out wait, the "sentinel" returned, saying, "Mr. Wilson will see you now. Please, follow me."

After Wilson greeted them and they were seated, the lawyer began. "Detective Wicks, I have your messages. I apologize for not responding—a combination of traveling and avoiding an unpleasant topic. I understand you want information on Thomas Bell, as you consider him a material witness in a possible homicide. Is that correct?"

"Yes. We're also concerned for his safety, because a person of interest, who arranged a contract murder in an unrelated homicide, is trying to locate him," Frosty answered.

"You're referring to the other call we received about him from a private investigator?"

"Yes."

"All right. In anticipation of your request, I met with several senior partners and was authorized to use my judgment as to whether we should cooperate without a court order. I will, yet you'll need such an order if you want his file."

"May we review it in house?" Ronnie inquired.

"Yes. I have it here. I'm not convinced I can be helpful, because we have lost track of him," Wilson replied.

"If you could just go over your relationship from the beginning?"

"Okay. When he applied in 2007, I wasn't the managing partner. But I was head of the hiring committee, a small group of partners that reviewed applications for further action and afterward participated in the interviews of those we chose. Bell's application and résumé intrigued me, since he submitted both names. I didn't recognize *Bellotti*, although it didn't take me long to check out who his father was. I investigated the businesses Bell represented, which appeared to be legitimate."

"That didn't bother you?" Frosty inquired.

"I was wary, yet it was easy to infer that Bell was honest and wanted to cut his ties with his father and *la Cosa Nostra*, regardless of how independent his clients were. He had relevant experience with the firms he'd represented. So, we hired him as Thomas Bell and sealed his application, et cetera, in his personnel file."

"How did it go after that?"

"Fine, in the beginning, but then Bell developed a drinking problem. At first, he started coming in late, then missed deadlines and had too many sick days. Finally, he showed up at a hearing under the influence. The judge adjourned the court and called me, because I was the managing partner then. When Bell returned to the office, I sent him home. The next day I read him the riot act. After that, things started to turn around. He was married in 2009, but in 2010 Bell pled guilty to a DUI, losing his driver's license for a year. Following his plea, the firm sent him to an inpatient rehab center for a month. Once more, he seemed to shape up. He and his wife had a daughter in 2010 and bought a home in Paoli early in 2011. But in March 2013, Bell showed up at court again—drunk. We couldn't tolerate it any longer and cut him loose."

"Do you know his wife's name or where they were married?" Ronnie asked.

"Carol; I don't know her maiden name. I think she came from near Wilmington. You might check Delaware's records."

"And you have no idea what Bell's doing now or where he lives?"

"No. But the house in Paoli was sold in 2014. I know because we handled the closing for him and his wife. He was out of work then; it was the last time I heard from him."

Frosty and Ronnie briefly reviewed Bell's personnel file, and as Wilson showed them out, he said, "When I see the private investigator, I'll require a judicial order to cooperate."

On the way back to northern New Jersey, Ronnie called Judy and brought her up to date, concluding with, "I'm suspicious there was a divorce also—probably in late 2013 or 2014. Check Delaware as well. If you can determine her maiden name, search all three states for a current address."

"Will do. I did additional investigating in New Jersey and Pennsylvania about the status of his law licenses. In NJ, it was under the name of Bellotti and lapsed in 2011. In PA, it was under Bell, first with a Lansdown address, then with a Paoli one. That license lapsed in 2011 as well. Afterward, Bellotti/Bell didn't renew his bar association memberships in either state," Judy concluded before ringing off.

***

Later in the evening, Petra and Henry had a good time at dinner, and Evie was excited that Petra was finally moving into her house. "I can come and spend the night sometimes," she said, looking at her father for approval.

"Well, only if you're invited."

"Don't worry about it," Petra interjected. "You're always welcome."

"Maybe I could spend a weekend now and then."

"Of course. I have three bedrooms, so we can set one up as yours."

"The Evie Conklin Room in the Evie Norris House," Henry quipped, and they all laughed.

When they returned to Henry's house, Evie went to her room to finish a reading assignment for school, and Petra went upstairs to change. In her terry robe, she returned to the den, where Henry had set out coffee.

"You must feel relieved now," he said.

"I do, yet I still have the issue of how to repay you. It's two hundred twenty-five thousand, correct?"

"Yes, but we don't have to deal with it now. It may work itself out if we stay together."

Then Petra's phone rang. Retrieving it from her pocket, she answered and listened. "That's right. Fine; tomorrow about ten o'clock."

When she'd rung off, Henry asked, "Who was that?"

"The driver from the storage company is confirming my address and time," Petra responded, taking Henry's hand. "Let's go upstairs."

***

Petra and Henry fell asleep late, and when they awoke the following day, Evie had already caught the school bus. They cuddled until Petra jumped out of bed, saying, "I need to get going. I'm meeting the storage guy."

Petra showered, put on her robe, and returned to the bedroom. Now it was Henry's turn for the bathroom, and soon she heard the shower.

Since Petra had received her book's advance check, she had been mulling over doing something nice for Henry. Something for Christmas, maybe; she was considering cuff links. So when Henry was showering, Petra looked through his jewelry box, gazing at the links and rings arranged in the slots. Taking her phone from her robe's pocket, she snapped a picture, thinking, *I'll take this with me when I go shopping.*

As Petra pocketed her phone and was closing the jewelry box, Henry walked in.

"What're you doing?" Henry spoke sharply, startling Petra, who hemmed and hawed while searching for an excuse.

"I was looking at your jewelry. That's all."

"What the hell for?"

"I like looking at your things," Petra responded, warming to a line of explanation. "It makes me feel closer to you."

"Oh, bullshit. You're snooping," Henry persisted, raising his voice.

"Henry, don't yell at me. I didn't mean anything by it. Don't get so pissed."

"I don't like anyone poking around in my stuff."

"Please. Mrs. Olsen will hear us. You're not being reasonable."

Henry shouted, "I'll be as unreasonable as I want, you stupid cunt!"

Petra burst into tears. "No, Henry. Don't call me that. If you must know, I was looking at your cuff links; I fancied buying you a pair for Christmas. Now you've ruined it."

They were close to each other, breathing hard. Henry reached out.

She pulled away.

"I'm sorry," he said tentatively, thinking, *Why am I so fuckin' upset? Maybe it's Evie's recent news flash that Petra plans to pitch her book on TV. She'll sit there gorgeous as ever, running her mouth with a cute French accent. If it's before my confirmation, it'll be a friggin' disaster. She'll freak out the senators. But more important, it's her nosing around in my jewelry box, seeing those two rings side by side. Fuck, what if she puts two and two together? What happens if the cops question her? I gotta prevent her from blabbing. Dammit, I don't need this shit along with Roberta.*

As Petra left, Henry said, "I overreacted; I'm really sorry. Will you come back tonight, please?"

"No, I don't think so. I'm too upset. Give me time. I'll pick Evie up Saturday morning. She's coming over to help around the house . . . remember?"

CHAPTER FOURTEEN

Thursday, September 15, 2022

Petra was confused. *Has Henry been gaslighting me? Why was he furious? Last night was terrific, so how could he be so nasty and cruel this morning? Granted, he's stressed about pressures I can't do anything about: Hank Conklin's saga, the court appointment, the police inquiry, and even Roberta. But is there another possibility— my book? I can do something about that. Ought I reconsider finishing it?*

Petra met the storage company, and Lucas showed up unexpectedly. "I thought I'd help direct traffic," he joked. By late afternoon, everything was offloaded and in place. Lucas and Petra did a walk-through. "It doesn't look like we'll need to do much," he observed. "I'll come over with a few guys tomorrow. We can rearrange anything you'd like and do the touch-up." Then they had an early supper at a diner on Route 46 before she returned to the Hampton Inn.

***

Once Petra had left the house, Henry took a while to settle down. But by the time he'd headed out, he'd decided to dispose of Hank's original ring—stat.

He drove to Grace Lord Park in nearby Boonton and made his way along a footpath to the Rockaway River. At this point, nearly fifty feet below the Boonton Gorge, the river had already passed over a dam and several waterfalls before beginning another steep descent to the downstream Boonton/Jersey City Reservoir. Henry gazed at the fast-moving water, thought about the ring's provenance, and tossed it in, thinking, *Bye-bye, hard evidence.*

Before going to the office, Henry resolved to deal with his mobile phone. Even though he'd already deleted his call logs and Jan's photos, voice mails, and so on, he was convinced the cops could recover all of it through forensic analysis. *So I won't make it easy. I'll destroy my phone as I did Jan's. Then they'll need a court order for my provider, which I'll challenge.*

Henry stopped at Best Buy and sat in the parking lot, listing his apps. Next, he bought a new phone—using his existing number. He left it at the store to have his email set up and contact list transferred.

When he arrived at the office, Henry said, "'Mornin', Ella, I need to work on motions. Would you hold my calls?"

"All right. Did you have coffee?"

"No, not yet. Do you mind?"

"Uh-uh."

Ella brought coffee, and Henry began sorting through his difficulties. It wasn't like him to be confused or indecisive, letting his emotions get the best of him. He needed to stop worrying about Hank's story and Jan speaking to the police. So it was time to devise a strategy.

After a while, he took a break, picked up his new smartphone from Best Buy, disposed of the old one, then had a late lunch. Returning to the office later, he handed Ella his new mobile as he said, "The old one was acting up. Here's a list of my apps. Please set them up and enter my appointments from your calendar."

"Sure, but why didn't you have the store transfer all that?"

"The sales guy suggested this was better because I might have corrupted files in my apps, causing problems."

"Makes sense—I guess. Give me an hour or so."

Henry resumed cogitating until Ella buzzed. "Tammy from the governor's office is on the line; I thought you'd want to talk to her."

"Yes, put her through."

"'Afternoon, Henry," Tammy said. "I want to update you on where the voting stands."

"Okay."

After giving him the rundown, Tammy summed it up: "So the senators with whom you've already met are on board. But you require two more from the five you'll be meeting with. Otherwise, we'll have to rely on Republicans."

"You sound concerned."

"Well, I'm encountering problems in scheduling appointments."

"Even for after the senate is back in session?"

"Yes."

"What does it mean?"

"Don't know—maybe nothing."

"Can the governor help?"

"It isn't his style to jump in yet. Let's keep this to ourselves until we have a problem. I only meant to give you a heads-up. In your remaining interviews, sell like hell."

Jesus, Henry thought. *"Not his style." Another friggin' problem. And there's still Roberta, Tommy, and Petra.* Henry sighed, trying to avoid thinking about what he should deal with immediately—Petra.

***

By Saturday morning, September 17, Henry had decided. He called Giuseppe. "We need to talk."

"How about lunch?"

"No. We can't risk being seen together."

"So the senators are still prickly?"

"More serious than that. Can we meet at the Headquarters Plaza like last time?"

"Okay, how's two thirty? I'll wait a little while to confirm you weren't followed."

"See you then."

Later, Henry drove down to the same level as before and parked. Giuseppe approached the front passenger's door in a few minutes and got in. "What's up?"

"I need the guy we used before," Henry replied.

"I'm not sure we can hire him again; he's retired. Massimino had to lean on him hard before he'd do the other job."

"Do what you can. We need to move fast, okay?"

"Yes, give me the details."

Next, Henry called Saul for an update on Tommy. "'Afternoon, Counselor."

"Hey, Saul. Do you have anything for me yet?"

"Yes, but it's been a slog. I don't know if this guy fell off the grid or went underground intentionally, but Bellotti has succeeded. I've confirmed a lot of what was rumored or common knowledge." Saul then updated Henry about Bellotti's name change to Thomas Bell and his DUI conviction. "Then, because Bell isn't listed in any directories now, it took me a while to locate the Philadelphia law firm he used to work for. Moreover, I'm still trying to reach their managing partner. He's the key to the next step. Finally, I've contacted my mob snitches, who are all low-level. Nothing's shakin' yet."

"First-rate work. The name change and DUI are new."

"I'll keep digging. Do you want to give me a budget? This is gonna take longer than I expected."

"No, not yet. Keep working on it."

***

That afternoon, Judy called Elizabeth with more information about Thomas Bellotti/Bell. Her search in Delaware for a marriage license had revealed that Thomas Bell and Carol Shipp were married near Wilmington, Delaware, in 2009. Further inquiries using his wife's maiden name had uncovered a birth record for a daughter, Kathleen Shipp, with Thomas Bell recorded as the father. The baby was born in 2010 at ChristianaCare Hospital in Newark, Delaware. Then in 2013, there was a record of a divorce. Carol had used her parents' suburban Wilmington address for her wedding license and her daughter's birth record but, for her divorce pleadings, an address in Delaware Water Gap, Pennsylvania. Judy had also found a mobile number on the internet and opined that Carol had never taken Bell as a last name.

***

Once again after church on Sunday, Evie caught up with Elizabeth at coffee hour and asked if they could talk.

"Sure. Let's go to the office."

Evie closed the door. "I'm worried. I was at Petra's house yesterday, helping her get settled. She's upset because she and my dad had a falling-out. I think he hurt her feelings badly, and I'm scared it's over between them."

"When did this happen?"

"The best I can figure out is Thursday morning after I left for the school bus."

"Did you ask her about it?"

"Yes. Then Petra started crying and said it was just a disagreement. But I don't think they've talked since. And Petra didn't come in when she picked me up or dropped me off at the house yesterday. Plus, when I got out of the car, Petra said, 'We'll still be friends—no matter what.'"

"I know how close the two of you are. I hope it works out."

"I don't know what to do."

"I don't think there's anything you can do. Just don't take sides. Be there for them if they need you."

After Evie left, Elizabeth returned to the rectory. Church was walking Jacques, so she changed her clothes and called Carol Shipp, who agreed to meet on Monday during her lunch break at the Village Farmer and Bakery in Delaware Water Gap.

CHAPTER FIFTEEN

Monday, September 19, 2022
Kill Devil Hills, North Carolina

Olivia had been up early this morning. She let Jimmy sleep, deciding to surprise him with fresh bagels and cream cheese from Sal's Brooklyn Bagels & Pizza. She showered quickly, dressed quietly, and was at the shop by seven thirty.

Sal's success story was the kind that warmed your heart. Sal, a bachelor, had tended bar at a Brooklyn tavern his entire life and was a well-loved fixture there. But at age fifty, he'd decided to pack it in and take his substantial nest egg to the Outer Banks, where he had bought a summer place years ago. At first, life was grand: the beach, fishing, reading, and even an occasional hookup with a woman. Yet after six months, Sal was bored off his gourd. He also missed being able to have a decent bagel. He tried, searching north and south, but they couldn't be had for love or money.

So back to Brooklyn Sal went, staying for three weeks with a friend who owned a bagel shop. Afterward, he returned to North Carolina with the know-how, the recipes, and a list of the equipment needed, the most important of which were the ovens and a water softener—*bye-bye, calcium and magnesium.* Then Sal bought a bagel shop on North Carolina's Route 12. It was priced for a quick sale by the former owner's estate, and one of the attractions was that it had a new four-deck oven. He bought a water softener, and within six months, Sal's Brooklyn Bagels was a success. *Life's even grander when you work for yourself.*

But Sal wasn't satisfied yet. It irked him that the store was closed so many hours a day after the lunch crowd left. And then the solution dawned on him. He put the shop in charge of his manager and was off to Brooklyn again, this time staying with a buddy who owned a pizzeria. When he returned home, he had recipes, a list of the equipment needed, and more. The good news was that he already had the ovens. But most important, Sal had two trade secrets: high-gluten flour and soft water, which he'd already solved. And soon Sal's Brooklyn Bagels & Pizza was open from five a.m. to ten p.m., with extended weekend hours, and was an even bigger hit. *And now life's the grandest: raking in the dough and attracting more women than ever.*

"'Mornin'," Sal greeted Olivia. "Haven't seen you in a long time; Jimmy usually comes."

"I let him sleep."

"You didn't wear him out again, did you?"

"I might've," Olivia laughed, returning Sal's banter and putting a container of veggie cream cheese on the counter. "Let me have two sesame-seed and two poppy-seed bagels, please."

When Sal returned with her order, he said, "I put in two new twenty-seven-grain bagels that I'm trying out. They're on the house—let me know."

"Thanks, will do."

When Olivia returned to the condo, she could hear Jimmy on the phone. He sounded peeved. "No. I told you last time, no more. Didn't I make myself clear? . . . Well, I am pissed . . . No, there isn't a need for me to think about it . . . You can call me back, but don't count on me changing my mind!" Jimmy rang off, muttering, "Fuckin' boss," while entering the kitchen as Olivia set out the bagels.

"And a good morning to you," she joked, kissing him.

"It isn't funny. I'm through with that shit. I'll make coffee," he said, putting out the French press.

"The boss wants you for another job?"

"Yeah. Can't be done by anyone else and all that nonsense— bullshit."

"Can you refuse him? Doesn't he have you by the balls?" Olivia and Jimmy had never talked about what he'd done for a living, yet Olivia had a good idea after his last job and what she'd surmised over the years.

"Probably."

"Maybe we should think about moving away from the Outer Banks, at least for a while—leave no forwarding address."

"You'd be okay with that?"

"As long as we're together."

***

At eleven on Monday morning, after dropping Billy at the church's office for a "play date" with Amy, as she referred to these times, Elizabeth and Church set out for the fifty-mile drive to Pennsylvania. They chose an outside picnic table, and soon an attractive woman in her late thirties arrived, spotted them, and came over to introduce herself. After Carol was settled, she said, "So have you been here before?"

"Elizabeth hasn't, but I was here once with a buddy. I fell in love with their hot dog/apple pie lunch combo," Church said.

"It's amazing," Carol said. "Even with the pandemic and inflation, they still keep it under five bucks." Everyone ordered the combo despite Elizabeth's unspoken apprehension about what might've been done to the hot dogs to keep their prices down. As they finished and had coffee, Carol said, "I haven't heard from Tommy in years. I don't know if I can help, but I'm concerned because you said he might be in danger."

"I'm consulting with the Morris County Prosecutor's Office on a twenty-four-year-old cold case," Church continued. "Our main person of interest in this disappearance/homicide investigation was a good friend of your former husband, who might be a material witness and in danger."

"Who's this good friend?"

"Please keep this confidential—Henry Conklin. He was Tommy's roommate throughout college and law school."

"Tommy never mentioned him. Never heard of him."

"As Elizabeth told you when she called, we can't locate your ex-husband. We've searched under the name you know him by, Bell, and his name before he changed it, Bellotti."

"Tommy changed his name? I never knew that. Why does Bellotti ring a bell? No pun intended."

"His father's the number-two in New York City's Genovese crime family."

"Oh, Jesus. Things make better sense now: why I never met any of his family, why no one came to our wedding, even all his drinking. I always knew Tommy had demons, but he wouldn't talk. Is he in danger from the mob?"

"No. His former roommate is a powerful man, and your ex-husband might have information that would be detrimental to him. We're concerned that our suspect might try to tidy up loose ends. So when was the last time you knew where your ex lived?"

"Kathleen, my twelve-year-old, and I moved back with my parents in early 2013, then we were divorced later that year. Tommy stayed in the house until it was sold in 2014. I don't know where he went after that."

"What about child support? Did you see an address on his check?" Elizabeth asked.

"No. He sent money orders from Philadelphia for a while, although the last one was from Camden. I haven't received anything since sometime in 2015."

"How are you getting by?" Elizabeth probed.

"Sometimes it's hard. I met Tommy when I was a legal secretary, so I have excellent office skills. After the divorce, I landed a local job with a regional trucking company. I'm the office manager now."

"How about your parents?"

"I can't rely on them, because Dad lost his business in the pandemic. Thank the Lord, my employer made it through. And I still have a chunk of money left from the house. I guard it judiciously, because that's for Kathy's college."

"Anything else about Tommy?" Church said.

"Yes. Concerning his background, there's something else falling into place now. We paid cash for the house. I didn't think much about it then, but after what you've told me, I wonder where all that money came from?"

"I take it, then, that you didn't contribute anything?" Church observed.

"That's correct."

"How does your daughter deal with all of this?"

"Well, Kathy knows about her father, but I never told her how bad it became with his drinking and job loss. I said we had fallen out of love and had to split up. Yet now that she's older, it doesn't fly anymore. She wants to know why her father doesn't love her and why he won't come to see her. It's tough."

"One last thing," Church asked. "Did you ever hear of Roberta Allen?"

"No?"

As Church and Elizabeth returned to Morris County, Elizabeth rang Tom, updating him on their meeting with Carol Shipp. "I also talked with Judy," she finished. "She's at a dead end, unless you want her to do what she does best. However, she thinks no one in your office will be the wiser if you run Bellotti/Bell through New Jersey and Pennsylvania DMVs after hours. I also asked her to take a closer look at Camden."

***

Later that Monday afternoon, after landing at Newark's Liberty International Airport, Jimmy rented an SUV and drove to a small Italian restaurant on Terhune Avenue in Jersey City. He parked and met the boss in the foyer.

"Our table's ready. It's in the rear—follow me," the mobster said. As they walked over, he continued, "It's hectic so that we won't be noticed or overheard. That's why I like it here." After they were seated, he explained the job. "So you see, this broad could fuck everything up; then the other job you did would be for naught. We can't afford to pass on this opportunity."

"Boss, you know I don't want to. I'm trying to retire. Plus I don't do women."

"Jimmy, do I have to spell it out? You can't retire—not really."

"Are you threatening me, Massi?"

"Take it however you like. But I need you to get with the program. Let's not squabble—do the fuckin' job! But be careful. My source in the Morris County Prosecutor's Office reports that they're treating Vanderveer's death like a homicide now, and your name came up as a possible hitter. Call me if you need ordnance—you have ten days," the boss said, passing Jimmy an envelope. "You can find her photo on the internet."

Driving to Morris County, Jimmy thought, *Fuck him. Olivia may be right: we should change zip codes.*

***

Late Wednesday morning the twenty-first, Karl and Klaus talked about Yankees baseball while sitting by the river. "Quite a game at the stadium last night," Karl said.

"It sure was! Giancarlo Stanton's walk-off grand salami was enormous: over four hundred feet into the left-field stands."

"Yeah. And Judge hit his sixtieth, tying the Babe."

"That puts him ten games ahead of Ruth's pace. He's gonna break Maris's record. With sixteen games left, don't see how he can miss," Klaus opined.

"Me neither."

"Did you hear anything new about Vanderveer's death from your neighbor, Joan?"

"No. But Amy at the church says the chief has been meeting at Saint Andrew's with Reverend Elizabeth and her husband."

"That's odd. Maybe Tom's concerned about eavesdropping?" Klaus suggested.

"Could be."

Changing subjects, Klaus asked, "Have you been following this tropical depression forming in the South Atlantic?"

"No."

"The weather pundits are talking about it becoming a big hurricane, Ian, hitting Florida before moving up the East Coast. It's supposed to be a real rainmaker with a landfall around the end of the month."

"Well, maybe we'll get a good soaking and finally end this drought!" Karl observed. It was a little after noon, and he pointed to

Jimmy, who had just entered the park carrying a Luigi's Italian Deli bag again. "Isn't that the guy we met here six weeks ago?"

"Yeah. I think so. He was on his way to Pennsylvania," Klaus said, as Jimmy spotted the old cronies and nodded. It was time for Karl and Klaus to leave, so they gathered their canes. As they approached Jimmy, Klaus spoke up. "Just passing through to Pennsylvania again?"

"No, I may be here for a couple of days."

"Business?" Karl inquired.

"Yeah. I'm a manufacturer's rep—visiting a few clients. By the way," Jimmy stated, changing the subject before the old farts became too inquisitive, "I tried that ice cream place you mentioned—perfect. I'll stop there after I'm finished here."

"We thought you'd like it. Well, we'll see you next time," Klaus said.

As they doddered toward the parking lot, Karl commented, "Nice guy."

***

After his ice cream, Jimmy returned to the mall to surveil his mark, a woman called Petra. She'd arrived at Macy's a little before eleven thirty a.m., so Jimmy had grabbed lunch while she shopped. He'd been shadowing her since yesterday and would keep it up through Friday morning. By then, the inkling of a plan he was mulling over should have fallen into place. Jimmy didn't like this job at all, but if his plan gelled as he hoped, he could solve his problem.

***

Meanwhile, as Henry left his office, Giuseppe called. "It's worked out for you; the guy you wanted is already here."

"That was fast."

"Yeah, but I won't have any additional details. So stay visible over the next ten days, understand?"

"Yes, and thanks."

CHAPTER SIXTEEN

Friday, September 23, 2022

First thing Friday morning, the governor called Henry. "Tammy and I have been putting our heads together. Here's an update on the senators you've met with since we last talked: one yea, one undecided, and one nay."

"So, I need another yea."

"Correct. Tammy's working on appointments now for when the senate's back in session. Just keep doing what you're doing, and don't discount the undecided vote or the possibility of Republican support. Let's hope there's no more damning news."

After Henry hung up, he called Saul for a report on his investigation into Tommy's whereabouts.

"I haven't turned up much. I finally saw James Wilson, the managing partner of the Philadelphia firm where Bellotti used to work. He reluctantly revealed that Bell had worked there for six years ending in March 2013. If we want additional information, we'll need a court order."

"Nothing else in the public record?"

"No. I've searched under both names in New Jersey and Pennsylvania—nada. I have a source in NJ's DMV. He's checking for any recent information. If that doesn't turn up anything new, I'm dead-ended."

"All right. Keep at it a while longer."

***

At the same time, Ronnie phoned Tom, Elizabeth, and Church. "I received troubling news last night from my DeCavalcante snitch. Jimmy Zee's back in the area. He arrived this past Monday afternoon and had dinner with Massi Rizzo."

"Any idea what he's up to?" Tom asked.

"No. But my informant said the boss was pissed with Jimmy afterward. It doesn't sound like they're on the same page."

"Isn't Jimmy trying to retire?" Elizabeth inquired.

"It seems like more than that."

"Then should we assume Conklin's behind it?" Church asked.

"Absent further information, I think so."

"So, who's the mark this time?"

"I don't have a clue yet," Ronnie continued. "Additionally, I spoke with Frosty. While Judy's doing her thing, he'll follow up on the Camden clue you obtained from Bellotti's ex."

***

Jimmy spent Friday morning and early afternoon following Petra. After that, he had lunch at a diner on the west side of Route 46. When he returned to the SUV, he called Olivia. They chatted briefly until Jimmy got around to what he wanted to discuss.

"Listen, this job is taking longer than I planned. And with Hurricane Ian strengthening, I don't think I'll be able to get home before the end of the month."

"I haven't been following it."

"The Weather Service predicts at least a Cat 4. The current track is for landfalls in Cuba and the West Coast of Florida before crossing into the Atlantic and moving up the coast to the Carolinas on the thirtieth. Ian will be a monster: high storm surges, winds, heavy rain, and flooding."

"Wow."

"I'm worried . . . Would you drive to your parents in New Jersey? Leave ahead of the storm on Monday the twenty-sixth, and I'll meet you at your mom and dad's when I'm done. You can have a visit. Then afterward, we'll take a road trip to New England."

"If you're that concerned, I'll do it. A trip down east will be fun."

"Great. Here's what you need to do," Jimmy said. "I'm not worried about the condo: it's rented, and the furniture came with it. So pack your valuables and clean out the safe. I'll give you the combo." Following that, Jimmy explained everything, including handling the cash and disposing of his gun. "Any questions?"

"No. Call me at my parents. I love you."

"I'll call . . . Love you too."

Now on to the next step, Jimmy thought as he pulled out of the diner's parking lot.

***

Later that afternoon, when Elizabeth had finished polishing her sermon, she heard the parish hall's door open. A man she didn't recognize walked into the outer office and up to her door and tapped on the jamb. "Reverend Elizabeth, may I talk to you?"

"Sure, come in. Sit. Have we met?"

"No, but I thought we should talk, because we can help each other."

"How so?"

"I'll show you," the man said, passing Elizabeth a phone. "The only things on it are my burner number and some photos you should look at."

As Elizabeth reached for the phone, she said, "You didn't tell me your name."

"No. I didn't."

"Well?"

"Just look at the photos. You'll figure it out."

Elizabeth was already becoming uncomfortable, but her apprehension increased as she scrolled through the pics. "I'd like my husband here," she stated, reaching for her phone.

"No. I don't want Church here. The two of us facing off in such a small space would be too much testosterone. I chose you because you're friends with Petra and handled the Doc Piscator episode well."

"You know about that? As well as my husband's name and what he did for a living? Who the hell are you?"

202

"Someone who does his homework. Relax. You have nothing to fear: I'm not armed. Please, look at the photos."

"Get up and stand away from my desk," Elizabeth demanded. After Jimmy complied, she continued. "Lift your shirt so I can see your waistband . . . Turn around slowly . . . Raise your pant legs so I can see your ankles." Jimmy wasn't armed. "Okay, you can sit again."

Jimmy smiled as Elizabeth returned to the photos. About fifteen were of Petra going through her daily routine: around the house, in town, shopping, and such. But there was another, and Elizabeth looked up when she saw it.

"Is that the picture when you were jogging on the towpath with Jacques?" the man asked. Elizabeth nodded, and he continued. "You aren't the target; I was cutting sight lines when you stumbled by. I didn't know you ran the same route as Petra."

"So much for your homework. These are surveillance photos. You're going to kill her. Are you Jimmy Zee?"

"I said you'd figure it out."

Elizabeth returned his phone; he wiped it with tissues from a box on her desk before handing it back.

"Keep the phone; you'll need it later."

"So, what do you want from me?" Elizabeth asked.

"I'm here because I don't want to do this job, and we can prevent this if we work together. But we don't have much time: after the twenty-ninth, my hands will be tied."

"What do you have in mind?"

"If Petra disappears and goes into protective custody, I'll take credit for completing the job. All I need is her phone as proof. That should give you and the cops time to put your ducks in line."

"Who contracted for the hit?"

"I don't know. I can tell you from where it originated, that's all."

"All right. Tell me."

"Not until I know you're on board," Jimmy said.

"Slow down," Elizabeth responded. "You know I don't have that say-so. I'd need to sell it to Petra, my husband, Chief Johnson, and the Morris County prosecutor."

"Fine. But I'll only meet with you."

Elizabeth nodded again, and Jimmy continued.

"It was a Morris County referral to the DeCavalcantes."

"Will you identify your mob contacts and give us a statement?"

"No. I'm not snitching."

"How about Jan Vanderveer: Who did that?"

"I don't know anything about it," Jimmy lied.

"Why are you helping, then?" Elizabeth asked as he began to leave.

"I don't do women. Call me when you have Petra's phone," he said, and left.

Elizabeth locked the parish hall and started toward the rectory. Billy, Church, and Jacques were about a third of the way across the parking lot. When they met, Elizabeth rustled Billy's hair, and Jacques began jumping while Church kissed her.

"I didn't think you had office hours today," Church said. "Who was that?"

"Jimmy Zee."

Church stiffened. "You're shitting me!"

"No. I'm okay, but we need to talk. Tonight, after Billy's asleep."

Later, once Billy was in bed, they sat at the kitchen table with coffee, and Church scrolled through Jimmy Zee's phone as Elizabeth told him what had happened.

"The picture of you and Jacques is across from where Doc Piscator's guys dumped Nancy Clarke's body, isn't it?"

"Yes."

"Ironic. Look, I don't want you meeting with him again."

"But he said he wouldn't meet with anyone else."

"He will," Church said. "We have something he needs—proof. And if Jimmy's so concerned about my testosterone, it's easy enough to park somewhere, facing each other—driver's side to driver's side—and hand the phone off through the windows. What was your impression of him?"

"It's hard to explain. He seemed so ordinary, so matter-of-fact."

"I had friends at Central Intelligence who were snipers. They were the same way: it was just a job."

"How can they keep doing it?"

"Some don't. Some crash and burn, and others opt out because of a bad experience. I feel that's where his comment about not doing women may come from."

They sat and talked briefly until she said, "Let's pick up the kitchen and go up early."

After they were in bed, Church hugged her. "Were you scared?"

"Yes, when I realized how much he knew about all of us. But mostly when I figured out who he was."

"You probably weren't in danger," Church reassured her. "Even though he's on the wrong side of the law, he's a pro."

"Easy for you to say."

"It is, and that's why I don't want you close to him again. You know, Ronnie's correct, you're 'one tough broad.'"

"Did he say that?"

"Yes. It's a compliment, so don't be pissed."

"I'm not. I know it's just Ronnie." Then, chuckling, she added, "Sexist though he is."

"And proud of it," Church bantered as Elizabeth snuggled closer.

CHAPTER SEVENTEEN

Saturday, September 24, 2022

Elizabeth announced at breakfast the following day, "I'm bothered about something. How did Jimmy Zee know I would figure out who he was? He counted on it, and there's just one way Jimmy could have known that."

"Well, only Tom, Ronnie, you, and I know about him, besides the prosecutor or attorney general," Church answered.

"Exactly. Once Ronnie's confidential informant leaks intel to him about Jimmy, it's passed on to the prosecutor or the AG. Then someone from their offices must be tipping off the mob. It's logical."

"Disturbing," Church said.

"Also, I've been thinking about where we might stash Petra. That would give Tom and Jon Anderson time to work out logistics," Elizabeth continued.

"Where?"

"Carmen's Beauty Salon."

"Your hairstylist? The one who kept an eye on Doc's pharmacy for us?"

"Yes. I'm sure that her second upstairs apartment is still unrented. So why not hide Petra there?"

"It's a workable idea. Call her while I phone the team."

Elizabeth went to their home office and called Carmen before the salon's opening.

"Hi," Carmen said when she answered. "What's up? You're not due for an appointment yet."

"No, I'd like to talk to you about something else." Then Elizabeth explained.

"Wow, sleuthing again. That's cool, and you say I know her?"

"Yes, but I don't want to disclose who it is until we've spoken with her."

"You're in luck. When the pandemic struck, I was about done furnishing the apartment. There's even cable TV. But nothing else happened after that until I bought a refrigerator last week. It's ready to go now; you're welcome to use it."

"Thanks. How much?"

"Don't worry. I've never rented it, so it isn't a big deal."

"Perfect. I'll let you know the details," Elizabeth finished her business in the office and returned to the kitchen.

Church had been successful. "The men suggest meeting after services tomorrow. Tom likes your idea about Carmen's apartment, because the county can't protect witnesses for long. We decided that Frosty would skip the meeting but be available by phone; we don't want to pile on Petra. And I mentioned your concern about leaks at Anderson's or the AG's."

Afterward, Elizabeth called Petra, who agreed to meet with them. Later, Church and Jacques headed out for a walk, and while they were gone, Elizabeth's mobile rang. It was Ronnie.

"Hiya, kid. Are you all right?"

"Yes."

"You were just a bit afraid, huh?"

"Yes, but I'm fine now. Church and I talked it through," Elizabeth replied.

"Do you need anything?"

"No."

"Elizabeth, you handled it like a pro. You're one tough lady."

"Not 'one tough broad'?" Elizabeth quipped.

Ronnie stopped, then burst out laughing. "That too, Lizzie! That too."

***

Petra attended church alone on the twenty-fifth, then idled about through coffee hour. When only a few parishioners remained, Elizabeth collected her, and they repaired to the conference room. The men were chatting around a long table, where coffee with trappings and a plate of cookies had been set out. Elizabeth introduced Tom and Ronnie, following which, Petra remarked, "This must be important to get all of you out on a Sunday."

"It is," Tom said. "I'll be direct. We've uncovered a plot to kill you, and the assassin is already here."

"What? You can't be serious."

"I am."

"Why?"

"I don't know." Tom explained Elizabeth's meeting with Jimmy Zee and handed her Jimmy's phone.

After Petra scrolled through his photos, she said, "And you say he's a mob killer. This can't be right . . . I don't know any mobsters . . . I don't understand."

Petra was dumbfounded when Tom told her they suspected Henry Conklin of being behind the threat. Then, as the shock wore off, tears welled, and Elizabeth put her arm around Petra's shoulders, saying gently, "We don't understand either. So we need to talk about that and Jan Vanderveer's murder; we're convinced Henry contracted for that killing also. Then we'll go over our plans to keep you safe."

As Petra calmed down, Tom said, "You're not in any trouble; we're simply looking for information. We also want to see if you're a material witness, because, even if you are only tangentially, it seems like events in the 1860 cold case and Jan's murder are swirling around you. First, do you have any questions?"

"I thought Jan's death was an accident—a botched robbery."

"No, we've determined otherwise," Tom said. "Why don't you start by describing your relationship with him, then afterward with Henry Conklin? How it developed, what's happening now, any points of conflict, and so on."

"May I have a break first?" Petra asked. "I'd like to go to the ladies' room."

"Sure."

"I'll show you," Elizabeth said, escorting Petra into the corridor and pointing. "It's down there on the left."

As she waited in the hall, Elizabeth looked through a window at the church's Memorial Garden, which formed a courtyard between the office/parish hall complex and the sanctuary.

When Petra returned, she stood beside Elizabeth, looking. "It's attractive."

"Well, it's not at its best between seasons; it's changing," Elizabeth commented.

As they walked back to the conference room, Petra joked, "You didn't need to wait. I wouldn't have run away."

"Oh, it wasn't that," Elizabeth said. "I didn't want you to feel alone, that's all."

As Elizabeth and Petra entered, Ronnie sensed a change in Petra's attitude. And after settling, she began taking charge, bit by bit.

"Well. Following the mayhem of my career and divorce, I sought to live in a quieter place than Manhattan. I looked in the tristate area at towns less than fifty miles from midtown. Canal Ville was one of the first I visited. It was perfect: accessible, a genuine village with shops and restaurants, a hospital, and so on. So I found a real estate broker and started house hunting."

"How did you end up with the Norris place?" Church asked. "It must've been a major undertaking."

"I spotted it and asked my real estate agent about the property. They were the listing broker, so they put me in touch with Jan Vanderveer to find out the cost of renovating the house. It seemed doable."

"You said you ran into problems with Jan," Elizabeth said. "Tell us about them?"

"I had three sources of money: First, some funds left from my career. It was enough to buy the house, because it was a handyman's special. Then there was the cash my ex gave me when he realized I was otherwise practically penniless. According to Jan, that should've been enough for the renovations. And lastly, my modeling and royalty income. So I went ahead, but things became screwed up after I closed. There were delays and cost overruns. I had been paying Jan cash as we went along, but I ran out of money. Jan was threatening to stop work and sue. I looked into raising funds, but it would take too long. At the same time, the unexpected happened: both my royalties and modeling income dried up.

"By then, I was dating Henry. He and Jan were acquainted through Masonry, and Jan pressured me to hit him up for money. I didn't want to, because our relationship was too new, but finally it all came out. I offered Henry a mortgage on my property to pay my debt to Jan. Then, while Henry remained in charge behind the scenes, he referred me to Murray Kriegman, who renegotiated my deal. That resulted in a discount of fifty thousand dollars on the final price."

"How'd that work out with Jan?" Ronnie asked.

"He was pissed. But Jan told me that finding that gold ring in the foundation of the old lodge was a windfall—a bit of an offset."

Tom spoke up. "Is that the one he came to police headquarters to see about claiming as lost treasure?"

"Yes. Jan was disappointed, because your officer said there wasn't a ring and showed him the evidence folder. Later, Jan told me that he had talked to Henry again and Henry had agreed to make good on the fifty K."

"Why did Henry change his mind?" Church asked.

"Jan texted him pictures of the ring."

"Hold on," Tom interjected. "Are you saying Jan photographed it?"

"Yes."

"We didn't know about that."

"I assumed you did," Petra lied. "He photographed it in the dirt at the excavation. Jan showed me the pics, then later emailed them to me for backup. They're on my phone. Would you like to see them?"

"Yes."

Petra scrolled through her phone before handing it to Tom.

As the team looked at Jan's pictures, Ronnie smiled. *This is no dumb redhead. In one fell swoop, she has sidestepped any implications of withholding evidence about what she knew and when. She flipped Henry the bird as well.* He looked along the table to Petra, who smiled at him. *She knows exactly what she's doing.*

"Henry understood the damage to his career if it became known that he'd removed the ring from the crime scene," Ronnie commented.

"Not to mention the possibility of ongoing blackmail. All that goes to a motive for Jan's killing," Tom said, and looked at Petra. "Let's move on to Henry."

"It's hard to sort it all out—keep it straight. We clicked so fast, and now it seems like we're breaking up just as quickly. I met Henry at Rod's on the evening after Memorial Day. We hooked up that night, and we've seen each other since. That Friday, the governor called Henry about appointing him to the supreme court. Henry was excited. Next, around the middle of June, I brought Henry a copy of Clara Norris's diary. That's the one that Jan had found while renovating. It contained information about Zeke Norris's gambling away his daughter, which you know about. Henry and I had been happy before that, yet it seemed like Zeke's tale started troubling him."

"Was he concerned about how it would affect his confirmation?" Elizabeth asked.

"I think that was it," Petra continued, "My past lifestyle seemed to be perturbing him as well. I started feeling like a liability. Despite all that, things were mostly normal until the beginning of July, when I started working on my book deal. Henry wasn't happy about that and started pressuring me to hold off."

"Was that the same issue as before?" Church asked. "Worry that it would throw a monkey wrench into his plans?"

"Yes. Henry was concerned that the combination of my earlier lifestyle, the Zeke Norris saga, and my book might be too much to overcome. And then other things started piling up on Henry. Around July twentieth, the governor called, suggesting that if Hank Conklin were Zeke's murderer, it might cause problems with his confirmation. Next, his father's DNA was returned, establishing Zeke's identity relative to Henry. Then came Jan's threats and the texted photos I showed you."

"How did Henry react to your having those?" Elizabeth asked.

"He doesn't know," Petra replied. "After that, our relationship became increasingly stressful. Henry was controlling and never realized that I wouldn't be dominated any longer. Then he wanted me to move in with him permanently. Henry talked about it frequently, not realizing that the house had become emblematic of my freedom. Additionally, he persisted in pressuring me about the book, even though it was important to revitalizing my career."

"Anything else?" Tom probed.

"Well, Jan seemed apprehensive after threatening Henry with the ring's photos. Then he was killed on August tenth. Afterward, Henry handled everything correctly, saying the right things, attending the memorial service, and picking up Jan's secretarial duties at the lodge. He acted sad, yet honestly, I think Henry was relieved. Following that, things became worse. The governor said Henry's confirmation was running into resistance. Then I signed a book deal and was awaiting an advance check. He became more stressed out—not sleeping well, talking in his sleep."

"When was that?" Elizabeth asked.

"Around the middle of August, at the same time as Henry arranged for Kriegman to buy his practice and take over Doc Piscator's case. But those two things didn't seem to relieve him."

"Could you make out any of Henry's sleep talk?" Elizabeth persisted.

"Nothing except the name Roberta, and only once. I asked him who she was, but Henry didn't answer. He was even more upset about ten days later. I think that's when he met with you, Tom."

"Correct," Tom spoke up. "We met on August twenty-fifth. I told him about Jan coming to HQ regarding the ring, although Henry claimed ignorance of it. I also said we knew about Roberta, and then he threatened me with slander."

After that, Petra resumed her narrative. "At the beginning of September, Henry learned I would be doing talk shows about my book. We had our blowup on Thursday, September fifteenth, and I moved into my house that afternoon. I haven't talked to Henry since."

"Before we go on, Petra, do you have any other questions?"

"Yes. I never did find out who Roberta was. Can you tell me?"

"I can't say much," Tom said, "because it's an ongoing cold case. Roberta Allen disappeared in March 1998. Henry had been dating her before that, but he was confirmed to have been in Florida at the time of her disappearance. That's all I'll say. Tell us about your quarrel."

"It was over something silly. Henry blew it all out of proportion."

"It seems that he tends to overreact," Church interjected.

"Probably," Petra agreed. "Henry was nasty. I've never seen him like that; I was only trying to do something nice for him. But he kept shouting, so I stormed out. Yet despite everything—now that I've calmed down—I've been thinking about how we can reconcile. Maybe if I put my book on hold? And what about Evie? She's shaken up. I told her we'd still be friends no matter what, but it wouldn't be the same."

"Petra," Elizabeth urged, trying to refocus her. "Tell us why the quarrel happened."

"Notwithstanding his control issues, Henry has been good to me. Besides helping with the house, he straightened out my hotel bill and gave me an allowance. I wouldn't have made it through without him. I was planning to give him cuff links for Christmas as a thank-you. So when he was in the shower that morning, I looked in his jewelry box to see what he had. He walked in as I was closing the lid. He yelled that I was poking around in his stuff—snooping. Then Henry called me the vilest name."

"Why was he so angry?" Church asked.

"I don't know. I hate to think how he would've reacted if he'd seen me photograph the jewelry."

"You took a picture? Why?" Elizabeth said.

"I meant to bring it with me when I went shopping. I haven't looked at it since."

"If you still have the photo, may I have your phone?" Ronnie asked.

After Petra handed it over, Ronnie enlarged the photo she'd taken. Then he began flipping between other pictures. Finally, he looked up. "I know why Henry was so mad. Look: his jewelry box has two identical gold rings beside each other. They're Masonic, and you can see a scratch on the band of one. Now enlarge the pictures of the ring Jan sent to Petra. It's one of the rings in Henry's box. See? It's Masonic and has the same scratch." While the others were studying the photos, Ronnie continued, "Here's the proof that Henry removed the ring from the crime scene. He made a mistake by keeping it; he ought to have ditched it straightaway. If Petra knew about Jan finding the ring, Henry was scared she'd eventually put two and two together."

"I told him that Jan found it. I don't remember when, but Henry seemed disinterested at the time. Is that what this is all about? Henry's trying to kill me before I realize what I saw?"

"Yes, and stopping your book," Tom said. "Let's talk about what comes next. Lizzie, would you tell Petra about what you've worked out?"

"Sure." Elizabeth told Petra about Carmen, where the apartment was, and the rest. "We still need to resolve details like shopping and so on, because you won't be able to go outside. But we have a little time, since Jimmy doesn't need to report back to his boss until Thursday the twenty-ninth."

"So here's how I foresee this playing out," Tom continued. "First, we'll download those photos, then delete them from your phone so we can deliver it to Jimmy Zee. I'll talk with Jon Anderson ASAP to get his buy-in. Then we'll move Petra, discuss security, and arrange for a formal statement. Does that sound about right?"

Everyone nodded except Petra. "I think it sounds fine, yet I'm uneasy," she said. "I grew up in France, and they have a completely different criminal justice system. So I'm not entirely certain what is the proper procedure here. I'm not a native speaker either and am leery about signing anything."

As she was talking, Ronnie thought, *Son of a bitch! Here it comes.*

"Would it be all right if tonight I called my attorney, Murray Kriegman?" Petra continued. "If he's on board, I'll email the photos to him to hold in escrow. Then I'll delete them, and you can have my phone. Afterward, Kriegman can meet with us when I make my statement. I want to help, but I need to be comfortable."

By now, Ronnie was grinning broadly. *Touché—nicely played,* he thought, noticing Petra avoiding his glance.

Then Elizabeth spoke up. "Petra makes sense, don't you agree, Tom?"

"All right. Let's do that."

As they left the building, Elizabeth muttered to Ronnie, "You were smiling—more than once. You saw all that coming, didn't you?"

"Petra has street smarts—shrewd like a fox."

"And you'd know all about that, wouldn't you?" Elizabeth quipped, and they both laughed.

***

That evening, Jimmy called Massimino. "Boss, I'll need a Tactical Solutions semiautomatic twenty-two-caliber LR rifle, a scope, and ammo. Can you have it delivered tomorrow evening?"

"Yes . . . is everything on track, then?"

"Yeah, we should be able to meet Thursday morning at the Tick Tock."

CHAPTER EIGHTEEN

Monday, September 26, 2022

J on Anderson entered his office just as the phone rang. Picking up, the prosecutor thought, *Murray Kriegman. What the hell does he want?*

"'Mornin'. Have you spoken with Tom Johnson yet?" Murray asked.

"No, what's up?"

"Jeez, I don't know where to start."

"Kriegman at a loss for words? Will miracles never cease," Anderson joked. "Hold on. Tom's on my other line." Anderson connected the three of them, and Kriegman spoke up.

"Tom will run it down for you. But first, my client, Petra, has retained me to represent her in discussions with your offices about her relationship with Henry Conklin. I've represented her before at the suggestion of Henry, with whom I have other business dealings, nothing I'd consider a conflict. I've disclosed everything, and she'll sign a waiver."

Then Tom summed up where they were for the prosecutor.

"So you're suggesting that her photographic evidence of the ring and corroborating testimony are sufficient to issue an arrest warrant for Conklin on obstruction of justice?" Anderson asked.

"Yes, don't you?"

"I'm a little worried about the chain of custody."

"I'm expecting Jan's texts from his mobile carrier any day now. I know where to look for those pictures," Tom answered.

"That'll work for me."

"How about Jan's murder and the conspiracy to kill Petra?" Tom asked. "Jimmy Zee's forcing our hand."

"Look, guys," Murray interrupted. "Those aren't my problems. My concern is that Petra will provide sufficient credible evidence for you to enter into an agreement granting her immunity from prosecution and providing for her safety. Are we there?"

"Yes," Jon said. "Subject to seeing the photos, we have a deal. But if she needs immunity from federal charges and protection for longer than a few weeks, I'll have to involve the US attorney in Newark and the US marshals. The WITSEC program is the only viable long-term solution."

"Are you concerned that the feds won't file?" Tom asked.

"Not really," Jon replied. "But even if they don't, we should have Petra covered. Don't you agree, Murray?"

"Even if only state charges are filed, Petra should qualify for WITSEC. That's because a witness testifying in a state case 'of a similar nature' to an eligible federal one is also entitled to federal protection," Kriegman responded. "Also, I can't imagine the US attorney wouldn't file. A conspiracy to commit murder using an out-of-state hit man with ties to organized crime provides ample cause under the RICO statutes."

As soon as the call was disconnected, Jon rang Church and Ronnie, bringing them up to speed, then called Tom back. "I didn't want to talk further with Kriegman on the line. You guys have done a fine job. We're in good shape on the obstruction charge, but let's hold off on all of them."

"Why?" Church asked.

"As we've said, once we go for an arrest warrant, even if only for obstruction, the cat's out of the bag. The governor will find out immediately and pull Henry's nomination. And then Conklin will have nothing to lose. You know he'll get bail and has the dough to make it. I don't think we'll ever get an ankle bracelet, house arrest, or the like, so he'll disappear. Henry has the mob connections to do it."

"What about Evie?" Ronnie asked.

"He would most likely take her along. I'm also concerned about leaks," Anderson continued. "Elizabeth suspects one here or at the attorney general's office, and I think she may be correct. So we'll continue to meet at the church or the apartment, and I intend to keep our agreement in the safe in my office until the feds take over. I'll only report what's necessary to the AG. I'm sure he's not the problem, but who knows about his staff."

"So we'll keep Petra under wraps for at least two or three weeks while we bear down on Jan's killing, the conspiracy to murder Petra, and the Roberta Allen case?" Ronnie summed up.

"Yes," the prosecutor agreed. "Maybe something will shake loose, and we can go for arrest warrants on everything simultaneously. With the murder and conspiracy to commit murder charges, there won't be bail."

"It makes sense," Tom said, ending the call.

***

On Monday, Petra mused about Sunday's meeting and her situation. Tom's plain speaking had stunned and confused her, but after his reassurance that she wasn't in trouble, she'd settled down and begun answering questions. Even so, she had been wary about the number of inquisitors ganging up on her. She knew she needed to change the dynamic. So she'd asked for a break and, in the ladies' room, peed and thought. *Tom and Church seem like straight shooters; Elizabeth will support me*, she decided. *Yet, despite that, I need to go cautiously. And then there's Ronnie: code red—cunning. I need to manage the rest of this interview. No missteps. And I need Murray Kriegman.*

So when Petra returned to the meeting, she'd acted accordingly. And Ronnie didn't let her down; he was smiling.

Later, Murray Kriegman rang with the news that his call with Jon Anderson had gone well. "I'll pick you up tomorrow morning, and we'll go to Saint Andrew's to iron out the details." *Good, but now's the tricky part*, Petra thought. *Calling Evie.* She picked up her phone and entered Evie's number.

"Hi. I missed you at church yesterday. How are you doin'?"

"Dad and I drove to Cape May for lunch and a visit with Mom's parents."

"That sounds nice. Was it fun?"

"It was a bit strained. You were like the eight-hundred-pound gorilla in the car."

"I'm sorry. It's not only your dad's fault. It takes two to fight. Work hard at giving him the benefit of the doubt. He's a wonderful father and deserves that from you."

"I will. When can I see you?"

"That's why I called. I'll pick you up after school tomorrow if you like, and you can see what I've done around the house. Afterward, we'll have supper."

"That would be great. Can we go to the pizzeria?"

"Sure. I haven't had pizza in a long time. See you then."

***

Jimmy's burner rang at about eight thirty Monday evening. It was Olivia calling. "Hi," he answered. "How was your trip?"

"Slower than I'm used to."

"What time did you leave?"

"Before seven this morning. I arrived a while ago," Olivia said.

"A lot of traffic on Route 12 out of Kill Devil Hills?"

"Yes. People were leaving ahead of the storm, but I sailed through to Demarest once I was on I-295 and the NJ Turnpike. As you asked, I stopped at banks along the way and bought four prepaid Visa cards—nine thousand dollars each. That took time too."

"How much money do we have?"

"Fifteen thousand in cash. Do you want me to start planning our trip?"

"No. I have it all figured out. It's a surprise," Jimmy responded.

"Cool. I'll talk to my parents for a while; then I'm off to bed. I'm tired. Let me know when you'll arrive, okay? I love you."

"Me too."

Then, about half an hour after their call, a messenger dropped off the ordnance Jimmy had requested.

***

Tuesday morning the twenty-seventh, Murray Kriegman and Petra met Tom, Elizabeth, Church, and Jon Anderson at Saint Andrew's. The discussion went smoothly, and Kriegman summarized as they wound down.

"Excellent. I'll draft an agreement and fax it to you by the end of business today. If that's agreeable, I'll email you and Tom the photos now?"

Jon nodded, Petra handed Tom her phone, and Kriegman continued, "When will you move Petra to the apartment?"

"Tomorrow," Church replied.

"How about getting her phone to Jimmy Zee?"

"Elizabeth will call him when we're finished. I'll probably hand it off sometime tomorrow afternoon."

"All right, let's sign the paperwork on Friday. We should probably meet at the apartment," Kriegman said, concluding the meeting.

After the others left, Elizabeth asked Church, "Are you worried about Kriegman pulling a fast one before the deal is signed?"

"No. Tom, Ronnie, and Jon agree he can be difficult, but they all say you can trust him. Tom and Jon have the photos, and Jimmy will have the phone. Petra's the only one with something to lose now, and Kriegman won't screw his client. I'm okay."

Later that day, Elizabeth called Jimmy. "Is everything all set?" he asked.

"Yes. Tomorrow, Wednesday afternoon, at four thirty, go to the Rockaway Mall. Do you know where it is?"

"Yes."

"Park in the center of the big lot in the northeast corner. There are hardly ever any cars there except on holidays or weekends. What are you driving?"

"The same as you saw the other day: a black Lexus SUV."

"Okay. Church will wait a couple of minutes before pulling next to you—driver's doors abreast. Then open your window; he'll pass you Petra's phone."

Jimmy was silent. Elizabeth thought he might balk, but instead he said, "That'll work," and rang off.

***

Petra and Evie were seated in the Canal Ville Pizzeria by six o'clock Tuesday evening. It was across the street from the apothecary and Carmen's Salon on Grist Mill Road near its busy intersection with Central Avenue. Anna, the co-owner with her husband, Giovanni, had greeted

Joseph B. Hodgkins

them and supplied menus. "How are you, Evie? It's been a long time," she asked with a slight Italian accent.

"Too long, Anna."

"And how's your father? I haven't seen him in a while either."

"He's fine—busy. This is my friend Petra. She's new in town."

"I know—everybody recognizes you." Anna extended her hand. "I think you'll be happy here."

"I'm certain I will."

"What would you like to drink? I'll fetch those while you're looking at the menus."

Petra ordered a bottle of San Pellegrino and Evie a Diet Coke. "What kind of pizza should we have?"

"A Margherita."

"Good," Petra laughed. "It doesn't give me agita."

"Mom, Dad, and I used to come most Friday nights. That was her favorite pie also."

"You still miss her a lot?"

Evie teared a little, nodded, and sniffled. "It never seems to get better."

"It will, eventually . . . honest."

They were quiet for a while. It was an emotional moment for Petra as well. The more she thought about it, the more it sank in: this might be the last time she saw Evie. And there wasn't a solution. Evie wouldn't know what had happened when she disappeared. The cops would arrest Henry, Petra would testify, and Evie would feel betrayed. After that, Petra would require complete witness protection: a new identity, location, and so on. Why? Because Henry could take his revenge—even from jail. *I feel awful about not being there for Evie when she needs me. But I don't have a choice; doing nothing is suicide.*

Petra picked up their conversation. "Whatever happens, you know how much I love you, don't you?"

"I do, but I wish you two would get back together."

"I'm not sure that's possible any longer."

"Why?"

"Relationships ebb and flow. As you get older, you'll realize that lovers and friends fall apart for no reason, even if nothing bad has occurred between them. It's the way it is. But your father and I had a serious bust-up. I wish it were different. But none of that means we love you less. You weren't responsible."

"I wondered if I might've been underfoot or wanted too much of your attention."

"Don't think that, not for a minute. Ask your father. He never thought that either."

"We'll have to try hard to stay in touch," Evie snuffled.

"Absolutely, but be realistic. It can never be as close as if I were living with you guys, even if only part-time."

"I know."

They finished their pie, and later, as Petra parked in Evie's driveway, Evie asked, "Can we do something this weekend?"

"I don't see why not. Now come over here." They hugged across the center console. Then Petra lied and said, "I'll call you."

"Love you," Evie said, and Petra drove away, fighting tears. *This sucks!*

***

On Wednesday afternoon, Petra sat on the couch in the apartment she'd just moved into. It had been helter-skelter since her meeting at the church on Sunday, Murray Kriegman's phone call on Monday, another meeting at Saint Andrew's yesterday, and supper at the pizzeria. Everything had happened so fast that she'd only had time to reflect on Evie, so now she mulled over her other circumstances.

On Monday and Tuesday, Petra had prepared to vanish. She supposed that if the mob, Henry, or others questioned her disappearance, they'd find a way to follow the money. Petra was lucky, because years ago, while living and working in Manhattan, she'd opened a trade name checking account called Salacious at the Chase Bank. Lately, it'd been inactive, but once she received her fifty-thousand-dollar advance, Petra had deposited it at Chase's local branch. She was convinced no one would look under that name. Next, she'd packed, using cast-aside boxes from her recent move. Elizabeth had told her that Carmen had a washer and dryer at the salon, so Petra took only ten days' worth of clothes, toiletries, and a few sentimental items. Then she'd packed the last pad of checks from her regular account and the Salacious checkbook. She'd abandoned her purse and laptop on the kitchen counter. Finally, Petra had left her car in the garage to complete the charade.

This morning, Petra had put her cereal bowl and spoon to rinse in the sink, showered, and dressed in sweats and sneakers. Elizabeth had food shopped for her, and later, she and Church had picked Petra up for the move to Carmen's. They'd parked in the back lot and entered through the salon's rear door.

I've thought of everything to create the illusion that I disappeared while jogging. Tom, Church, and Ronnie will work out a security scheme tomorrow. But I have questions: I don't fully understand the implications of the WITSEC program, and notwithstanding Henry's loan, I can't walk away from my house, because it has too much equity. So, before I sign their deal on Friday, I'll talk to Murray Kriegman and Jon Anderson about everything.

***

Later Wednesday afternoon, Jimmy arrived at the Rockaway Mall a few minutes early. He quickly located the area Elizabeth had described and parked in the center, pulling through one spot into the next, nose out. He gave the site a quick look-see. There was no one around, so Jimmy popped the hatch, left the SUV, removed the rifle, scope, and ammo, still packaged in brown wrapping paper, and slid them under the vehicle. There was no need for them now, because they had served their purpose—hoodwinking the boss.

While Jimmy was doing that, Church, using field glasses, surveilled him from a distant crowded lot. *I wonder what that's all about. I don't see him planting a bomb under the car to blow us to smithereens.* So Church drove to meet him as they'd agreed. The men lowered their windows. "What's in the package under your car?" Church asked.

"It's a rifle, scope, and ammo. I didn't want to leave it lying around or waste time ditching it safely. Get rid of it for me, all right?"

"Okay."

"Did you relocate Petra?"

"Yes, earlier today." Then Church passed her phone to Jimmy, who pulled away immediately. Church picked up the package before leaving and thought, *I'll turn this over to Tom.*

***

Jimmy met the boss early Thursday morning and handed over the proof. "How'd it go?" Massi asked.

"Smoothly."

"Great. I know you weren't happy about this job." The boss gave Jimmy an envelope. "There's a little extra inside, a bonus. In the future, I'll try to use you only when necessary—*capiche*?"

"Okay."

"There's a big storm headed for the Outer Banks this weekend. Are you goin' home now?"

"No. I'm visiting family in Pennsylvania," Jimmy improvised.

"How about your ole lady?"

"She's cool—hunkered down inland with friends," he replied, keeping up the deception.

They finished breakfast, and as Jimmy left the diner, he called Olivia. "Hey, I'm on the way to Demarest. See you in less than an hour."

"That's great. You're finished earlier than I expected."

CHAPTER NINETEEN

Friday, September 30, 2022

Karl and Klaus were finishing their breakfast in the coffee shop. "Your Yankees had a good week," Karl said.

"Yeah," Klaus admitted. "They finally clinched the AL East on Tuesday in Toronto with a first-round bye in the playoffs, and Judge tied Maris's sixty-one homers on Wednesday."

"Do you still think he'll break the record?"

"Yes. I'm leery about the World Series, however. The Yanks will probably have to get past Houston first, and they're tough."

Karl changed the subject. "It looks like Hurricane Ian's coming ashore this afternoon near Georgetown, South Carolina."

"Florida's west coast already took a wallop," Klaus remarked.

"Yeah, and now they're sayin' that since Ian took so long to cross over the state and into the Atlantic, the total damage will be over one hundred billion."

"Jesus! But the good news is we'll get rain from its remnants next week."

"We need it," Karl concluded as they settled their checks and headed for the park.

***

Later that morning, Elizabeth, Church, and Ronnie met at Petra's apartment. They chatted until Tom and Jon Anderson arrived. "So, how did the move go?" Jon asked.

"Fine," Petra replied, and told him about the precautions she'd taken to make it look like she'd gone missing on her morning run.

"That was well thought out. Kudos. Do you need anything?" Jon asked.

"A burner phone and someone to collect the mail from my post office box. I didn't change it to delivery at the new house before this happened."

"I'll pick up your mail every couple of days. Just give me the combination," Elizabeth offered.

"And I'll see to a phone," Ronnie said, as Murray Kriegman knocked on the door.

Before they reviewed and signed the documents, Petra asked them about selling her house and the WITSEC program.

"What we're doing now is temporary. Once WITSEC is in play, the US attorney and marshals can answer your questions. They have plenty of experience," Jon reassured her. "I'm holding off approaching them until the last moment because of security concerns too."

"I'm nervous, though."

"That's normal," Elizabeth said, trying to comfort her. "Hang in there; it'll be okay."

After the documents were signed, Murray Kriegman and Jon Anderson left. Tom reported arranging increased overnight drive-by patrols past the salon. "You should be safe if you stay out of sight."

On the way home, Elizabeth asked Church, "Do you think she'll be okay?"

"Yes. Henry thinks she's dead. This subterfuge should hold for as long as necessary if Petra's careful."

"What if the mob finds out?"

"I don't think they care. They were paid, as was Jimmy. And what's Henry gonna do, sue them for breach of contract?"

"No. He'll hire someone else."

"That's why putting him in jail fast and getting Petra into federal protection is important."

"I'd feel much better if you'd also keep an eye on her."

"O ye of little faith! I've already decided we ought to supplement law enforcement's security. I'll work it out with Ronnie, then clear it with the chief."

***

Olivia and Jimmy slept in on Saturday morning. After lunch at her parents', they took a long walk, even though the weather wasn't ideal: overcast with temperatures around sixty degrees, a gentle breeze from the northeast, and an occasional light shower. Wearing jackets and armed with umbrellas, they strolled down Demarest's east hill, stopping when the village appeared. They looked across the park to the Duck Pond. "It was enlarged in the mid-1800s by damming the Tenakill Brook," Olivia explained. "Much later, the park became a popular setting for wedding party photos."

"Huh," Jimmy uttered. "Interesting. Nice looking. I didn't pay much attention yesterday when I came through; I was following the GPS with one eye on the screen."

Olivia pointed to the historic Demarest Railroad Depot, situated beyond the pond on Park Street, across from the shops. "Cleveland Cady, the designer of New York City's Metropolitan Opera House, drew the plans, and it was completed in the 1870s, then named after a railroad's director. It's a senior center now." Then motioning south along Park, up the hill, Olivia said, "Where the fire department and police station are now, the Tenakill Hotel used to stand. It was built when the Northern Railroad came through in the 1860s and was a popular summer resort for New Yorkers. The attractions were rowing on the pond and visiting the Knickerbocker racetrack, where the high school now stands. The hotel burnt down before 1900 but was never rebuilt."

Afterward, they continued past the Demarest Middle School, which Olivia had attended. She picked up her narrative, telling Jimmy about David des Marets (later known as Demarest), from Beauchamps, northern France, a Protestant Huguenot fleeing religious persecution. He had settled in the Hackensack Valley during the mid-1600s and had a large family that became influential statewide until after World War II. She continued to relate how this region of the Northern Valley— originally a farming area—had been part of two adjoining towns until 1903, when it was spun off, taking the name of the railroad depot and the Demarest family, and was now an upscale bedroom community, chiefly for New York City.

Farther along, turning into a side street, Olivia said, "I want to show you something unusual."

The Demarest Railroad Depot

After they'd walked a short distance, Jimmy stopped and pointed. "Is this it? It looks like a small park in a roundabout."

"Look closer," Olivia said, leading him through the entrance. "Sautjes Tave's Begraven Ground cemetery. It's from the Revolutionary War era. Very few people know it's here because of the hedges and trees surrounding it. Check this out," she said, showing Jimmy a grave marker. It read:

> *Here lies the remains of Douwe Talema, who died on the 11th day of May 1779 in his Ninetieth Year. This aged Man at his Residence near this Place was wilfully and barbarously murdered by a Party of Tories. Traitors to their country who had taken refuge with the Troops of Britain then in New York and came thence to murder and plunder. To pay a Tribute of Respect to his memory and also to commemorate the manner of his death, several of his relatives have erected this Stone.*

"Amazing," Jimmy said, and they began returning to her parents' house. "So the Tories crossed the Hudson River, then scrambled up the Palisades."

"Yes, at Lower Closter Landing, following a rough road that's no longer here."

"You know a lot about your town."

"I did a paper on it during high school."

Olivia had become pensive throughout the afternoon, and as they approached her parents', she sighed. "We aren't going on vacation, are we? We're not coming back."

"No. Not for a long time."

***

After services on Sunday the second, Evie hung around during coffee hour until she could speak with Elizabeth. "I'm worried about Petra. I can't reach her."

"Do you think something's the matter?"

"Don't know. We had supper at the pizzeria on Tuesday, and Petra said she'd call during the week to set something up for yesterday— but nada. My calls go to voice mail. Have you seen her?"

"Not since church last Sunday," Elizabeth answered, uncomfortably lying.

"Did she seem okay?"

"Yes. How about your father? Has he talked to her?"

"He says no. But I can tell he doesn't want to talk about it. Could we go to her house and check? I know where she hides a key. Petra might've fallen downstairs and be lying there, hurt."

"Fine. Call your father and tell him you're with me."

While Evie was on the phone, Elizabeth called Church from her office. "Evie's coming to the rectory with me while I change. She wants me to take her over to check up on Petra."

"Is she distraught?"

"Yes. It's gonna be tough."

"All you can do is be there for her. It sucks."

240

While Elizabeth was upstairs, Evie played with Billy and Jacques. In a few minutes, Elizabeth came down, saying, "Church, we're having lunch afterward, so it'll be a while."

"No problem," he said as they left the house. "The lads and I are all set to watch baseball this afternoon."

"They're cute," Evie remarked as they went to the car. "Church loves being a dad, doesn't he?"

"He wouldn't change it for anything."

A little while later, while parking in Petra's driveway, Elizabeth said, "Everything looks normal.

They exited the car, and Evie retrieved the hidden key. The women investigated before finally ending up in the kitchen—no Petra. Evie opened the garage door, and the Mercedes was there. Then they spotted her bowl and spoon soaking in the sink and a laptop and purse on the counter. "Let's check that," Elizabeth suggested.

Evie emptied the purse's contents on the kitchen table. "Her wallet, phone, and keys aren't here. She must have them with her."

"Did you notice her sweats and running shoes upstairs?"

"I didn't. But I know where she keeps them." Evie left and was back in a few minutes. "No running shoes. There are sweats in the hamper, but I can't find her second set. I think Petra went running but didn't return. We need to call the police."

"It looks that way, but let's not jump to conclusions. We'll lock up and discuss it over lunch."

Later that evening, talking in bed, Elizabeth told Church what had happened. "I finally calmed Evie down, but I had to promise we'd report Petra's absence to the police if she doesn't turn up by Wednesday."

"I'll give Tom a heads-up. You did a great job following through with our ploy. Are you okay?"

"Not really; I feel sorry for Evie. I know she seems mature, but fifteen's too young to be without parents. It isn't fair."

Hugging Elizabeth closer, Church agreed. "No, it's not. But it wouldn't be right to risk Petra's life if Evie slips up."

***

On Wednesday morning, October fifth, Karl and Klaus were at their usual spot in the coffee shop. "That rain from Ian sure came in as expected, "Karl said.

"We might have as much as three inches by the time it's outa here tomorrow."

"So we'll have to skip the park today—head home after breakfast. I heard on the news that Aaron Judge did it last night."

"Sixty-two at the Texas Rangers," Klaus confirmed.

"You seem bummed. Is anything the matter?"

"No. I'm a little nostalgic."

"How so?"

"I remember how much fun it was in 1961 following Maris's quest. Everyone was talking about it. Yet it was more than that. We were happily married, had decent-paying jobs on the railroad, and the lodge was full at every communication. Life was simpler—kinder. However, that didn't last long with the Cuban Missile Crisis, the civil rights march on Washington, DC, JFK's assassination, and all that followed."

"Baseball versus football," Karl quipped.

"Pastoral versus pugnacious: I like that."

"I didn't realize you were unhappy," Karl probed.

"Not unhappy. Bittersweet's a better word."

"Well, look at it this way: we made it to the extra innings."

"That we did, but I wish my wife were here," Klaus murmured.

"Me too."

***

Later that morning, Tom, Elizabeth, Church, Ronnie, and Frosty met at Saint Andrew's. Tom asked everyone for an update, beginning with Elizabeth.

"We moved Petra successfully last Wednesday, and she signed her statement and paperwork on Friday," Elizabeth said, then described her trip to Petra's house with Evie. "She's upset and wants to file a missing-persons report. I suggested she wait until today."

"All right," Tom said. "It makes sense now; enough time has passed. Evie's a minor and can't file it. So, Lizzie, would you? Then I'll hold it on my desk for the time being."

"Sure."

"Anything else?"

"Judy called," Elizabeth resumed. "She didn't turn up anything with her Camden investigation."

"I followed up with the DMV searches Judy suggested," Tom said. "Nothing new. How about you, Church?"

"I met last Wednesday with Jimmy Zee and handed off Petra's phone. He gave me the rifle, et cetera, that he acquired for the job. It's in the rectory. Tom, you should pick it up before you leave."

"All right," the chief answered, then addressed Frosty. "Do you have anything?"

"I followed up on the Camden angle—nada either."

"That leaves you, Ronnie."

"I'm still working on my snitches with the Genoveses and DeCavalcantes. I don't have anything to report either. But I've been thinking. Maybe we've been approaching things bass-ackwards—at least with the Genoveses."

"How so?" Tom asked.

"We've been focused on running Thomas Bellotti to ground because he was close to Conklin. Yet at the same time, we've never considered him an active participant, certainly not the hitter."

"So, where are you heading with this?" Frosty asked.

"I'm suggesting we take the opposite direction. See who Tommy's friends, associates, and acquaintances were in the crime families. We'll stand down on Tommy and interrogate our informants for his mob links."

"Agreed," Tom said. "Then we'll start pulling them in on bullshit charges and see what shakes loose."

Ronnie was watching Elizabeth, who was grinning. "What's up? You look like the cat that swallowed the canary."

"Why not use the leakers in the prosecutor's and AG's offices to launch a disinformation campaign? Make it well known that the prosecutor is fed up and is putting together a task force to crack down on the gangs, dragging everyone in for interrogation, and so forth. Use any excuse. We'll rile up the mobs beforehand. Who knows what might materialize?"

"That's wicked, Lizzie." Tom chuckled.

The chief spoke to Anderson, who supported their cage-rattling stratagem and offered additional investigators to assist.

***

The governor called Henry on October 6 as he drove to meet Giuseppe in Morristown. "The senate's back in session," the governor began, "and they've promised me a confirmation hearing before the end of the month."

"That's great. How does it look?"

"Tammy says we should have the required votes without any Republicans. That gives me confidence, because confirmations tend to be more bipartisan than regular business. I wouldn't go ahead if I thought you would flame out. You did a fine job with the difficult interviews. We'll make plans after I have a date."

When the call ended, Henry parked at Headquarters Plaza. The meeting with Giuseppe went the same as the previous ones, and Henry left in a few minutes with Petra's phone, which he destroyed, as he had the others.

That out of the way, he called Saul. "Anything new?"

"Do you remember the battle-ax in Philadelphia who kept me cooling my heels the two times I called on the managing partner?"

"Yes."

"Well, I chatted her up both times. She's not a bad ole broad. I think she's lonely. So I had an idea. I started staking out the coffee shop next to the law offices. Sure as shit, she stops in before work every day and gets takeout: a large sweet 'n' light with a crumb bun. So I went to the shop before she arrived and sat where I'd be noticed. The bottom line is we had coffee together."

"Didn't she ask why you were there?"

"Yeah. I told her I was working on a different case. Then we had coffee another time. She said she'd heard scuttlebutt that Bellotti wasn't well. And he lives and works with a significant other in Camden. I'll reach out to my contacts in the Philly Mob," Saul finished.

***

On Thursday the sixth, Ronnie and Frosty, along with the investigators assigned by Anderson, started interrogating Genovese and DeCavalcante mobsters. They used the phone, had clandestine meetings, or dragged them into police headquarters. Ronnie was in his element, being aggressive and intimidating. "A friggin' full-court press," he quipped.

By early Monday morning, the names of Thomas Bellotti's associates and other feedback were coming in, and the mobs were jittery. Ronnie was pleased, had another cup of coffee with his wife, and was reading the paper before heading out when something caught his eye.

"Hey, the Stop & Shop in Morris Plains is having a big sale on bell peppers—all colors," he announced. "Do you want me to pick some up?"

"Sure. Would you like sausage and peppers tonight? We haven't had that in a long time."

"You're on. I'll stop at Vespucci's in East Hanover, pick up sweet sausages, and then drop everything off before I hit the road."

At the supermarket, Ronnie went directly to produce. A large bin was piled with green, red, yellow, and orange peppers. He walked around, choosing. While Ronnie was doing this, a middle-aged man, well dressed in a navy chalk-striped business suit, white shirt, and red power tie, approached the other side of the bin and began perusing the produce. He looked up at Ronnie, commenting, "Quite a selection."

Ronnie acknowledged him, and after a brief pause, the man continued, "So, what do you want, Detective?"

Ronnie looked up. "Consigliere?"

"Good, you know who I am—it saves time. Call me AJ. I'll ask again, what do you want?"

"Are you here on behalf of your boss?"

"Does it matter? Let's not dance."

"Okay. It's you I want to talk to anyway."

"How so?"

"I'm looking for Thomas Bellotti."

"Good luck with that."

"You were one of his closest associates back in the day. If anyone knows where he is, it's you."

"You've been doing your homework. Yeah, Tommy and I grew up in the Bronx. We went through school together. I was a couple of years ahead of him. When he graduated high school, I was already working for Enzo. Then Tommy went to college and law school. We weren't close after that, although he did work for his dad for a few years after graduation. You know all that."

"Yeah, but why did he disappear?"

"That's personal. Family business."

"It's just odd. Didn't his father care when Tommy dropped off the map?"

"You're confusing the man with his profession. Maybe he cared more than you realize."

Ronnie wisecracked, "If you love something, let it go . . ."

"Exactly."

"We heard a rumor that he was in Camden using the name Bell. But we couldn't turn anything up," Ronnie continued.

"I heard the same story years ago."

"Didn't you have the DeCavalcantes or your buddies in Philly run it to ground?"

"No, the boss didn't want to. Why do you want to talk to Tommy?"

"We're investigating a 1998 Kearny cold case. It concerns the disappearance of a teenage girl, Roberta Allen. We think Tommy may be a material witness. We're also looking at Henry Conklin."

"The lawyer?"

"Yes. Do you know him?"

"By reputation."

"You never met him?"

"Once, I think, back in the day, when Tommy was in law school. They shared an apartment."

"What about Roberta Allen?"

"I've never heard of her."

"And you'd know . . ."

"If it were family business? Yes. Is that all?"

"Do you know Jimmy Zee? Have you met him?"

"He's a ghost—works mainly for the DeCavalcantes."

"You didn't answer my question." When AJ didn't respond, Ronnie pushed, "Have you ever met him?"

Finally, the tight-lipped gangster asked, "Is there anything else?"

"Not for the time being."

"Okay. And Detective, if you want to talk again, no need to go through the back door. Call," AJ said, handing Ronnie a business card that read ANTHONY "AJ" JACONELLI, PURVEYOR OF QUALITY ITALIAN IMPORTS TO FINE RESTAURANTS.

Ronnie picked up the sausages, stopped at home, and called Church when he was back on the road. After he reviewed his encounter with Jaconelli, Church said, "That must've been unnerving. Did he associate you with being undercover in their crew back in the day?"

"No. He was still in school then. I'm not worried; they won't do anything crazy. But I was surprised that they responded so fast. I had the impression he wanted to truncate our investigation ASAP. He sounded cooperative, yet he didn't tell me anything. He knows more—hiding something," Ronnie opined.

"And he doesn't want Enzo Bellotti involved," Church concluded. "While you're on the phone, there's something else." He explained his plan for additional security at Carmen's.

Ronnie thought briefly. "Well, it's a pain in the ass, but you're right. Tom can only do so much. We'll rotate randomly, several times a week. I agree it makes sense to set up when street traffic dies down after one a.m. and leave an hour before sunrise."

"Okay, Carmen's on board. She'll give us the keys to the back door, and we can park in the rear lot. The salon has two sides, so if we sit inside the one across from the second-story stairs, we can cover the killer's natural 'avenue of approach,'" Church said.

"And we can easily hear anyone entering through the front or back doors. It sounds like a plan. Let's start tomorrow; I'll take the first tour," Ronnie volunteered as they rang off.

CHAPTER TWENTY

Monday, October 10, 2022

Cortona, Italy

Olivia and Jimmy had made their plans before leaving her parents'. They'd shared the prepaid credit cards and cash to finance travel expenses. Then, saying goodbye to Demarest, Jimmy drove to Boston, dropping Olivia at Logan Airport, where she'd caught a Lufthansa flight to Frankfurt International Airport. She stayed overnight, then flew to Rome's Fiumicino Airport early the following day before heading to Cortona. Jimmy drove to Montréal and flew to Paris, where he stayed a few days before duplicating the rest of Olivia's trip. Along the way, they used fake IDs: Jimmy a different one than Nico Karras, Olivia one he'd obtained behind her back—all this to bamboozle would-be snoops.

Cortona, in Tuscany, had an Etruscan, Roman, and medieval heritage. It was an appealing walled hilltop town with a labyrinth of tiny lanes, shops, trattorias, historic churches, and important museums. Olivia had arrived on the sixth, staying at the modest Hotel San Luca on the Piazza Garibaldi. Its lobby, at street level, was on the top floor, since the hotel's other seven floors were built down the side of a steep hill, affording spectacular views of the Tuscan countryside.

Olivia wasn't sure when Jimmy would come, so she spent her time sightseeing. On Friday she walked to the Chiesa di São Francesco, a thirteenth-century Roman Catholic church, and had it to herself until a chubby, balding Franciscan from the nearby monastery came and greeted her. At first, Olivia thought he was coming to chase her away, yet instead, he started chatting in broken English before reaching into his cowl and retrieving a guidebook. The monk chattered enthusiastically, pointing to and underlining various sections about the church and its artwork with his finger. Olivia nearly laughed because the book was in Italian. Nevertheless, with her high school Spanish, they managed to communicate. As Olivia started to leave, she handed him twenty euros.

"*Mille grazie, mille grazie,*" he said, continuing with, "Signorina, you come this way." Then he led her to carefully preserved Saint Francis of Assisi relics, namely, a habit and an embroidered cushion on which the dying saint was supposed to have laid his head.

On Saturday morning, Olivia explored the town's medieval center—its narrow streets, alleyways, and shops. Then, during the afternoon, she relaxed, read, and thought. Later, in the bar that evening, she met another young woman, Janice, who was traveling on a ten-day college alumnae tour. It was based in Cortona with daily side trips. The two women hit it off, and when the tour's conductor came in later, they talked her into letting Olivia accompany Monday's coach trip to Assisi. *Fifty dollars well spent*, Olivia believed.

Then she went to mass at the Basilica di Santa Margherita on Sunday. The cobblestone pathway to the basilica, which began across the Piazza Garibaldi from the hotel, was about half a mile long, doubled back on itself with a fishhook left turn, and was one of the steepest hills in Italy. Stations of the cross had been fashioned along the climb, with stone resting/viewing benches across from them. The hike turned out to be a challenge, and Olivia wondered, *How can anybody who isn't in shape do this?*

After mass, she visited the sinner-turned-saint's remains in a glass case above the altar. Later, descending the pathway, Olivia glimpsed bird's-eye views of the ancient town.

Cortona

Monday was a long day. The forty-five-mile trek to Assisi was slow, and the tour wasn't as enjoyable as Olivia had hoped. She chatted with Janice. That afternoon, as the coach left for Cortona, she thought, *It killed a day, anyway.*

At about four thirty when the bus pulled in, Jimmy was sitting, his duffel at his feet, on the rocks at the base of Giuseppe Garibaldi's monument in the middle of the piazza.

As they walked to the hotel, Olivia said, "You should've gone inside. I left a key for you."

"I checked with the desk. They said your tour was nearly back, so I decided to hang around outside."

When they were in their room, Jimmy crossed to the two floor-to-ceiling casement windows. "Wow! What a view."

While he was still looking, Olivia quickly undressed, then teased as she lazed on the bed, "And how about this view? Isn't it time to pay attention to your lonely girl?"

Hours later, they ambled to a trattoria and took a long time over dinner. When they returned to the hotel, Olivia said, "We need to talk."

"I know. But not tonight. Is tomorrow okay?"

"Yes."

They were up early on Tuesday, packing before breakfast because Jimmy said they were leaving at noon. After their meal, they strolled through the narrow lanes and byways of the town's center, Olivia guiding him.

She resumed Saturday's stock taking as they wandered, beginning with their first meeting on the Kill Devil Hills beach. Jimmy had rescued her, and she still marveled at what had happened. Bang! In an instant, two spirits had collided, unexpectedly becoming one. They'd never looked back or explained, and neither gave a damn about the other's prior lives. Thoughts of equality, partnership, and fairness were irrelevant in their relationship, because they were one. And they were happy.

Despite that, confusion had begun when she'd shown him around her hometown. At first, it was a simple walk through Demarest, but by the end it had become something else—something worrisome.

Not only was Olivia a bright and observant woman, but she was intuitive. There had been hints and clues between their initial meeting years ago and this summer's first recall by the boss. That's when she'd seen what Jimmy removed from his safe and realized he might've been a mob assassin. She pondered it and thought she understood. It was a job; he'd compartmentalized it, like being an army sniper or a CIA black-ops guy. While not condoning it, Olivia didn't worry about his first call-up, because that wasn't her Jimmy. But now there'd been a second one. He was angry about it, not to mention apprehensive. This wasn't like him.

All of this was part of her discontent. And her solution had been to drop out of sight after Jimmy finished the second job. Yet, sitting in Cortona, waiting, Olivia realized that maybe never returning home wasn't what she'd envisioned. *But I could live with that. So it's something else that's needling me.*

Then finally, this morning, her feelings had become clear.

"Let's talk now," Olivia said.

"Do you want to go first?" Jimmy asked.

"Yes. I've been sad since Demarest."

"I know. Second thoughts?"

"No. I'm still okay as long as we're together. No regrets, only sadness. That's what's confusing."

"I understand. You wanted me to see what you were giving up."

"Yes. Yet it's not simply that. I need the reassurance of your love."

"I know leaving wasn't easy, but what'd I do to make you feel that way?"

"Something changed . . ."

Jimmy was silent, and in a bit, Olivia continued.

"I have to know what's happening, where we're going, what we're doing. And more important, how serious is the danger we'll be in? I feel left out, like a junior partner. Our oneness is gone, and I need it back."

"We've never talked about our pasts. I have secrets—"

"Never mind that," Olivia said, holding up her hand. "I know. Let me make this easy." She hoped that her analysis of his job was accurate. "You were a mob hit man. Let's move on."

"You knew?"

"An inkling until I packed up the safe: the cash, my fake ID, and later the stops to buy prepaid credit cards. Not to mention ditching your gun and ammo in the Atlantic. I was certain afterward."

"And you're still okay?"

"I'm here."

Jimmy paused. "You're right, of course; I wasn't forthcoming. I'm sorry." Then he told her about Petra, his inability to act, and the risks they would incur after his trickery was detected.

"Okay. As I see it, once Petra testifies, Conklin's the big threat."

"Yes. He has the money and connections to retaliate, even behind bars."

"How about the mob?" Olivia asked.

"Well, they were paid, and I don't see the boss getting too pissed off over being misled."

"What about her screwing up whatever the DeCavalcantes are plotting for Conklin?"

"I don't know. But there's no question Petra's testimony will fuck it up."

"Is there anything else?"

"Perhaps . . . a premonition. I keep worrying about something that happened nearly twenty-five years ago. Petra stirred it up."

"Having to do with why you couldn't do her? Will you tell me?"

"No. It's probably nothing. Only three of us knew, and it was off the books . . ." Jimmy shook himself. "Let's go over my plan now," he went on. "It's first-rate. Only you, me, and my cousin, Ciccio Amicucci, will know. He's my mother's sister's kid. Their family isn't involved with the mob. He'll pick us up at noon, then head to Montepulciano, about twenty miles southwest, where we own Amicucci's Winery and Vineyard together. Ciccio also has a second vineyard in Montalcino, about twenty miles west of Montepulciano. He makes two award-winning red wines, Vino Nobile di Montepulciano and Brunello di Montalcino, as well as other varietals such as Chianti. I'm a forty-nine percent silent partner. Years ago, I put up the dough when he moved to Tuscany and bought the business. I don't appear on the paperwork. But I have a signed and sealed side agreement in the stuff you collected from the safe. My only contact with him until recently has been a once-a-year telephone update on how the business is doing. The company has been growing, so I'll help him part-time.

"We'll live at the winery in a two-bedroom guest house. My cousin used to rent it to traveling wine aficionados by the week, but that business hasn't returned since the pandemic. I've always considered this as the bedrock of my fallback plan. And I have money stashed with Swiss banks and brokers. We ought to be safe and comfortable. Do you feel better?"

"Yes, but don't leave me out ever again. Do you understand?"

Jimmy nodded.

"Okay, then I'm cool. We'll be vintners instead of beach bums."

***

AJ wasn't happy on Tuesday morning as he drove the 110 miles down the New Jersey Turnpike to Camden. He'd asked the boss for a day off to handle personal business. Yesterday had been a bad one: first, that detective, Ronnie Gruenburg, then later in the afternoon, a phone call. AJ hadn't recognized the caller ID, so he'd let it go to voice mail. A few minutes later, after tolerating Verizon's never-ending mind-numbing introduction, he'd heard Connie Morales's message:

"Anthony, I'm Tommy Bell's—Bellotti's—companion. He asked me to call. Tommy's sick, dying—cirrhosis and liver cancer—and only has a few months left. He wants to patch things up with his dad and needs help arranging a meeting with his daughter. Can you come, please? It's hard talking on the phone. Thank you."

AJ had called Connie back and made plans to drive down this morning. He was upset over his old friend's health and apprehensive about his boss's feelings. Mixed, for sure—afraid for Tommy, surprised and happy about a granddaughter—but once Enzo moved past those emotions, he'd go berserk discovering the real reason for the father-son estrangement. A story AJ had kept locked away all these years.

Speeding past Princeton, he recalled what'd happened. It was as crystal clear and impactful as if it had all gone down yesterday. He thought about the cost: one dead girl, Roberta. And then there was damage to at least three of the four men involved. Tommy had been hurt the most; the diagnosis Connie Morales had just delivered was proof of that. Jimmy Zee had been fucked up as well—still couldn't do women. Luckily for him, there weren't many contracts on broads. And AJ had had his share of bad times until he turned the key. That left Henry Conklin. Who knew if he even gave a shit? *And why should he? He has what he wants. All of this, except for Tommy, has been caused by fucking ambition. And even now I don't understand the Tommy-Henry relationship. I guess today it would be called a bromance.*

***

Near the end of February 1998, AJ had gotten a call from his friend Tommy Bellotti. They'd grown up together in the Bronx. AJ was a couple of years older and, after high school, had gone to work for Tommy's father in the Genovese crime family. Tommy had finished high school, graduated from Princeton, and was now at the NYU School of Law. Not unexpectedly, they weren't as close as they had been.

Consequently, AJ was glad to hear from him. But the call hadn't been to catch up. Tommy was looking for a favor—a big ask. A hit gratis. And it wasn't even for him.

Initially, AJ had reservations, because he was still learning the ropes. Yet he was impatient to move ahead, and Tommy would be a valuable asset. So he called Jimmy Zee, with whom they'd hung out while growing up. He worked for a New Jersey affiliate, the DeCavalcantes, and was also a go-getter, already developing a reputation as a contractor, doing jobs quickly and quietly. And it made sense to use someone from out of state for the hit, because Enzo Bellotti would be less likely to hear about it.

On Friday, February 27, AJ, Tommy, and Henry met in a mob-backed *ristorante* on Arthur Avenue in the Bronx's Little Italy. It was full of activity, so the men weren't noticed or overheard. Henry provided AJ with the necessary information: a description, photo, and home and school addresses. When AJ learned Tommy and Henry were heading to Florida for a ten-day spring break beginning on March 13, he suggested, "That's the best time to do it. You guys will have ironclad alibis."

The next day, AJ met Jimmy and filled him in.

"I already know where and when to do it and how to dispose of her," Jimmy said when AJ had finished. "I'll surveil during the week of March second; then we'll plan on Monday the sixteenth. I'll confirm that it's before their spring recess, okay? You'll need to have a van with side doors—and bring a couple of shovels."

By the tenth, Jimmy's recognizance was finished and AJ had acquired shovels and a stolen van, switching the tags with those from an abandoned car.

They met up later that week to go over their strategy. It was simple. Roberta usually walked home from Kearny High School with friends. It was a short distance, but she split off from the others a few blocks before her house, then continued down lightly traveled streets. That's where they'd grab her. The beauty of the plan was that they could snatch her anytime during the week of the sixteenth if complications such as her getting a ride home, having a friend over, or the like arose.

On the afternoon of the sixteenth, AJ parked down the street from the high school. He quickly spotted Roberta leaving. After letting her get a head start, they trailed her from a distance. When she turned down a side street, AJ drove past her, parking at the curb. Roberta was isolated— no passing cars or people about. They exited the van, and AJ waited while Jimmy opened the sliding door and climbed into the back. Jimmy rummaged in his duffel, removed a syringe, and then took a marmalade tiger kitten he'd acquired from a shelter out of a cardboard box. As Roberta approached, they stood on the grass strip between the sidewalk and the street, Jimmy cuddling the kitten.

Roberta said, "Oh, he's so cute. Can I pet him?"

"Sure," Jimmy said, and she began fondling the kitten's head and scratching behind the ears.

"What's his name?"

"I don't know . . . just found him. He was in a box with four others by the side of the road. What do you think about Fred?"

"That's not a cat's name." Roberta laughed.

"You're probably right. Say, would you like to see them? Maybe you could take one. We gotta figure something out; we can't keep 'em."

"I couldn't. My father would kill me if I brought one home." Notwithstanding her protestation, Roberta moved past the men toward the van's open door and the box. Jimmy handed Fred to AJ, and as Roberta started to lean into the truck for a look, he swiftly injected her in the neck with a knockout drug, pushing her into the van. AJ tossed Fred into the box, then helped Jimmy zip-tie Roberta's hands before covering her with a tarp. Afterward, AJ began driving north to the other side of MetLife Stadium in East Rutherford, then onto Paterson Plank Road.

"Smooth," he said. "What'll you do with the cat?"

"Fred's cool. I think I'll keep him," Jimmy replied.

At Paterson Plank Road, they went east, eventually turning north into the Meadowlands, driving nearly two miles past fifty-five-gallon drums of toxic chemical waste scattered along the marshland's makeshift road. There was no need to worry about Roberta, because she was still out.

The weather had gotten warmer and the soil was workable, even though it was March, so it was easy to dig a shallow grave. Afterward, the men left the shovels and went to collect Roberta. She was coming around. The drug had worn off sooner than Jimmy had expected. A slight complication, because he'd meant for them to carry her while she was unconscious and put her in the grave before he shot her. Instead, Roberta was groggy and confused when they started to move her. "What's going on?"

"You fainted, that's all," Jimmy said, standing her up. "Come on, let's take a walk. Get some fresh air."

Jimmy and AJ guided Roberta to the foot of the grave, and AJ helped her lie down.

"Just rest," Jimmy continued.

"What are you doing?" Roberta cried out, wide-eyed. "I wanna get up." But because of her tied hands and the residual effects of the drug, she couldn't. She started struggling, and Jimmy moved to the foot of the grave, aiming a .32 semiautomatic.

"Stop thrashing about," Jimmy demanded. "Stay put!"

"Don't shoot." Roberta fought harder, wailing. "Why are you doing this? Please—stop!" Then, in the end, she grasped what was happening and crumpled. Tears streamed down her cheeks, and she whimpered, "It's Henry, isn't it?"

Jimmy fired two rounds into Roberta's chest. Then they buried her and headed off.

***

Connie had given him directions to a dilapidated bodega. She'd said they kept a small office on the second floor, living in an attached one-bedroom apartment behind it.

AJ parked on the street. Three young ne'er-do-wells were hanging out on the corner, eyeing his Escalade.

He took his compact .45 semiauto from the glove compartment, slipping it into his waistband.

"Nice ride, Señor," one of the kids said as AJ left the car.

Walking over to the group, he made sure they saw his gun as he reached for his wallet. Removing a one-hundred-dollar bill, he tore it in two, then handed half to the speaker. "Make sure no one fucks with it, and the other half is yours when I leave."

"Are you here for *el abogado*?"

"Yes."

"Right there," the kid said, pointing to a door beside the bodega.

Connie heard him climbing the stairs and greeted him at the top. "I'm happy you came."

"Me too, yet I wish it were under better circumstances."

"Let's talk in the office first. Tommy's showering and shaving—wants to put his best foot forward."

"Is it that bad?" AJ asked as she showed him to a chair before Tommy's desk, taking another side chair for herself. The office was orderly, although the furniture was well used.

"It is. What I told you is accurate. He doesn't have much time. Tommy still gets around a bit, but he becomes exhausted quickly and lives on booze and oxycodone. I don't know how long it'll be before his organs start failing and he'll have to be hospitalized with intravenous painkillers."

"How are you getting by?"

"We don't have much of a business anymore. I'm a bilingual paralegal, so most clients are pro bono or barter cases with immigration issues. I research and draft under Tommy's name. He goes to court if necessary, but he hasn't kept up his law license for years. No one ever asks, though."

"Money, insurance?" AJ asked.

"Not much. Enough for Obamacare. Yet that's even tough to maintain. He still has pride, so I don't know how forthcoming he'll be. Tommy isn't thinking about himself. He's looking to reconcile with his dad, see his daughter, and provide for her and me. I didn't know his real name until he asked me to call you."

"Do you know what caused his problems?"

"No, not really. Tommy talked about not being under his dad's thumb and leaving the family business. In any case, it's not merely that. Tommy's haunted—that's the only word that covers it. I think he feels responsible for something dreadful that happened years ago and can't shake it. Let's go through; he should be ready now."

The apartment was tidy, with worn furnishings like the office. Tommy was coming out of the galley kitchen. "AJ, it's been a long time," he said. "Glad you're here." Then, holding up a partially filled glass, he offered, "Wine?"

"No thanks," AJ answered. Tommy was thinner than he remembered. He'd appeared in sweats and slippers with his wet hair combed back, his sallow face nicked from shaving. Walking hesitantly, steadying shaky hands, he moved to his recliner.

"How about coffee?" Connie spoke up.

"That'd be great," AJ said. "Gee, it's good to see you, Tommy."

"Sit, please." Tommy motioned before taking a swig. "They become steadier, my hands, during the day," he quipped self-deprecatingly. "I gave up the hard stuff a while ago. It makes me feel like I'm doing something healthy. But it doesn't matter, since I'm thoroughly fucked."

"I hate to hear you talk like that."

"It's the truth, and I have no one to blame but myself."

Connie brought AJ his coffee and asked, "You'll stay for lunch, won't you? I planned on sandwiches and iced tea from the bodega downstairs."

"Yeah, I'd like to."

After Connie jotted down their choices, Tommy said, "Pick up white wine too and take your time. AJ and I have things to talk over." Then, spotting AJ's .45 as he reached for his wallet, Tommy remarked, "So, consiglieres carry now?"

"Only in combat zones," AJ chuckled, handing Connie a hundred dollars. After she left, he continued, "What can I do?"

"I aim to straighten out my life before I go—not for me but for others. I'll need your help with that. First, I intend to patch things up with Dad. I don't know how he feels, but I can't let him think it was his fault."

"I never bought that bullshit about you not liking the family business."

"There was a little truth in that, but not enough to leave home over. You know what it was all about?"

"Yeah, Roberta. Jimmy Zee and I had a rough time too, but it was worse for you."

"Well, I instigated the whole thing. I don't know what the fuck I was thinking. Afterward, the pain was so bad that I used booze to keep it at bay. Then I was hooked. How about Henry?"

"Who knows? He appears to be doing all right."

"The cops—did they ever cotton on?"

"Not a peep." AJ saw no purpose in upsetting Tommy about Gruenburg's snooping around. "What do you want me to do about your dad?"

"Get him here. I want to see him, do this face-to-face. And if Dad doesn't come, you'll need to tell him everything . . . and don't wait too long."

"Don't underestimate him. He loves you; I think he'll come. But you know what his first reaction will be?"

"Yeah, he'll explode. But he has a right to."

"What else?"

"I want to visit my daughter, Kathie. I know where she and my ex live. I haven't seen her in nearly nine years. Then I want him to provide for her, my ex, and Connie. Connie's important—my rock for a long time. And he has the dough. If he doesn't come to see me, you'll have to sell that too."

Connie returned, and they had lunch. The men discussed old times. Then, in a few hours, AJ handed the street-corner kids the other half of the hundred and was back on the road.

Retracing his route up the turnpike, he ruminated. *What a fuckin' shitstorm. I don't see a way out. If I do nothing, let Tommy think his dad abandoned him, then our secret goes to the grave. Yet if the boss ever finds out, God help me. So I gotta talk to him for Tommy's sake and mine, putting my best spin on it.*

CHAPTER TWENTY-ONE

Wednesday, October 12, 2022

Bronx, New York

AJ hadn't slept well and continued to be agitated all morning. Enzo Bellotti was recognized for his evenhandedness and viewed by many old-timers as a throwback to the godfather, Don Frank Costello—*capo di tutti i capi*. So, after the lunch crowd cleared out of the mob's trattoria, AJ sucked it up and went to the boss's office. He tapped on the open door and asked, "Do you have time for me? I must talk to you about something."

Enzo sensed his anxiety. "Sure. Sit."

AJ updated him about Ronnie Gruenburg.

When he was through, Enzo said, "Not surprised. The cops have been busting guys and grilling them about a twenty-something-year-old Kearny case."

"They are. That's the main thing I need to talk to you about." Then AJ began, concentrating on staying calm.

After a few minutes, inferring where AJ's story was heading, Enzo held up his hand, stopped him, and closed the office door. When he sat down, he said flatly, "Go on."

Nearly an hour later, AJ finished, and Enzo sat for a few minutes. "Jesus, Tommy's dying, and I have a granddaughter. How the hell am I supposed to feel?" he finally asked, struggling with his emotions. "And the rest of it: were you guys out of your friggin' minds? I have a real mess on my hands now."

"Well, at least the cops haven't caught on yet."

"Oh, don't even go there," Enzo ordered. "That's the least of your problems. Don't you understand? Tommy couldn't handle it, and it's killing him."

"Jimmy and I had problems too, but not as bad."

"I'll bet you did. I need to deal with Tommy and my granddaughter first. But we're not finished with the rest."

"Boss, focus on your granddaughter, Kathie; that's good news."

"Watch yourself, AJ. I'm spitting mad. This isn't the time to act like my consigliere. Here's what I want you to do. First, call Connie and make plans for me to visit ASAP; next, research the area's best long-term care or hospice-type facilities. If they don't have room, see if the Philly Mob can help. I'll pay what's necessary."

"What about the DeCavalcantes? They also operate in that area."

"Are you nuts? That's part of the problem I need to straighten out. I'll also talk to Tommy's ex, so ensure I have all her info. Then do a rundown on Grant Allen. Now go."

AJ started to leave, but as he opened the door, Enzo's rage finally boiled over. "Stop—close that door—get back here. I'm furious. And I'm gonna get it off my chest, and you'll listen, goddamn it! Why the hell didn't you talk to me? I could have set you straight. What'd you think I'd do, shoot Tommy?"

"I was confused."

"No shit! The outside world has its morals and values, and we have our code. Do you know why?" Enzo asked rhetorically. "In both cases, they are there for when we don't know what to do. Everybody gets confused: I do, the don does, and we rely on the code. You broke nearly every fuckin' rule. At a minimum, you needed permission to operate in someone else's territory, use their personnel, mess with a cop's family, use our people for personal business, and contract for a hit. Even I wouldn't have had the authority to whack a cop or one of his family without the godfather's say-so. And we didn't get anything out of it; it was bad business. For Christ's sake, we're not the cartels. Now get the fuck out of here: I need to think." Enzo shook his head, muttering after AJ closed the door, "What a friggin' catastrophe. An American tragedy."

***

The following morning Enzo left the Bronx early, driving to the godfather's townhouse on Manhattan's Upper East Side. He had texted AJ, saying he wouldn't be in until later.

A *soldato* waved Enzo into one of three empty parking spaces cordoned off by construction cones, then escorted him to the front door. The *don*'s wife greeted him. "Enzo, it's so nice to see you." They kissed on the cheek. "I was happy when my husband said you were coming for breakfast. I've already had mine. He's in the kitchen; you know the way."

Mrs. Hudson, their venerable cook-housekeeper, was stirring batter as the don waved Enzo to the table in the bay-windowed breakfast alcove.

"We're having pancakes with real maple syrup; you timed your visit well," the godfather said, indicating a chair. Mrs. Hudson carried over a tray with coffee and orange juice. "I'm glad you called yesterday. I'm sorry about Tommy; he's paid a high price. And you're right; our first concern is protecting him. He shouldn't be badgered to the end. But

I also agree that we have a problem. I like your strategy, so we'll talk when Mrs. Hudson is finished here."

When they were alone, the don said, "The Morris County prosecutor and the local cops have their teeth into it now. All this will come out eventually; let's get ahead of it and control it. So, talk to Grant Allen. Besides doing the right thing by giving him some closure, I don't want him going off half-cocked, taking payback where and when he pleases."

"You know what he'll want."

"Yes."

"I don't feel comfortable using Jimmy Zee—he's involved."

"I hear he's gone to ground anyway. We'll use Bermuda," the godfather offered.

"Is she back in your good graces after doing the wrong woman in Saint Martin?"

"She was never on my shit list. Massimino fucked up—gave her the wrong intel. But I had to let him save face. Bermuda took it like a pro and completed the job."

"About the DeCavalcantes—I'd like to let sleeping dogs lie," Enzo said. "But they're setting Henry Conklin up for blackmail over the two hits Jimmy Zee just made, so I need to give them a heads-up."

"That's not the whole story. Their crew is about to flip Henry Conklin after he's appointed to Jersey's supreme court. Anything we do about him will screw that up," the don responded.

"So they'll want something in return for their cooperation."

"Give them three percent more of your New Jersey operation. If that's not enough, check back with me."

"I guess that's fair, and I need them to arrange the Giuseppe Pappalardo end."

"You're really stretching his testimony, especially about the Allen girl."

"I'm confident we can persuade him to lie and swear to it. After all, Giuseppe's getting a golden parachute." Enzo chuckled.

"Are you convinced the Morris County prosecutor will play ball?" the godfather asked.

"Why wouldn't he? We'll be giving him a gambling bust plus solving two current murders and a 1998 Kearny cold case."

"Okay. Give him Jimmy Zee too. He doesn't need to know it's window dressing."

"Excellent idea. Thanks for your help."

The godfather walked Enzo to the front door. "Another thing. AJ has to go. He knows too much."

CHAPTER TWENTY-TWO

Friday, October 14, 2022

Canal Ville, New Jersey

Tom and Ronnie met with Elizabeth and Church at Saint Andrew's. When they were settled, Tom announced, "Jon Anderson called me. The senate has approved Henry Conklin's appointment this morning."

"How does that affect our investigation?" Elizabeth asked.

"I don't think it does. He probably won't be sworn in until year's end. We only need to be sure our case is airtight when we apply for warrants. How's Petra doing?"

"Okay. A bit stir-crazy, though."

"I guess that's to be expected." Then Frosty called in, and Tom continued, "Is there anything new since we met last week?"

"I still can't get anywhere with the Camden lead," Frosty answered. "The guys I've questioned don't know anything."

Ronnie reviewed Monday's meeting with Enzo Bellotti's consigliere. "Jaconelli was on top of what we were doing lickety-split. And he avoided answering whom he represented. Then I learned AJ received a call Monday afternoon, which upset him. After that, he took Tuesday off—for personal reasons—and drove to Camden. On Wednesday, AJ and the boss were behind closed doors. Enzo was pissed, raising his voice. I learned from another CI this morning that the boss breakfasted at the godfather's house Thursday morning."

"It's all pointing to Camden," Church observed. "And it sounds like AJ's trying to head us off at the pass, maybe keep our investigation from the boss. In any case, something's breaking loose. What's next, double down on the pressure?"

"Yeah, concentrating on AJ," Tom said. "Lizzie, will you ask Judy to run down everything on him in the public records of New York and New Jersey? And Frosty, contact the FBI's NYC field office and ask Grant Allen to check with his old informants."

Elizabeth agreed, and Frosty added, "I know agents on their joint Organized Crime Task Force. I'll call them."

"Fine. I'll update Anderson," Tom finished.

***

It was late Sunday afternoon, and Enzo was returning home from Camden. Earlier, when he'd arrived at Tommy's apartment, Connie had left the men alone for a long time. Their reunion was emotional; father and son had cried and said everything that needed to be said. And now, as he arrived in the Bronx, Enzo was still calming down. Yet under the circumstances, the meeting had turned out well. He had assured Tommy and Connie, without hesitation, that he would take care of Tommy's medical expenses, AJ was researching top local facilities specializing in palliative care and they'd have choices for him to review shortly; neither Connie nor Carol would ever need to work again if that were their choice; and Kathie's education would be taken care of, with an allowance to continue afterward. Lastly, they'd discussed the best way to arrange a meeting for Tommy with his ex and daughter and agreed that Enzo would call Carol this evening.

Now, sitting by the phone, Enzo was nervous. It was a lot to dump on someone with no forewarning, but based on his assessment of Tommy's condition, they ought not to waste time. Not if Tommy was to travel to them, which was what he wanted. He had pleaded, "Not in Camden, Dad. I don't want them to see what I've come to."

With his supper finished, Enzo finally rang Carol's number and hoped Kathie would be occupied with homework.

"Hello," Carol answered.

"Carol, this is Enzo Bellotti. Do you know who I am?"

After a pause, she replied, "Yes. I learned last month who you are and that you're Tommy's father."

"Good. That makes things easier. I have a lot to tell you, most of it unhappy. You might like to sit."

Carol pulled up a kitchen stool. "Okay, go ahead."

"Where to start? I lost track of Tommy when he disappeared in 2006. It's hard to believe, considering my line of work, but I could never find him, never knew he was married, had a child, or was divorced. I didn't know what Tommy was doing or where he lived either. I found out all on Wednesday. He's living in Camden, and earlier today, I saw him for the first time since he left home. Before I tell you what I've learned, may I assure you that I will do whatever it takes to make this right, at least as best I can. Practically speaking, that means you and Kathie no longer have any financial concerns. Her education—whatever she wants to do—is assured. No strings attached either, and I think you understand I have the means to live up to that promise."

After that, Enzo described the situation as kindly as possible without underestimating the seriousness of his son's condition. Carol was silent for a while.

"And Tommy only has a brief time left?"

"Yes. I'll get the best doctors, yet realistically, I don't think there's any hope. He isn't eligible for a liver transplant because of his drinking."

"If Tommy wants to see us, wouldn't it be better for us to go to him?"

"Yes, but he's insistent. Look at it this way: if you visit him after that, he'll be in a top-flight facility and might even be closer than Camden. Do you think you'll want to keep seeing him?"

"I don't know how I feel, but I think Kathie will. She's wanted this for so long."

"What's the best way to proceed? I could come alone beforehand and meet Kathie. It would be less taxing for her, because Tommy and his partner, Connie, would be with me otherwise."

"That's a sensible idea. She's usually home from school by three thirty in the afternoon. I can take a half day, and you could come earlier to talk."

"All right. Would you like to have lunch?"

"No, it's best if you come to the house. I should tell you that the cops visited me. They're looking for Tommy."

Enzo paused. "Will you tell me what they asked about?"

"They wanted to interview him as a material witness in a cold case. Something about Henry Conklin; I think he was Tommy's roommate in law school, but I never heard of him. Also, a girl named Roberta—I never heard of her either. They said Tommy might be in danger. I was upset afterward."

"I'm sorry that happened."

"Is he . . . in danger?"

"I don't know, but I'll take care of it—don't worry. Do you remember with whom you spoke?"

"Yes, I have his card. I'll get it."

"I'll make another phone call while you're doing that."

When Carol was gone, Enzo called AJ. "This is important. Call Thunderclap. We need security for Tommy and Connie in Camden—twenty-four-hour, high-profile—until further notice. They're not to allow law enforcement in without a warrant. I also want round-the-clock security for his ex and daughter in Delaware Water Gap. Tell them to keep a low profile and not to interfere with the cops if they show—*capiche*?"

"Yeah. What's the matter?"

"Tell you tomorrow," Enzo said, and picked up Carol again. "I'm back. I've arranged twenty-four-seven low-profile security, and they'll take Kathie back and forth to school. You should vary your route and time to and from work. They'll explain everything; you and Kathie will be safe."

"You're scaring me."

"It's only a precaution."

"What about Tommy?"

"We're getting him security too, but high-profile."

"Are these guys . . . crooks?"

"No—all legal. They're from a private military company like Blackwater. Try not to worry. I have plans to solve all of these problems and will accelerate them now. But under the circumstances, I'll come down tomorrow. Can you work that out with your boss?"

"Yes."

"I'll see you about one p.m. Let me have the name of the cop you spoke with."

"His name's Church Gagne, an investigator with the Morris County Prosecutor's Office, and he was here on September nineteenth."

On Monday the seventeenth, Enzo went to the office at about ten thirty a.m. to pick up AJ, who got behind the wheel. They headed across the George Washington Bridge, then west on I-80 toward Delaware Water Gap, Pennsylvania. The men stopped for lunch and arrived at one o'clock. AJ waited in the car with his thermos of coffee and a book.

The house was small, well ordered, and in a safe neighborhood. Carol let the boss in, and they went to the kitchen. They talked and got to know each other. Finally, as it grew time for Kathie to come home, Carol said, "I never told her about the cop that was here before. But last night, I said you were coming today and revealed what you did."

"How's she taking it?"

"She had mixed feelings about her dad—excited that she'll see him yet upset about his health."

"That sounds normal. And me?"

"Kathie Googled you."

"And?"

"All she said was, 'Gee, he actually is a gangster.'"

Enzo laughed. "I've been called worse."

They moved to the living room. When Kathie came in, the adults stood, then Carol said, "Kathie, this is your grandfather, Enzo Bellotti."

"Hi," was all she could manage.

"I'm happy to meet you after all this time," Enzo said.

Kathie looked puzzled. She hadn't dropped her backpack or taken off her jacket yet. Carol thought she might cry, but instead she said, "I don't know how I'm supposed to feel."

Enzo smiled. "Me neither."

"What do I call you?"

"Anything except Mr. Bellotti or Boss. Why don't you lose your backpack and we'll take a walk—is that all right?"

Kathie nodded, and they headed off. As they went down the front walk, AJ waved. Kathie hesitated before reciprocating, then asked, "Is he your bodyguard?"

"No, that's AJ, my consigliere."

"What's that?"

"An adviser."

"Is he armed?"

"No."

"Are you?"

"No . . . would it help if I told you about myself?"

Kathie nodded.

"Your mom said you Googled me, so you know a lot already. I'm the second in command in my organization. My job is almost entirely management and administration. I'm hardly ever in the field anymore. I can tell you're a smart girl—plainspoken too—so I won't buffalo you about our activities. All I can say is that I've worked hard to convert our business into a legal enterprise. When your dad worked for me after law school, he only represented my licit companies. Close to sixty percent of our business is legit now."

"Mom says you'll help financially."

"Yes."

"Will you promise me that the money will come from the legal side?"

"Yes."

They walked and talked. Kathie told Enzo about what she was doing in middle school—how she was on the field hockey team, how she wasn't sure what she wanted to do yet but planned on college. Then Enzo told Kathie about their family. How his father and grandfather had been in the "family business" and how he'd followed along. How Tommy was an only child and about his wife, Maria. "Your grandmother's eager to meet you."

After they returned to the house, Enzo stayed a few minutes, then Kathie walked him out. As he opened the car's door, he stood aside and said, "Kathie, this is AJ. You'll see him from time to time."

They greeted each other. Before Enzo got in, Kathie said, "I'll call you Gramps," and kissed his cheek.

She waved as the car pulled away, and AJ said, "Gramps . . . cool. Do you like her?"

"Very much. She's unquestionably precocious, though." Enzo chuckled.

***

Wednesday morning, October 19, Karl and Klaus met as usual. "It's cooler this morning," Karl said. "Breezy too."

"Time to put the heat on," Klaus replied.

"Yeah, I usually put it on about now. I heard Henry Conklin's appointment to the supreme court was approved Friday."

"I know. Rajathi at the pharmacy said she saw Henry, Evie, and Mrs. Olsen celebrating at that Italian restaurant that used to be Peer's. That's a feather in Canal Ville's cap."

"It is. I see your Yankees are still hanging in there," Karl commented.

"They beat Cleveland five to one last night to take the ALDS."

"So now it's on to Houston tomorrow for the league championship," Karl said.

"Yeah. But as I told you before, I'm not optimistic. Houston's a tough team. And Judge has only hit two homers in the postseason with a lackluster batting average." Then, changing the subject, Klaus asked, "Have you heard anything else about the investigation into Jan's murder?"

"No. All's quiet. Amy at the church said that the cops continue to meet there."

"They must still be apprehensive about leaks."

"I guess so," Karl opined.

***

The same evening, the boss drove his large S-Class Mercedes along the New Jersey Turnpike, returning home. He had gone to Camden that morning to pick up Tommy and Connie for the trip to see Kathie and Carol. Enzo and his wife had decided to visit Tommy and their granddaughter later to avoid overwhelming him today.

He stopped at the Richard Stockton Service Area near Hamilton Township for supper and called his wife. "How did it go?" she asked straightaway.

"I arrived about eleven. Two security men were outside, with another upstairs in the office. I have security at Carol's too, but it's inconspicuous. Tommy was finishing dressing. Connie told me he hadn't had a drink since last night. He was trying to make a good impression."

"Was he shaky?" Maria asked.

"He was okay but relying on extra pills. Tommy's ex took another half day, so we were on the road in time for him to talk with Carol before Kathie came home."

"So . . . tell me."

"Connie and I sat in the kitchen. We didn't hear any raised voices. Then later we moved back to the living room, and it looked like Carol had been crying. I think it went as well as we could've hoped."

"And when Kathie came home? Was it awkward for her?"

"No. I don't think so, because Carol, Connie, and I left them alone for a long time."

"How were they when you returned from the kitchen?"

"Their eyes looked red, but Kathie was sitting on his lap. And they were smiling and hugging. Honestly, I think it went well also. Kathie had time to adjust to the bad news before she saw him. She just looked happy."

"I hope that wasn't too much for him—her sitting on his lap. He's frail, from what you said."

"That was my first reaction, yet it didn't bother him. And he didn't mention anything on the trip back to Camden. Tommy did fine."

"I'm glad. And I want to visit them when we can without overloading him."

"Agreed. We'll talk more once I'm home. I'm a little less than an hour and a half away."

CHAPTER TWENTY-THREE

Thursday, October 20, 2022

Stone Harbor, New Jersey

Enzo and AJ had left the Bronx earlier this morning, heading to the Jersey Shore. Before leaving, Enzo said, "I want you to carry today—just a precaution."

AJ nodded.

They arrived before noon and parked where they could observe the front door of Nemo's Pizza and Restaurant on Third Avenue. Grant Allen ate lunch there daily. It was the highlight of his day. Otherwise, he spent time reading, shopping, or walking the beach with his wife until supper, after which they watched TV. AJ had Googled the retired chief, printing a photo.

In a few minutes, Allen arrived and entered. As Enzo and AJ walked into the restaurant, Enzo said, "Hang by the bar—keep an eye on us. I'll try to have him walk to the beach if he becomes agitated. It's not far. If we do, follow along at a distance."

Julie, Grant's regular server, spotted him before he entered and met him at his table in the rear corner, IPA in hand. The chief sat facing the door. As he settled in, the body language of two men coming in piqued his interest, especially given all his years of experience as a cop. The first was a younger, taller man who remained by the bar. Allen noticed he was carrying. Then the second older, shorter man approached. There wasn't much doubt about what was happening when he opened his suit coat surreptitiously, showing that he wasn't armed. *What the fuck is this?*

"Chief, I'm Enzo Bellotti. May I join you?"

"Damn. I knew I'd seen your picture, but I couldn't place you. Sit."

The *capo bastone* waved Julie over and ordered. "I'll have the same as the chief."

The men sat quietly. When Enzo's ale arrived, they ordered lunch, and Enzo took a sip before saying, "I need to talk to you."

"This can't be good," Grant answered.

"No. It isn't."

"Roberta?"

"Yes."

"After all these years?"

"Do you want to talk here or take a walk?"

"Here's fine. I accepted the inevitable years ago. Tell me up front. Did that prick Henry Conklin kill her?"

"Yes, but he didn't pull the trigger. There were others."

"When? Was Roberta abused? Why?"

"The day she disappeared. No abuse, just two quick shots. Roberta was pregnant."

"Oh, Lord, a grandbaby. Her mother and I wondered. Was Conklin the father?"

"Yes."

"Do you know where her remains are?"

"Yes and no. She's buried in the Meadowlands north of Paterson Plank Road, east of the football stadium. But after all these years, we'll never find her."

"Christ, that's a toxic waste dump. Couldn't they have done better by her than that?"

"Look. I'm not mincing words. It was a colossal, unauthorized fuckup. It should never have happened."

"Well, that sure as shit doesn't make me feel any better. I want to hear all about it. You owe me that."

"I do." Then Enzo told the retired chief what he knew.

"I'm sorry for you . . . about your boy. He has paid, yet it doesn't seem like enough," Allen said vindictively.

"He'll probably die before Christmas."

"They all deserve to be dealt with. You know that's the right thing."

"No. It isn't. There are bounds. That's why I'm here. I want to work out what's fair."

AJ continued watching, and Grant Allen's face showed his anger. The boss wasn't facing AJ, but his body language revealed he was fuming. Even so, both men kept their voices down. Then, after twenty minutes of bitterly butting heads, they stood up, shook hands, and Enzo left abruptly, snapping, "Let's go," as he passed AJ.

In the car, Enzo continued, "What a bastard. He wants everybody's head on a platter."

AJ didn't respond, since his head was one of the ones in question.

"Don't worry; I didn't tell him about you and Jimmy. I'm still not convinced Allen won't go off half-baked. Christ, he even wanted me to kill Tommy."

That evening, Enzo spoke with the don, who thought briefly before saying, "Jesus, that old prick went Old Testament on you—tough son of a bitch. Are you on board?"

Enzo hesitated briefly before answering, "Yes."

"Fine, I'll bring Bermuda here right away. I want her in place. What's next?"

"The DeCavalcantes, Saturday."

"Keep me posted."

***

Recently, something had been nettling Elizabeth about her interview with Carly Johansen. Finally, this morning at three a.m., it came to her with a start. But she chose not to mention it to Church yet, because it was a long shot. So late Friday morning, Elizabeth called her.

"Hey, Elizabeth," Carly said. "I'm glad you called. Anything new about Roberta?"

"Not much: two steps forward and one step back. In any case, I have a question about our interview. Do you remember telling me you went on a triple date to a blues club along the Palisades with Henry, Roberta, Tommy, and his date?"

"Sure."

"Can you recall when that was?"

"It was on a Saturday, shortly before Roberta disappeared."

"So that would be March seventh or thirteenth?"

"Probably the seventh. Why?"

"It struck me as odd. I mean, it was out of everyone's stomping grounds. Why were you there?"

"I think a buddy of Tommy's recommended it . . . Yeah, that's right. An up-and-coming young singer was there. I remember she was tiny but could belt it out; brought the house down with 'Ball and Chain'— like Big Mama Thornton."

"Was anyone else there that you guys knew?"

"Now that you mention it, Tommy's friend, who recommended the club, was there. He had the hots for the singer. Tommy said hello when he spotted him sitting with her between sets in a corner booth."

"Would you recognize him?"

"No. Roberta and I had our backs to him."

"Do you remember his name?"

"No. Not really. I think Tommy called the guy by his initials, though."

They talked briefly before Elizabeth said, "You've been helpful. Thanks. I'll keep you up to date."

***

Later in the day Friday, Elizabeth, Church, Tom, and Ronnie met at Saint Andrew's with Frosty on the phone. "Frosty, why don't you go first?" Tom said.

"I have a mixed bag. Regarding Camden, I finally picked up rumors that Tommy Bellotti lives there but is gravely ill. Then I checked with NYC's FBI Organized Crime Task Force and had a rundown on Enzo Bellotti and AJ. Neither one is a person of interest in any ongoing investigation, but both men are on the FBI's radar and have been investigated and interrogated sporadically. Enzo has a spotless record, having never been arrested, and has been number-two in the Genovese crime family for years. AJ had a few minor scrapes in the day, but the charges were always dropped. He started working for Bellotti early on, riding his coattails, and AJ has been his consigliere since Enzo became the *capo bastone*. Plus, just before you called, I talked to Grant Allen. It was an odd conversation. He was indifferent when I asked if he had anything new from his confidential informants. Then later he said, 'I know you guys are doing your best, but nothing's happening. I can't do this anymore, getting my hopes up. Just leave me alone.' Ronnie, you and Church were there when we met. Does that sound like Grant to you?" Frosty asked.

"No," both men responded.

"Maybe Allen was threatened," Elizabeth suggested.

"I think that would've made him mad, not apathetic," Ronnie opined.

"Well, something's happening," Tom said. "Church, do you have anything?"

"Judy's still searching the public records of the men. Just what you'd expect so far; I'll follow up."

"Ronnie?" Tom continued.

"There's chatter. Enzo Bellotti drove to Camden on Sunday the sixteenth. It was probably to see Tommy, if Frosty's info was correct. Then he and AJ went to Delaware Water Gap, Pennsylvania, on the seventeenth, I assume to Tommy's ex's. And on the nineteenth, Enzo drove to Camden again, this time alone."

Elizabeth went next, telling them about her call with Carly. When she finished, Church said, "That was a terrific idea. It must be about the Roberta case because of the date; it fits perfectly and is the only clue pointing to AJ's involvement."

"We ought to drag his ass in for an interrogation. We don't need to handle AJ with kid gloves," Ronnie said.

Recalling Ronnie's heavy-handed grilling of Bobby Wagoner and his underage stripper-prostitute and "girlfriend" Annabelle in the Doc Piscator case, Elizabeth cautioned, "Ronnie, mind your p's and q's."

"Elizabeth," he exclaimed, faking astonishment, "you know I'm by the book."

"Okay," Tom said, fighting a smile. "I'll bring Anderson up to date. Let's regroup when we have additional information."

***

On Saturday morning, Massi Rizzo, the DeCavalcantes' acting *capo bastone*, waited for his visitor, Enzo Bellotti, at the union's local near Port Elizabeth. Massi preferred meeting in public spaces, notably crowded restaurants or diners, because electronic eavesdropping was difficult. But in any case, his office and conference room in the union hall were routinely swept for bugs. *So, no harm.*

When the godfather's underboss arrived, he expected the meeting to be about the recent police activity targeting the New Jersey operations of their two crime families. Instead, he learned there was another agenda—Henry Conklin.

"Look. You'll have to tell me more if you want me to scrap our plans to flip him," Massi said, after listening to Enzo.

"Isn't a request from the don sufficient?"

"Well, of course—no disrespect intended—but this is a big fucking deal. For Christ's sake—a sitting supreme court justice in our pocket."

"He understands, but that's not all," Enzo explained, telling the acting underboss what Giuseppe Pappalardo needed to do.

"I'm speechless. You're putting him out of business. He'll have to disappear after he testifies."

"The godfather greatly respects him, but Giuseppe has been doing this for a long time; perhaps he should retire. There'll be a substantial payday. Giuseppe will be well compensated."

"It doesn't matter. This will look terrible," Massi complained. "And what about Jimmy Zee?"

"From what I hear, he's vanished. You'll have to trust us. Focus on Jimmy being form over substance, and neither will be hurt."

"Well, what about my crime family? We need something in return."

"I'm listening."

"Jesus, so that's what this is all about, what it'll cost you?" Massi negotiated hard, and after half an hour, the men shook hands.

Driving back to the Bronx, Enzo thought, *The godfather was correct: three percent was the right amount.*

***

Henry was also busy Saturday morning. He'd asked Ella to work, and they were tidying up loose ends on their cases, organizing, and cleaning out in anticipation of Murray Kriegman's takeover. The sale had been signed and sealed, with the funds in escrow until the fourteenth of November.

Ella came in and announced, "Saul rang while you were on the phone."

"Okay, thanks," he said, before returning Saul's call.

"'Mornin' Counselor," Saul said when he picked up. "Congratulations."

"Thanks. Anything on Tommy?"

"Finally, I have new information. With help from a Philly snitch, I was able to locate Tommy yesterday. He's living over a bodega in a rough part of Camden. I noticed what looked like a security team outside when I drove by. A few street kids were hanging at a nearby corner, so I parked and went over. Fifty bucks loosened their tongues. Here's the deal: *el abogado*—that's Tommy—lives and works upstairs with a broad. According to the kids, he's ill and looks like shit. They haven't seen him lately because he no longer comes downstairs. Then recently, there's been activity with well-dressed guys in expensive cars coming and going. Probably his father and his cronies. And a few days ago, security showed up, ensuring they were noticed."

"The mob?"

"No. I don't think so. They looked professional."

"Why?"

"It's a guess. I think to prevent anyone from talking to Tommy, especially law enforcement, unless they have a warrant."

"So what's next?"

"Frankly, nothing. I know you want to talk to him, but he's off-limits now. And if he's as sick as the miscreants say, you may never have a chance."

"All right. Excellent job. Please send me a final invoice. Ella and I are working today on wrapping things up. I'll head for Trenton in a few weeks to familiarize myself with the terrain. But let's keep in touch. I recommended you to Murray Kriegman; give him a call."

As the call ended, Henry thought, *If Saul's correct, I don't need to worry, because the mob doesn't want what happened twenty-four years ago to get out. Why else would they keep Tommy under wraps? In any case, I only have to wait a few months before Tommy's dead.*

CHAPTER TWENTY-FOUR

Tuesday, October 25, 2022

K arl and Klaus had saved toast from their breakfast, and after arriving at Riverside Park, they tossed torn-up pieces to a raft of ducks floating past. When they finally sat on "their" bench, Karl said, "Sorry about Houston sweeping the Yanks in four games last night. I didn't see that coming—thought it would be closer."

"Embarrassing . . . but I told you so. So it'll be the Phillies at Houston for the series—first game Friday,"[1] Klaus responded. "I'll route for Philadelphia. I don't like the Astros, since they've been caught stealing signs. It's an ongoing problem."

Changing the subject, Karl said, "Did you hear anything about Petra?"

"No. What's happening?"

"I stopped by the church last week to pick up another directory because I lost mine. When we chatted, Amy told me to keep it under my hat: Petra's gone missing."

"How did she find that out?"

"Tom, Elizabeth, Church, and the others still meet at Saint Andrew's. Passing their conference room as she went to the ladies', Amy overheard that Evie and Petra had made weekend plans during supper at the pizzeria on a Tuesday. After Evie hadn't heard from her, they went to Petra's house on Sunday, and it looked like she hadn't returned from a morning run. And finally, Elizabeth filed a missing-persons report on October fifth," Karl reported.

"Maybe she took a vacation or is visiting friends. Or Henry might know?"

"I don't know, but it seems odd that we haven't heard anything; no one in town is talking about it. You'd think the cops would ask around, visiting merchants, trying to track Petra's movements."

"You're right. It's strange," Klaus opined.

***

At dusk that evening, Enzo picked up AJ and drove to an inactive pier on Brooklyn's Red Hook waterfront. They went by warehouses, cranes, and docks handling containers or bulk cargo. When they parked, Enzo said, "We won't be long; just picking up Bermuda."

"What's wrong with the 'friendly skies'?" AJ quipped.

"Who knows."

"Probably wants to stay under the radar."

The men walked down the dock, past dilapidated storage sheds and makeshift offices, and stopped. Then they heard the sound of engines as a forty-two-foot Hatteras fishing boat lying offshore came alongside. AJ watched. "Boss, I don't see her."

"I'm right behind you," Bermuda said, stepping from a shed before nudging AJ with her .22 LR silenced semiauto. "Hands on top of your head." Then she rapidly patted him down, continuing, "Let's walk to the boat."

AJ was momentarily befuddled, then turned to Enzo, imploring. "Boss—please."

"I'm sorry, AJ."

Bermuda prodded, they boarded, and the boat drew away. AJ looked back at the boss as the dock grew smaller, and she said, "It wasn't his call; the don made it." Then, aiming at the back of AJ's head, she fired two hollow-point rounds, and he collapsed on the deck. Despite minimal blood, she withdrew a thirteen-gallon garbage bag from her jacket and pulled it over the dead man's head.

Later, Bermuda tossed the gun the captain had provided overboard, went to the flying bridge, and drank coffee. The Hatteras sailed toward the Verrazano-Narrows Bridge, Lower Bay, and the Atlantic. They would dump the body at sea and continue to South Amboy, New Jersey, where after landing at Newark that afternoon, Bermuda had parked her rental and boarded the forty-two-footer. Once they docked, she'd drive to the Sheraton Parsippany Hotel, her usual haunt when working for the Five Families, then inventory her nearby self-storage locker. *Easy peasy.*

***

Later, when the boss arrived home, he called the godfather on a burner. "I have an update for you."

"Tell me about Tommy first."

"Security's in place at both locations. We're moving him by ambulance tomorrow. It's a top-rated facility about halfway between Camden and his ex on the Pennsylvania side of the Delaware. I took an adjoining room, so Connie won't have to schlep back and forth if she doesn't want to."

"Is security in place there also?"

"Yes. Twenty-four-seven in the corridor."

"The hospice seems accommodating."

"Well, money talks," Enzo remarked.

The don chuckled. "Don't put off taking Maria to visit Tommy."

"I'm planning to see Jon Anderson on Thursday. If that works out, I'll have breathing room," Enzo said.

"Anything else?"

"Massimino's on board—unhappily."

"As you said, money talks."

"He'll speak to Giuseppe tomorrow."

"And Bermuda?"

"She arrived this afternoon."

"AJ?"

"It's taken care of."

"I'm sorry, Enzo, but we couldn't take the risk. It sounds like you're moving right along," the godfather said, and rang off.

CHAPTER TWENTY-FIVE

Wednesday, October 26, 2022

Massimino had asked Giuseppe to arrange lunch at Emil's restaurant on Route 10 in Whippany. It was his *capo*'s favorite spot and practical because, after their meal, they could move to Emil's office for what Massimino imagined would be a difficult conversation. And now, heading back to Elizabeth, he was relieved. *Despite Giuseppe driving a hard bargain, it went better than I'd hoped.*

Even though his job was demanding, Massimino liked being a boss. He enjoyed the recognition, prestige, perks, and pay. But he didn't like personnel issues, most notably when he disagreed with the godfather, as in this case. But Massi felt obligated to support the don's decision nonetheless. *After all, if I can't do that, I should pack my bag.* So today was problematic. In corporate parlance, it was effectively the "downsizing" of a trusted friend, a loyal second-generation DeCavalcante crew member, as was he. Hence Massimino had argued against the load of crap Enzo was dumping on him. But the godfather's *capo bastone* assured him things were happening behind the scenes that he wasn't privy to. Necessary things. Or in other words—corporate bullshit.

***

Heading home, Giuseppe was happy. He couldn't wait to tell his wife, Angie. *She'll be tickled pink.* He chuckled silently.

Earlier, sitting in Emil's office after lunch, Giuseppe had sensed where the conversation was headed, even though Massimino had wandered around Jack Robinson's barn for quite a while. So Giuseppe shammed a devastated mien, concealing that he was tired and wanted to retire. *I've had a good run, never been arrested, and the mob isn't what it used to be—not with the Russians and the cartels moving in.* But actual retirement was a constant problem because of the Michael Corleone conundrum: "Just when you think you're out; they pull you back in."[2]

They wanted him to take the rap for a gambling bust of his November card game and spend a night or two in jail. During that time, a plea deal for time served would be worked out with the Morris County Prosecutor's Office. Giuseppe would testify as a state's witness in an upcoming trial and reveal damaging information about the mob and one of its clients. He'd be a first-class snitch in open court. *I'll have to split after that—no if, ands, or buts.*

So this was his opportunity. Acting discombobulated, Giuseppe negotiated what Massimino called a "package." They agreed he would be provided with a Johnnie Cochran–caliber lawyer, have the feds sign on to his plea deal, be reimbursed for all expenses, and receive a generous pension and "severance" pay of two hundred thousand. Then, finally, the pièce de resistance: a DOJ Gulfstream would fly him and Angie to Rome immediately after the last day of his testimony. *Then we'll disappear into the airport before heading to our villa near Nice, which no one knows about.*

CHAPTER TWENTY-SIX

Thursday, October 27, 2022

E nzo Bellotti left the Bronx at three p.m. for the one-hour drive to the Morris Museum in Morristown, New Jersey. He had learned from one of his sources that Jon Anderson would attend a New Jersey Bar Association tour and cocktail reception that afternoon and evening. It was scheduled to begin at three, followed by the reception at five, once the museum closed.

Enzo pulled into the Normandy Heights Road parking lot, paid the twelve-dollar admission, and roamed the museum until he spied the bar association's escorted tour. From his Google search, Enzo recognized the prosecutor, but he kept his distance, mixing with the crowd until he accompanied them for cocktails. He had a scotch on the rocks from the bar and mingled until he maneuvered into a conversation with Anderson, who was standing alone.

They chatted, and Enzo was confident the man had no idea who he was. Before long, the prosecutor said, "I'm being rude—Jon Anderson," and extended his hand.

The underboss took it, saying, "Enzo Bellotti. Let's find a quieter place and talk for a few minutes."

Enzo had no doubt the prosecutor recognized his name. Anderson was nonplused but finally said, "This is inappropriate. What could we possibly have to talk about?"

"Give me five minutes. If you don't think continuing is worth your while, I'll leave."

The men left the reception and found a seating arrangement in the closed museum. Enzo talked for nearly an hour, with Anderson occasionally interrupting with a question. Finally, the gangster asked, "So what do you think?"

"I'm sorry about your boy. But you're going to great lengths to shield him briefly. What aren't you telling me?"

"Don't you think I'm offering you enough of a quid pro quo?"

"I think that's what bothers me. I'll ask again. What aren't you telling me?"

"The Roberta Allen killing was an unauthorized hit—never should have happened. I have internal issues."

"After all these years?"

"Yes. This isn't negotiable. It's a take-it-or-leave-it offer."

"I'll have to discuss it with my investigators. And if you're insistent on a DOJ sign-off, I have to run at least the big picture by the US attorney."

"Do what you must. But if it leaks, you'll fuck everything up. Don't take too long. Here's my number, and let's meet Saturday," the *capo bastone* concluded, handing Anderson his card.

***

Friday morning Jon Anderson was in his office first thing. He intended to rethink the strange offer that Bellotti had made yesterday afternoon. After a while, he decided what he would do: verify what he could.

The prosecutor looked at his watch. Nearly nine, but he'd wait until after that before making the calls he planned. Since he'd brewed coffee earlier, he headed to the break room for another cup, greeting his staff along the way, who had been arriving for the last forty-five minutes.

When Anderson returned to his office, he closed the door and began making phone calls, the first to his wife.

"'Mornin'. Did I wake you?"

"No, I'm having coffee."

"Me too. Something has come up; I'm driving to Delaware Water Gap, Pennsylvania. Do you want to ride along? We can have a late lunch there. Then I'll do what I need to, and we can look around afterward."

"I'd like that. There's a place I've read about—the Asparagus Soufflé. It's a specialty cookware and gift shop; we could check it out."

"Fine. Pick you up at noon."

Next, he called the Camden County prosecutor. They'd met a year ago at a continuing education seminar. Jon asked him if he would have the Camden PD drive by Tommy Bellotti's address and confirm that security was in place, as the underboss had claimed. "No problem," the Camden prosecutor responded. "Call you back later."

Then Jon called the hospice where Bellotti's son was purported to be a patient. At first, the administrator he spoke with was reluctant to cooperate. Anderson had anticipated this. He turned on the charm and finally said, "I don't need any medical information. Google my office and look up my number. I'm using that line, and your caller ID should verify."

In a few seconds, the administrator responded, "Okay, I have it. I can confirm that he's here. Anything else?"

"Is there private security outside his room?"

"Yes, round the clock."

"What's Bellotti's prognosis?"

"All I can say is that this is a hospice facility. You must know what that means."

"Yes, I do. Thank you."

After that, Anderson returned calls before picking up his wife. They headed west and reached their destination in an hour. After lunch, they drove to Bellotti's ex's address, parking up the street. Across the road, in front of the house, was another car with a man inside. After a few minutes, Jon observed another man exit the front door, taking a post on the stoop. Then the man in the car got out and started walking toward them. *They're communicating*, Jon thought before saying, "Time to leave." The prosecutor held his badge against his window as they drove past the approaching man, who waved.

"Did you find out what you needed to know?" his wife asked.

"Yes. Security's in place."

Later that afternoon, the Camden County prosecutor called on their way home, reporting that there was also security at the bodega. "Why are you concerned with security issues in Pennsylvania and Camden?" his wife asked.

310

"I'm not. I'm verifying that a man I met yesterday was telling the truth."

"Well, was he?"

"Yes."

"Who was this guy?"

"Between us?" Anderson asked, and his wife nodded. "The number-two man in the Genovese crime family."

"Swell friends," she joked.

***

Jon Anderson contacted Tom Johnson late Saturday after meeting with Enzo Bellotti. "Tom, we need to convene first thing Monday morning. It's important."

"What's up?"

"I don't want to talk on the phone—too complicated. But suffice it to say that Enzo Bellotti has handed Henry Conklin to us on a silver platter."

"Which case?"

"All of them. And with evidence to boot. But we need to discuss it, because his proposition is odd."

Everyone except Frosty, who was on speakerphone, was assembled by eight o'clock Monday morning in the Saint Andrew's conference room. Ronnie brought bagels and their trimmings, and Elizabeth had made coffee. Jon had prepared a bullet-point memo of his discussion with Bellotti and faxed one to Frosty. "Enzo Bellotti is willing to do this because his son, who is dying from liver cancer and cirrhosis, doesn't have much time left, and the old man doesn't want his boy bothered by the police. So look this over; then we'll discuss it." He handed over the paper.

> *The Morris County Prosecutor and the U.S. Attorney for the District of New Jersey will agree not to prosecute Thomas Bellotti, also known as Thomas Bell, for state or federal crimes. In exchange, Enzo Bellotti, as an anonymous tipster, will:*
>
> - *Provide information allowing law enforcement to raid a high-stakes monthly poker game run by Giuseppe Pappalardo, the Morris County Capo for the DeCavalcante Crime Family.*
>
> - *Arrange for Pappalardo to plead guilty to a gambling charge and pay a fifty-thousand-dollar fine.*
>
> - *In exchange, Pappalardo will:*
>
>   o *Receive a suspended jail sentence and an immunity agreement for any crimes mentioned herein.*
>
>   o *Testify how Pappalardo met with Henry Conklin and James Zappulla, also known as Jimmy Zee, regarding the murders of Jan Vanderveer and Petra.**

- o *Testify how Pappalardo met with Bell and Zee regarding the murder of Roberta Allen.*

- *Additionally, Enzo Bellotti will provide a sworn and witnessed deathbed confession from Bell:*

  - o *Corroborating Pappalardo's testimony mentioned in the previous point.*

  - o *Verifying that Bell was acting on behalf of Conklin.*

  * Enzo Bellotti is unaware that Petra is alive and in hiding.

"What about Giuseppe? Will we allow him to stay in business while waiting to testify?" Ronnie asked.

"Bellotti says Giuseppe will remain the titular Morris County *capo*, continuing to run his legit businesses. But otherwise, Tony, his erstwhile bodyguard and present-day number-two, will take over. That's all he'll say."

"Do we trust him?" Ronnie continued.

"Remarkably, I do," Anderson replied.

"Wow. He must've paid dearly for Giuseppe's cooperation," Elizabeth commented, then asked, "Why such an elaborate plan? Why not just keep his son sequestered with security?"

"Bellotti blames Conklin for all of Tommy's problems. His son couldn't cope with his participation in Roberta's death. Hence the booze:

self-medicating to kill the pain." Anderson then explained how Tommy had been living, giving details about Connie, Tommy's wish to patch things up with his father and see his daughter before he died, and the hospice facility and professional security. "The old man's convinced that Roberta's murder will come out because of our beefed-up investigation. So he's killing two birds with one stone: protecting his son and taking revenge on Conklin," the prosecutor said. "I verified what I could on Friday," he concluded, and explained what he'd done.

"How'd you convince Bellotti to get a deathbed affidavit from his son?" Ronnie asked.

"When I met with the old man on Saturday, I was truthful, telling him that Pappalardo's testimony about Roberta was hearsay and probably inadmissible. Bellotti understands that our case is much stronger with it."

"Do you think we can prosecute him?"

"No. Our conversation only amounted to 'I said, he said.' I wasn't wired, so as long as Pappalardo sticks to his story, Enzo's bulletproof," Anderson stated.

"Regarding Petra," Church said. "I'd like to bring her out of hiding after she testifies—give her life again. But I'm still concerned about Conklin, even from jail. Do you think Enzo Bellotti can guarantee her safety?"

"I talked to him about witnesses in general," Anderson continued, "but not Petra specifically; I didn't want to give her away. He says the godfather will put out the word to the Five Families and their DeCavalcante affiliate not to take any contracts from Conklin. There are also the Russians and the cartels, but their cooperation is anyone's guess. That's the best we can do."

"We should probably leave it up to Petra," Church suggested.

"It sounds like you have it tied up as best you can," Frosty interjected. "I have a few updates. These are not necessarily linked. The FBI's NYC task force picked up chatter: AJ has gone to ground, and Jimmy is thought to have left the country."

"It sounds like the mob's circling the wagons. Maybe Enzo isn't giving us as much as he appears to be," Ronnie observed.

"Also, Bermuda's back in town. Why?" Frosty wondered.

"And what about Grant Allen? Mention of him is conspicuous by its absence," Elizabeth commented.

"I don't know," Anderson admitted. "But we should decide if we're proceeding, because I need to read in the US attorney. I also want to talk to Judge MacKenzie. He's presiding in the superior court. I must be certain we're all in sync with timing, warrants, and pleas."

"One last thing," Tom added. "In light of Bellotti's disclosures, we can have Judy stand down. Lizzie, would you tell her and have a final invoice sent?"

In conclusion, Jon asked, "Should we go ahead?" Everyone agreed.

***

On Tuesday morning, November 1, Tony picked up Giuseppe at his home in Mountain Lakes. They headed for the AMC Theatres building in the Rockaway Mall. Giuseppe kept an office in the rear of a travel agency where he was a silent partner. As they drove, the *capo* asked, "Give me an update on tomorrow's game?"

"Everything's set. The suite's rented, the food's ordered, and I'll send the texts tomorrow morning with the hotel and room number," Tony replied.

"We're using the Sheraton Parsippany this month, right?"

"Yeah."

"Let me look at the players list before you send the texts. I may want to tweak it."

"Sure, boss."

"You know, I've been thinking. We've been putting in long hours lately. Why don't you skip the game tomorrow, take a night off? I can handle it myself."

"I like to watch the action."

"Yeah, well, you shouldn't neglect your wife, or you won't be getting any action. *Capiche?*"

"She's cool with my hours."

"So, when did you last take her out to dinner?"

"Jeez, boss. I don't know."

"My point exactly. I insist; here's some dough," Giuseppe continued, handing Tony three hundred dollars as they exited the car.

On Wednesday evening, November 2, Giuseppe arrived at the hotel half an hour before the card players would come. Tony had the room prepared: the bar with plenty of ice in the fridge and the table with unopened cards, ashtrays, and poker chips. Long ago, Giuseppe had devised a procedure whereby no cash was used and the players settled up at the night's end using banking apps on their smartphones.

Giuseppe called room service, telling them to bring the cold cuts, salads, and sodas. Then he fixed a scotch and settled down, waiting for a night of cards and to be arrested.

CHAPTER TWENTY-SEVEN

Thursday, November 3, 2022

On Wednesday evening, the gambling bust had gone off as planned. Giuseppe was detained, but the players were released with a warning.

On Thursday morning, Isaac Aaronson, one of the country's top two or three defense lawyers, a Harvard Law School professor emeritus, and a Fox News contributor, met with his new client, Giuseppe Pappalardo. Later, the Morris County prosecutor came in, and they finalized their agreements. By midafternoon, Anderson had called the US attorney, filled him in on the one-hundred-thousand-foot view, and suggested the federal lawyer accompany him to see Judge Harold MacKenzie at his home in Mendham that evening.

MacKenzie was eccentric, recognized for coloring outside the lines: wearing T-shirts, shorts, and flip-flops under his robes in hot weather; his devotion to bebop jazz—on vinyl; and keeping a wee dram of Bushmills ten-year single-malt Irish whiskey on hand. Jon Anderson had contrived to meet at the judge's home because of potential leaks. When he called, MacKenzie had responded acerbically: "I don't like your characterization of a potential leak in my office. But more important, this better be good enough to disrupt the Eagles and Texans football tonight."

The men arrived at seven thirty. MacKenzie greeted them at the front door and proceeded to his study. He indicated chairs and removed a disc from the turntable, inserting it in a sleeve before taking two glasses and a bottle of Bushmills from a drinks trolly. He poured three fingers neat in each, matching what was in his own glass, then passed them to his guests, sat, and waited.

An hour later, much better informed, the jurist spoke. "Son of a bitch. You know Conklin's just been confirmed to the supreme court?" he observed rhetorically. "All right. What you're asking is unusual, but that doesn't mean we shouldn't do it. Before we proceed, let's confirm what you want me to do tomorrow: you want his bail hearing moved to my court, placing it first on the docket. Then counsel will approach, asking for an *in-camera* hearing in my chambers. After that, we'll run through all the regular hearings, Pappalardo will plead guilty at a sentencing one, pay his fine, and I'll approve the deal you've worked out?"

"Yes, Your Honor, and sign the arrest warrant."

"Yes, which you propose to execute Monday morning, first thing."

"Yes."

"Will you be applying for an arrest warrant for Jimmy Zee at some point?"

"Yes."

Turning to the US attorney, the judge asked, "Are you on board? Will you be filing federal charges?"

"Yes. As soon as Conklin's incarcerated without bail, we'll sort out jurisdictions and who will prosecute which charges."

"All right, I understand your desire to act now because of potential leaks. I'm sure federal and state grand juries will indict, so let's not eff around. Your obstruction case is solid. You should prevail on Jan's murder case as well, because you have a body, a motive, Giuseppe's testimony, and Jan's text to Henry containing the ring's pictures. But your case would be enhanced, as would the others if you arrested Jimmy Zee and made a deal for him to testify. The conspiracy to murder Petra has strong evidence with Rector Williamson's testimony and Jimmy Zee's surveillance photos, although the motive might be a little fuzzy. You'll prevail in the Roberta Allen case if you obtain that deathbed confession. But if you don't, you're left with hearsay and a preponderance of circumstantial evidence."

"Agreed. In any case, we continue to work on the investigation. Whatever happens, we'll keep Conklin off the bench if we get a conviction on the obstruction case, albeit with minimal jail time," Anderson concluded.

"Jesus, what a friggin' fiasco," the judge said, walking the men to the door.

***

Henry dropped Evie at the rectory at two o'clock Saturday afternoon. Elizabeth had invited her to spend the night, and then Henry would pick her up after coffee hour on Sunday. This had all come about because Evie was going on what appeared to be an actual "first date" tonight and needed . . . well, Henry wasn't clear. *It's not the birds and the bees, because I ensured she was up to speed years ago.* But whatever it was, Dad wasn't the ticket. When these times popped up, he missed Hannah terribly. Petra had started to fill that void, but *oh well; she isn't around.* When Elizabeth had gotten wind of the situation at church Sunday, she'd stepped up.

Jacques alerted Elizabeth to Evie's arrival, and they went outside. Henry pulled away, and Evie came up the walk with a small overnight bag. They planned on an early supper, so Church and Billy went shopping. Billy had become fascinated with all the colors and shapes in the supermarket and now never missed an opportunity to tag along, riding in the shopping cart while pointing to merchandise, frequently asking, "What's that, Daddy?"

After they left, Elizabeth and Evie watched TV and later talked. Elizabeth learned that Evie's date, Tim, and his older brother, who had his license, were double-dating. They intended to go to a seven-thirty movie at the Rockaway Mall and afterward to the Canal Ville Pizzeria. "Would you like me to put on a little makeup for you after your shower?" Elizabeth asked. "We're both blonde, so my colors should work."

"Please, I never use it—don't have a clue."

That evening, while Elizabeth was upstairs lightly applying eye shadow and blusher to Evie's face, Evie said, "I don't know why this feels different. Tim and I have been friends for a long time. We'll probably end up hanging with our usual group."

"Did Tim ask you out?"

"Yes. He was cute . . . nervous."

"That's why you feel different. It isn't casual, like running into each other. It's a statement that he wants to be with you and a step up in your relationship, albeit small. Dating wasn't so complicated in my day. If a guy asked you out, you knew he was interested," Elizabeth said.

Evie giggled.

"What?" Elizabeth asked.

"Or at least wanted to . . . well, you know," Evie joked.

"That too. And on that topic, do you want to talk about anything?"

322

"No. I'm up to speed."

Before Evie arrived downstairs, Tim knocked on the front door. Church let him in and introduced himself. They sat in the living room, and Tim seemed shy, so Church kept up a patter; "Evie's about ready: shouldn't be long. You know the ladies always keep us waiting— standard operating procedure."

Tim laughed, then asked, "Mr. Gagne, what time do you want me to bring Evie back?"

"Hmm . . . I don't know. I haven't done this before. What do you think?"

"Is midnight okay?"

"That sounds fine."

Elizabeth came down, followed by Evie, who left with Tim shortly after that. Church and Elizabeth watched from the front stoop. Then, as they turned to go inside, they overheard Tim say, "You look very pretty tonight."

"It sounds like your makeup was a hit," Church joked softly. They had coffee in the kitchen, and Church continued, "Did you help Evie through whatever was worrying her?"

"She had trouble understanding that Tim was ratcheting up their relationship."

"Does it bother her?"

"No, she's happy. Just a little confused, that's all."

"One of us should wait up."

"I'll do it," Elizabeth offered, then changed the subject. "I'll be glad when Monday's over. I'm upset and worried about Evie."

"I know. Should I stay down?"

"No, I'm okay . . . you go up."

Church hugged Elizabeth, and she settled on the sofa with a book, Jacques curled beside her.

Around midnight, the dog's ears perked up, and he moved to the front door. When Evie came in a few minutes later, his tail wagged happily.

"I think Jacques missed me," Evie said.

"I'm sure. Did you have a good time?"

"Yes. Tim's fun. We're going out again."

"I'm glad. Do you want anything from the kitchen before I lock up?"

"No, I had pizza." Evie dallied with Elizabeth as she made the rounds before finally hugging her. "Thanks for being there. Sometimes I'm lonely and confused. Dad tries his best, but I need a woman," she said, before hurrying upstairs.

Even though Evie had made her happy, Elizabeth had trouble falling asleep, fretting about Monday. But despite a restless night, she cheered up the following day as she watched Evie play patty-cake with Billy while Church fixed breakfast.

They went to church, and Henry collected Evie after coffee hour. While driving off, they waved their thanks to Elizabeth.

***

On Monday, November 7, at six in the morning, Tom Johnson and another uniformed officer, Ronnie, and Church met Jon Anderson at the Canal Ville Coffee Shop. Anderson had called Tom on Saturday, reporting that Judge MacKenzie had signed the arrest warrant for Henry Conklin on Friday. Following that, Tom had arranged the breakfast strategy meeting ahead of the arrest.

When coffee had been poured and orders taken, Anderson began. "Our surveillance shows that the house's routine on Monday morning is ideal. Mrs. Olsen, the live-in housekeeper, has Sunday off and spends the day at her sister's, staying the night. She returns to the Conklin household at seven, then enters through the back door using her key. Within fifteen minutes, Conklin comes down, and breakfast gets underway. Evie usually arrives later. I think this is our best window of opportunity. Tom, station your officer outside the front door in case he does a runner, then enter through the back one."

"Fine," Tom agreed.

"Are you expecting any trouble?" Ronnie asked.

"Not really," Anderson replied. "We have surprise on our side, and I checked gun records—nada. Here's a floor plan from the town's Building Department. We'll wait quietly in the kitchen. Hopefully, there won't be any hullabaloo."

After they reviewed the house's layout, Church said, "It's too bad, but Evie's becoming collateral damage."

"Don't forget about Mrs. Olsen," the prosecutor commented. "Also, there's a retired local grandfather and her mother's parents in Cape May, so there's plenty of support and dough."

"I know, just sayin' . . . I have Elizabeth standing by. It's her day off, so I'll call her as soon as we have Conklin in custody."

When they left, the uniformed officers were in a black-and-white, Ronnie and Church in Ronnie's car, and Jon Anderson in his own. They parked a couple of blocks away, where they could watch the house unobserved. Anderson moved to Ronnie's car, and everyone waited.

A few minutes after seven, Mrs. Olsen arrived, parked on the street, and went around back. The arrest team waited five minutes and drove to the house, parking across the street. The uniformed officer was posted at the front door, and the others went to the rear.

The men drew their guns—all except Anderson, who was unarmed. Mrs. Olsen was the only one in the kitchen, beginning to move around, starting coffee, and so on.

Tom tapped on the door. When she opened it, he said, "Step aside, Mrs. Olsen. We have an arrest warrant for Henry Conklin."

"Oh no," she reacted. "He isn't down yet." Then, hesitating, she continued, "It's funny, because I always hear him stirring by now. But there's only noise from the front of the house this morning. There it is again; did you hear it?"

"I don't hear anything," Anderson said.

Tom responded, "Okay, Jon, take Mrs. Olsen outside and wait with her while we clear the house."

Using hand signals, Tom, Ronnie, and Church began moving through the downstairs rooms. As Church approached the den's closed door, he heard the noise, waited, and heard it again. Turning the doorknob quietly, he entered low, taking a combat-shooting stance.

Rapidly assessing the room, Church holstered his gun, shouting, "Guys! In the den—now!"

EPILOGUE

After breakfast this morning, Bermuda had driven from her Spanish Point home to Hamilton. At first, she meandered along Front Street, window shopping at a few places while stopping in others before entering a favorite: the English Sports Shop. She perused different sweaters: Scottish cashmere, Irish, and merino wool, finally settling on a mauve cashmere turtleneck. The day was lovely so far, mild, and the summer tourists had nearly all gone home.

Bermuda continued walking until she came to Brew, an up-and-coming coffee shop with grab-and-go or eat-in sandwiches and salads during lunch. It was eleven thirty, so she stopped in.

Despite the busyness of the eatery, she was shown to a table. After ordering a salad with iced tea, Bermuda started thinking about the primary reason for her trip to town. She was flying to Charleston tomorrow for Thanksgiving with her brother's family. She'd already purchased small gifts for the kids but needed a hostess gift for his wife. Hence, she planned to take the harbor ferry to the Royal Navy Dockyard, where the cruise ships tied up. Those cruises were finished for the season, so the yard wouldn't be crowded. Bermuda thought a hand-blown vase or bowl from Dockyard Glassworks would be in order.

While crossing the harbor, Bermuda began reflecting on her recent New York metro area trip. Even with the excellent pay, it had been aggravating from the beginning. The first hit was on October fourteenth, only hours after she'd arrived in Newark, and the second one was around noon on November sixth. As a result, she'd been away from home for a long time, about three weeks, and it hadn't been necessary.

She'd surveilled the second mark for a week and concluded that Sunday morning was optimal. Bermuda had suggested the twenty-third with the thirtieth as a fallback, yet the godfather wouldn't authorize the hit until after the end of the month. So why all the hurry-up-and-wait?

Then, because of the screwup in Saint Martin, Bermuda had still been apprehensive about her relationship with the client, so she didn't complain. But mostly, she was apprehensive about the second job. She didn't like it, especially what they'd asked her to do at the end.

Leaving the ferry, Bermuda muttered, "Not *easy peasy* this time."

***

On Sunday morning the sixth, Bermuda had been in place by nine, parking down the street from the house. She'd surveilled their routine three times. Henry and his daughter left home at nine thirty, and he returned alone before ten. Then he went again at eleven fifteen, and they came back together before noon.

Following them the second time, she learned Henry was busing Evie back and forth to church. So this morning, Bermuda waited, yet he didn't leave. Her plan revolved around entering the house while Henry was gone. If he didn't depart, she would have to abort and try next week. That would piss the don off, because now everything was *hurry up* again.

Bermuda was about to break off when Henry came out, leaving alone. She checked her watch: eleven fifteen.

She drove closer to the house before parking and putting on a token disguise: a dark wig and large, lightly tinted shooting glasses. Exiting her car, carrying a kit bag, the assassin went around back, pulled on gloves, and entered through the unlocked door.

She listened for a few minutes in the kitchen, then quietly cleared the house. Evie wasn't there. So now they were back to the original schedule.

The client had provided a floor plan, so Bermuda set up in a large walk-in pantry off the center hall between the kitchen and den. The killer function-checked her .22 LR semiauto, screwed on a silencer, inserted a full magazine of hollow-points, racked the slide, and waited.

A few minutes before noon, she heard father and daughter return. "I'm going up to unpack and call Tim. He should be up by now," Evie said.

Henry smiled. "Okay, I'll be in the den watching the Jets pregame show. How about having lunch out?"

"Can we go to the diner?"

"Sure, don't be too long," Henry replied, and Bermuda heard the TV switch on.

When she entered the den and pointed her gun at Henry, he didn't notice her until she said, "Stand up, hands on top of your head."

"What the—"

"Shut up. Sit in that side chair." She motioned to one next to a desk. After he obeyed, Bermuda handed him three zip ties. "Tie your ankles to the chairs' legs first, then your left wrist to that arm of the chair."

Henry finished. "What do you want? I have money in the safe."

"Quiet!" the killer snapped, slipping her gun into her waistband before quickly zip-tying his right wrist to the chair's right arm.

"Please, I'll do whatever you want."

Bermuda ignored him, checked the other zip ties, and duct-taped Henry's mouth before turning off the TV. Then she took a position along the den's wall away from Henry, putting her finger to her lips and shushing him, then drawing her gun.

Shortly afterward, Evie called from the foot of the stairs, "Dad, I'm ready." When Henry didn't answer, she persisted. "Dad?" and walked into the den.

"Evie, I have a gun. Put your hands on your head, kneel, and stay still," Bermuda commanded.

Henry struggled, but the killer paid no heed and stepped behind Evie, aiming at the back of her head.

Through the tape, Henry strained to shriek, "No! No!"

Then the assassin fired two rounds, replaced the gun in her kit, turned to Henry before leaving, and said, "Compliments of Grant Allen."

THE END

NOTES

1. The Houston Astros defeated the Philadelphia Phillies in six games on Saturday, November 5, 2022.

2. *The Godfather Part III*, written by Francis Ford Coppola and Mario Puzo and directed by Francis Ford Coppola, Paramount Pictures, December 20, 1990.

ACKNOWLEDGMENTS

With thanks to my wife, Ann, who cheers me on; my sister, Pamela H. Rappolt; my friend, Michael F. Shepherd, who is always my first beta reader; and the Reverend Jim Petroccione. And a special thanks to Rachel Keith for her first-rate copyediting combined with excellent comments and suggestions.

ABOUT THE AUTHOR

Joe Hodgkins and his wife of over fifty years, Ann, live in Morris County, northern New Jersey.

He graduated from Fordham University's Rose Hill Campus in the  Bronx. He was a member of the Fordham Alumni Support Team, FAST, representing the university at college fairs and nights held by local high schools. After attaining his undergraduate degree in liberal arts, he attended New York University's Graduate School of Business Administration in Manhattan.

Hodgkins was a senior manager in both commercial banking and corporate finance. He was a member of the Commercial Finance Association, now known as the Secured Finance Network, and was a frequent presenter at continuing education seminars for the New Jersey Society of CPAs and the New Jersey Institute for Continuing Legal Education on topics such as crisis management, asset recovery, and secured lending. He took early retirement in 2002.

He is currently a eucharistic minister at his local Episcopal church, where he also served as treasurer and chairman of the finance committee. Hodgkins has been active in Freemasonry for nearly forty years and has been an Officer or Grand Officer in all bodies of the York Rite. In 2015 he received the First Masonic District of New Jersey's Distinguished White Apron Award for his service and contributions to the Craft.

Other interests include traveling with Ann, reading, and handgun target shooting.

Made in the USA
Coppell, TX
26 July 2023

19602167R00198